TOM PHELAN

TOM PHELAN was born and raised in Mountmellick, County Laois, in the Irish midlands. He attended St Patrick's Seminary, Carlow, was ordained, and worked in England for several years. He later emigrated to the United States, where he earned a master's degree from Seattle University and eventually left the priesthood.

Phelan's earlier novels, the critically acclaimed *In the Season of the Daisies* and *Iscariot*, have been published in four countries and three languages. In addition, *In the Season of the Daisies* was chosen by Barnes & Noble for its Discover Great New Writers series. The father of two grown sons, Tom Phelan and his wife live in Long Island, New York.

"Writing seems to come as naturally to Tom Phelan as breathing."
Books Ireland

"Phelan's talent is immense."
Book Lovers

"Phelan's exquisite economy of form is akin
to musical composition."
Discover Great New Writers

"A writer who understands the concept of craft."
Examiner

DERRYCLONEY

Also by Tom Phelan

In the Season of the Daisies
Iscariot

Derrycloney

Tom Phelan

To Cynthia
With best wishes
Tom Phelan

BRANDON

A Brandon Original Paperback

Published in 1999 by
Brandon
an imprint of
Mount Eagle Publications Ltd
Dingle, Co. Kerry, Ireland

Copyright © Glanvil Enterprises Ltd, 1999

The author has asserted his moral rights

ISBN 0 86322 253 6
(original paperback)

10 9 8 7 6 5 4 3 2 1

Published with the assistance of the
Arts Council/An Chomhairle Ealaíonn

Acknowledgments

Thanks are due to the following people who supplied me with information while
I was writing *Derrycloney*: Mike, Mary, Anne, Tina, Teresa, Martha, Kathleen and
John Phelan; Theresa Hourigan; and John Hourigan. I also appreciate the assistance
of the staff of the Freeport Memorial Library. Special thanks to my wife Patricia.

Author photo: Seamus Clarke
Cover design: Public Communications Centre, Dublin
Typesetting: Red Barn Publishing, Skeagh, Skibbereen
Printed by The Guernsey Press Ltd, Guernsey, Channel Islands

In memory of Martha Geoghegan Hayes
To Pat and Joe and Mike with love

About the name *Derrycloney*

My maternal grandmother lived in a place called Derrycloney. 'Granny' and 'Derrycloney' were interchangeable. I was six years old when she died, and my childhood ended with her death.

Although there is a real place called Derrycloney, the 'Derrycloney' in this novel is fictional. It never existed and neither did its inhabitants.

1. Liam Glanvil

Dear Sister de Monfort,

Thanks for *The Ski Patrol.* I read it in seven days. I learned a lot about Lapland.

The name of the composition is "An Old Woman".

I remain, Your nephew, Liam

AN OLD WOMAN

Every day an old, grey woman limps down Derrycloney Lane with her white enamel bucket in her left hand and her blue jug in the other. Cinders always walks behind her, like a queen's husband who isn't a king. The jug has small flowers on it, red and yellow, growing on a vine with no beginning and no end.

Missus Brady is the woman's name.

Her hair is wound into a bun that's stuck to the back of her head with wire clips shaped like staples with long legs. If all the clips fell out at the same time, the long hair would fall down her back and she'd look like a witch. But that never happens, only children are afraid it might.

Missus Brady dresses in black clothes all the time, except when she wears her green coat with the two dead foxes in the collar when she goes up town. Her stockings are always wrinkled around her ankles because her legs are too thin to fill them. In the heel of her left hand she keeps her handkerchief ready, in case she sneezes all of a sudden. The handkerchief is a piece of a flour sack with the u in ODLUMS on it in faded blue. Her face is wrinkled like a potato that got lost in a dark corner a year ago, so wrinkled it's hard to imagine that it was ever smooth.

When she comes to the wicket door in our wall, she holds the bucket and the jug and the handkerchief in the same hand while she opens the latch with the other. Cinders is not allowed into the farmyard because he runs after the hens.

My mother and the children know from the sound of the latch who is coming into the yard. Whenever my mother hears Missus Brady's latch-rattle, she goes to the little hob, clears away the drying socks and gives it a rub with the corner of her apron. The little hob is where Missus Brady sits, because it is higher than a chair for her bad hip, and it's the warmest spot in the kitchen. Missus Brady broke her hip when she fell off her bike. My father said her bones are so brittle that they break easily. "She's cold to the bone," he has said many times about her when she's not there.

Missus Brady knows so much and is so wrinkled she must be a hundred years old. She cooked lobsters when she worked in de Lacy Hall. When the lobsters were put into the boiling water, they used to cry. Missus Brady can imitate the crying of the lobsters.

2. Johnny Glanvil

It's a quarter after two on the dot and, if I look, Missus Brady with her bucket and her jug will be hobbling out through her door.

And yes! thar she blows, all to one side as she limps out on to the lane. She's a ship listing in the water, either lying away from the wind or into it, or getting ready to sink. Up and down, from the long leg to the short one. And, of course, she stops to look at her flowers in the chicken-wired garden. If it's not the onions in the back garden, it's the flowers in the front one she's working at, her arse off up in the air because she can't bend right at one of the hips. I always thought she was a bit mad with her flower garden, but then one day when I saw her looking at it the way I'd look at a field of growing wheat, it struck me that the flower garden gives her great satisfaction. What else does she have?

Missus Brady is a little bit nervous of me; not that I blame her. She nearly jumps off the hob when I go into the kitchen. But, for Kate's sake, I like to see her limping down the road. She's a great gossip, the way she makes it into little stories and imitates the one she's talking about. In the few hours she spends cleaning Doctor Mansfield's clinic every Monday, she hears enough gossip to keep her going for a week. But she can sting, too, and rip and tear with that tongue of hers. She can turn into a spitting and scratching cat in the blink of an eyelid if she thinks someone's trying to get the better of her, like she thinks Paddy Burns is. The way she's always reminding poor oul Paddy about the twelfth of November, you'd think he was going to cheat Benny Cosgrove out of his farm.

I only go into the kitchen when she's been there long enough, when I know Kate would like to get the supper ready, or feed the turkeys or the calves.

The minute I appear in the door, Missus Brady's off the hob like a snipe out of a ditch. She didn't take the hint the first time I went in to flush her out, when Kate and I were first married, me rattling the tongs against the grate. The next time I brought in two galvanised buckets. She got the hint real quick when I dropped them on to the concrete floor in the middle of a story she was telling, the one about the time the electricity came to de Lacy Hall.

It's nineteen years since she and Jim came to live in the house above; the first wife died on Jim, so she's the second. He didn't marry her for her legs: they're like two dry sticks; and she didn't marry him for his good humour. He must have piles to be always so contrary. They were only married a week when they came to Derrycloney looking to rent, and he was cross with her even then, treated her like she was his maid. You'd wonder why she married him at all, even if it was her only way out of Irish Slavery, as they call it. She must have been living in a woeful situation altogether if she married Jim to escape from it. And, even though no one would ever say she is a saint or a martyr, she has never been heard to say one bad word about Jim.

There's Crip Quigley's cow bawling from the pain in her elder, waiting for Crip to milk her, the lazy bugger.

Missus Brady sways and waddles up to the place where

the hedge is low. Cinders is with her, like he always is. The day he's not with her is the day he'll be dead, that's if she doesn't die first from drinking all the dog pee he squirts into her water bucket. I don't know why they just don't drown the dog. With Jim drinking everything he makes at the stonework, they can't afford to feed themselves, never mind a bloody dog. Maybe she should put Jim in a sack with a rock and drown him, keep the dog.

But at least that little job in Mansfield's gives her a few bob every week and a chance to wear her good coat with the fox-head collar. It's the one decent thing she owns. She's been dressed in the same clothes for as long as I can remember: black cardigan, black dress halfway down her stick legs. She's as poor as the church mouse, but like a lot of poor people she's very proud and thin-skinned. The only way you can give her something is to put a few extra spuds in the bag when she comes to buy a stone or for Kate to give her an extra drop of milk every day and some blue duck eggs. Kate pretends no one will eat the blue duck eggs, and she more or less begs Missus Brady to take them. Jim is such a cranky old bastard that he'll only eat a boiled brown hen's egg. But, unbeknownst to Jim, his Missus has been boiling the blue duck eggs in old tea for years. I'd give him a brown hen's egg! Give him a hard-boiled one in each ear at the same time, the contrary old bollicks.

There she is, putting the bucket and the jug in the one hand so she can open the wicket door. She probably likes going down to our house to get away from Jim as much as Kate likes to hear her latch-rattle. She'll have Kate in kinks in a few minutes, after she fills the white enamel bucket and puts it on the lane.

Now that I know for sure where she is, I'll snake around by her house and look in at the flowers through the hedge.

I love the colours, but I wouldn't want her to know the
flowers give me any pleasure. She might think I owed her
something.

3. Crip Quigley

Who made the world? "God made the world."

Why did God make the world? I know the question, but I forget the answer.

Why did God make man? "God made man to know, love and serve Him here on earth and to live happily with Him for ever in heaven."

We had to know all the answers for the priest-inspector coming to the National School once a year. We got all dressed up in our best clothes that were too small for us, everyone's suit sleeves at their elbows and the seams in the back split.

I knew the answers, but not what they meant. Consubstantiation. Constantinople. Constipation. Transfiguration. Transcontinental. Transubstantiation. Transatlantic. Transmutation. Convocation. Concelebration. Colcannon. Concannon. Seamus Concannon. Poor Seamus, he died when we were seven, a week after our First Communion. Whooping cough. We all dressed up in our best clothes for his funeral. White coffin.

The priest's clothes were so black and his collar so white, they all looked new. His skin was so clean you wanted to feel him.

How do I feel? I feel very bad.

How does it feel to feel very bad? It feels like the sky's so low that I'm bent over all the time.

What is it I hate the most to do? I hate getting out of the bed.

What is it I like to do the best? I like to sleep, and I wish I could sleep for ever.

Why don't I sleep for ever? Because I wake up, and then I have to lie here with the pains in my back and legs. I have to jow, too. I can move over and do my water in the mattress on the other side of the bed, but I'm not able to think about jowing in the bed. A pig doesn't jow where it sleeps. As it is, every time Bride comes down she says the house smells like a blocked-up piss-wall in a public house. You'd think I was still a child – and I fifty-two when Mud died.

I hate when Bride comes. "What's wrong with ya?" she screeches like a pheasant in stubbles.

"There's nothing wrong with me," I tell her. How many times does she have to hear me saying it?

Bride peeps out of the corners of her eyes, and she thinks I can't see her doing it. She says she'll clean the place up. I tell her it's not dirty. Every frigging time she comes down, I have to tell her it's not dirty. She talks a lot of jow, and the worst is when she asks me, what would Mud think if she walked in through the door?

I don't know that she'd get the fright of her life, like Bride says she would. At least she wouldn't sit there and tell me how bad the place is. Mud would say nothing; she'd just roll up her sleeves and do whatever she thought had to be done and not make me feel bad about it.

Bride got notions about herself when she married your man Lehan. He's nothing but a frigging conductor on the electric trams in Dublin. Only he wears a uniform and a cap with a shiny peak on it, he'd be nothing but an old jow like the rest of us.

"There's not the laste fear of that, of Mud coming in the door," I told her the last time. "It's hard to get up after being six foot under for eleven years."

Then she says, "Don't talk that way about Mud." Then she tells me how the place was when we were young; how Mud used to keep the walls whitewashed, and the floor swept, and the cobwebs and dirt out of the windows, and the fly jow off the panes, and the ashes emptied out of the ashpit, and the chicken jow swept off the floor and scraped off the half door, and how Pops used to keep the place thatched, and that no part of the roof ever fell in and looked like the devil from the outside when he was alive. She never worries at all that the roof could have killed me, only about how bad it looks from the outside.

The last time she started, I got so fed up with her that I said, "Yarra, will ya whist yerself, woman. What yer telling me is how bad ya think the place is now, not how good it was when we were young."

She left in a huff, but she always has to have the last word. "Well, I hope Missus Brady never sees the inside of the house," she said. "It's bad enough she sees it from the outside, like it's abandoned from the time of the Famine."

"To hell with Missus Brady," I said, as Bride got up on her bike. I made myself sound like I didn't care what Missus Brady would say. But at the same time I wouldn't let Missus Brady cross the invisible line between Derrycloney Lane and my front yard, never mind let her into the bedroom to see where the roof fell in. I've often talked to her out there on the road in the spills of rain, the water running down her face like she was the stone angel on Mick McGrath's grave on the wet day of a funeral. But no matter how many hints she gave me, I never offered to let her into the house. Beware a mule's hind foot, a dog's tooth and a woman's tongue, as old Mangan taught us.

I hate getting up. The room's colder than a cowhouse without a door in March, but at least it's not raining. The one good thing about the roof falling down in here in the bedroom is that I can tell whether it's raining from the drips in the basin and the chamberpot. I don't even have to open my eyes. Bride would never think the roof's any good sagging in like that. I should tell her that old saying: it's an ill wind that, it's an ill wind that . . . Frig. Isn't that a good one! I can't remember it. It's an ill wind that . . . That's going to bother me all day now.

Good God, it's nearly one o'clock, and if it wasn't for that frigging cow bawling to be milked I wouldn't get up at all. I wish she could squirt out her own milk. The Glanvils and Missus Brady and the Burnses can hear her, and Cha Finley, too, only he's deaf. As long as she bawls with the pain in her elder, they all know I'm not up yet. It wouldn't please them to know I'm still in bed in the middle of the day.

I'll have to put my feet on the cement floor.

They're the only reason I go to Mass on Sundays, too: so they won't be able to say I don't go. If they only knew that I never even get as far as the church door; that I stop on the River Bridge and talk to whoever else is dodging Mass, standing there looking down into the water. Sometimes I don't even know who it is, and they look at me like I'm mad when I start talking. The floor is terrible cold. It's an ill wind that . . . Jow! I thought I might snake up on it from behind all of a sudden and say it before it got away again.

4. Paddy Burns

Ah, Jazus! Wouldn't you know it! Every time I start to go up the lane, there's the old bitch limping along like an overworked hure.

It happens every fecking time. I peep around the corner of the henhouse before I come charging out in d'ass-and-cart to make sure Missus Brady's not on the lane, and there she always is, going up the town or down to Kate's, and I have to wait. Will you look at her swaying from side to side like a soldier with two wooden legs! If I do manage to get up the lane without running into her, she's bound to be standing in her doorway just to let me know she's seen me trying to snake past.

Why did she ever start hating me? Has she been hating me all these years and only letting it all out now? Of course, the cow breaking into her flower garden didn't help matters, but it wasn't as if she were depending on the flowers to keep her alive. Those accusing eyes of hers, as if I'd done something wrong, and it doesn't take much for her to break into words. But they're more than words. It's spikes they are, spikes of a harrow inside my head, ripping me apart.

There's no beating around the bush with Missus Brady. Straight for the balls she goes, and when she's got them in a twist, there's not much I can say to defend myself. It's only after the whole thing is over, and I'm still boiling mad, boiling like a forgotten pot of spuds, that I think of the things I should have said.

If she was only a man! With a man, you could tell him to go and feck off, or threaten to knock his block off. But a fecking woman! You say "feck off" to a woman, and the next thing she has cousins you never knew about, and one fecker bigger than the next.

There's Crip's cow bawling to be milked.

The Missus and myself had barely settled into Derrycloney, fifteen years ago, when Missus Brady started talking about Benny's rights! And now that it's getting near his twenty-first birthday, she's at it non-stop. Benny's fecking rights! Jazus! "And what about my rights and the rights of my wife and my own two daughters?" I roared back at her a few weeks ago, and the noise in my ears was so bad I didn't hear what she was saying. It was like looking at her through a wall of water, her lips and face moving real ugly-like, and I not hearing one word she was saying, that finger of hers cutting up the space in front of her face like a nun dressing down a child. But I knew well enough what she was saying, because she'd said it to me a hundred times before; aye, and to Lizzie too. "It's yer nephew, Benny Cosgrove, who owns that farm," she'd say, "and ya not even letting him sleep in the house at night."

Forty-one acres, but by the way she says "farm" you'd think there were forty-one thousand of them. Forty-one miserable fecking acres, a cold house with three rooms altogether, the water running down the inside of the walls in the winter, aye, and for most of the rest of the year too. What am I supposed to do with Benny? Let him sleep in the same bed as my daughters, his first cousins, and the whole lot of them with hair under the arms?

Just because Missus Brady took care of Benny for a few months after his mother died, you'd think she was related to him. The father was all over the place like a madwoman's shite when the wife died, and all Missus Brady did was feed Benny and bring him to school. But if you ask me, the only reason she looked after him was so everyone would think she was Florence Nightingale.

When Mick Cosgrove got back on his feet, and said Benny could stay home from school for the one day of the threshing, Missus Brady got all contrary and wouldn't take care of Benny any more. She was such a stubborn old cow. Every child in the world stays home from school for the threshing. If it was Benny's interest she had at heart, she could have fought with Mick and left the child out of it. But no. If *she* was going to take care of the child, then it would be up to her to decide when Benny should and should not go to school. If only Mick Cosgrove had kept his mouth shut, she would have let Benny stay home. Talk about contrary! She's the contrariest woman I ever met. No wonder Jim is such a miserable old shite. If I was married to Missus Brady, I'd hang myself first thing, and I wouldn't care a feck if they wouldn't bury me in the cemetery or if I went to hell for ever.

She's so fecking slow! I'm still waiting for her to get off the lane. But at long last there goes the hand with the bucket over to the hand with the jug. She's getting ready for the latch on the wicket door. The way she goes about it, you'd think she was getting ready to steer a ship through the Suez Canal. She's gone into the yard now, and Cinders upends himself and looks at the door. He'll wait till she comes back out with the bucket full of water. She always fills the bucket before she goes into the kitchen for the milk and the chat with Kate. There she is now; she puts the white enamel bucket beside the wall so no one'll fall over it. And the minute she goes back in through the door, Cinders goes over and lifts his leg to the bucket. Half his piss goes into the water. Maybe she'll get a disease from it and die all of a sudden. Wouldn't that be great? The great dog-piss disease.

Jazus! The waiting games a man has to play before he can go up his own fecking lane to get the messages. And then my own Missus scalds me for being afraid of Missus Brady, for trying to dodge her. When a man is caught between two women, he can never be right about anything.

I'll get d'ass-and-cart.

5. Missus Brady

Wasn't I coming down the lane yesterday from doing Doctor Mansfield's clinic when Bride, Crip's sister, rode up behind me on her bike and let a screech out of her worse than an oul hen bit by a dog. She nearly frightened the life out of me.

"Missus Brady, Missus Brady, me knit's in the ditch," she shouted, with her hair all over the place, and for a minute I thought someone was after her with a cross-cut saw. She jumped off the bike and got so close to me I could smell the mothballs off her dress under her coat.

"Me knit's in the ditch, Missus Brady," she shouted in my face. Breathless she was, and the veins in her nose looked like they'd burst any minute. I can't stand the smell of camphor, so I had to back away from her, but she followed me like a calf thinking I'm its mother.

"In the name a God, Bride," says I, "but what's wrong with ya?" She pointed back up the lane and screeched again. She kept pushing her hair out of her eyes. "Back there, Missus Brady, back there where the big briar's coming out. Me knit's in the ditch."

Only for her hair all over her face, I would never have known what she was talking about. The briar had snagged her hairnet and ripped it off as she rode by.

Then she says, "I declare to God, Missus Brady, but for a minute I thought there was a man in the ditch making a grab for me. I was terrified, and only I knew ya were up ahead a me, I'd a died on the spot. Oh thank God and his blessed mudder ya were here." She had her hand on her heart like she was keeping it from jumping out of her chest. Then she asked me would I go back with her to rescue the hairnet. "I can't let Crip see me looking like a scarecrow," says she. As if Crip would notice the difference! I said to myself.

I thought to myself that if the net was wrapped around a thorny blackberry briar, there wasn't much chance of picking it off without putting holes in it. But, I have to say this for Bride: she might have the face and moustache and hairy arms of a man, but she has dainty fingers.

Bride examined the hedge to make sure there wasn't a man hiding in the bushes. Then she leaned the bike against a whitethorn and told me to hold the end of the briar. Well, with the patience of Job she picked the net off the thorns without pulling one stitch.

And all the time she talked ninety to the minute, told me about Crip. If she hadn't been serious, I would have died in knots. "Well, ya know, Missus Brady, I try to come down to Crip once a month since Mud died. To be honest with ya, the conductor," as she calls Pad Lehan-the-husband, "doesn't like it at all that I come back to Derrycloney so often. He spends so much of his time in Dublin on the trams in his uniform, that when he comes home he has to get used to the dirt and the smells of the country all over again; ya know the smells I mean, Missus Brady, and the dirt too, the dunghapes outside the kitchen doors and cow plops all over the place no matter where ya step."

Suffering duck! That's what she called them: cow plops!

Such refinement you never heard in your life, and her nose a little bit up in the air when she said it – cow plops.

"I can never fool the conductor," says she. "He can smell it offa me – Crip's house, I mean." Then she lowered her voice to tell me things every one of us knows for the last hundred years. "Missus Brady, ya couldn't believe the state of Crip's house. There's dirt and ashes all over the place. Everything's black with damp soot. Ya can scrape it off the back of the chairs with yer nails. Between the soot in everything and the bits of rotting straw floating down from the thatch, I wouldn't even drink a cup of tea if he offered me one. I'd let on I wasn't thirsty; it's so easy to make him cross. I'd swear the place hasn't seen a brush or a rag since the night we waked Mud. The roof caved in beside his bed nearly a year ago. It could have killed him."

Then Bride lowered her voice so far I could hardly hear her at all. "Missus Brady, don't tell anyone this, I'm so ashamed of it, but the smell of the place is terrible. The house smells like a chamber pot that wasn't brought out to the dunghape for ages for emptying. What's wrong with him at all, Missus Brady? He never says a word to me, just sits there at the corner of the table staring into the pile of ashes in the ashpit. He's not taking care of himself. He only shaves for Mass on Sunday, and all he ates is bought bread. The conductor says that's what gave the English sailors the scurvy, when their teeth fell out and their gums got so long they had to cut them out of their mouths with a knife. No vegetables. Crip won't even let me wash his Sunday shirt. He won't let me do anything for him. But I had to come down today to look for a clocking hen. I couldn't wait another day because d'eggs'll go bad. So, down I'm going to see him, smelly chamber pot and all."

Well, I was having a terrible time trying to keep a straight face. Going down to get a clocking hen from Crip beat the band altogether. I was going to tell her what happened Crip's hens, but then I said to myself, why should I spoil it for her? Can you imagine what the conductor will have to say about Crip when he hears about the hens?

I was dying for her to tell me more about the conductor and Crip, but who comes up on us without making a sound only Crissy the Widda and the butt of a fag hanging out of the corner of her mouth. "Curses and blazes on ya, Crissy," says I to myself. "Ya couldn't have timed it worse." But then, everything about Crissy's timing is bad. She'll even die at the wrong time – when someone's having a threshing or when everyone's at a wedding.

Of course, Crissy shot her left arm up in the air to push her wrist out of her sleeve. "I have a new watch," she says. "I got it with me honey money."

"And what time is it, Crissy?" I snapped at her, telling her with the sound of my voice to go away and drop dead. But a wink is as good as a nod to a blind horse, as Crip would say. Crissy stood there looking at the watch and saying nothing, holding it up to her ear to hear it ticking.

"Do ya want to hear it ticking, Missus Brady?" says she. I nearly cut the nose off her, but Crissy didn't even notice. She started off about her bees. God! Crissy the Widda and her blessed bees. If it's not the bees, it's the watch. If it's not the watch, it's the knitting. If it's not the knitting, it's Lieutenant Colonel Edwin Pickwoad's letter. Bride wouldn't gossip in front of Crissy, so we had to listen to bee-talk till the last thorn was out of the hairnet.

I stood in the kitchen door for ages, waiting for Bride to come back from Crip's. I thought I might hear her version of how the hens lost their beaks. But I couldn't wait any longer, and the minute I went out to the back garden to pull onions for the supper, didn't she go flying up the road. There was nothing in the basket on the front of her bike. She'll never get her eggs hatched.

6. Billy Bates

The bawling of the cow must have only got as far as my ears because, when I wakened in the fierce dark, it was the Hippwell One who was in my mind, put there by the patch of wet shirt stuck to my belly, the smell, too, coming up when I moved the sheet, warm damp.

I lay there, remembering how I'd done it to her before I fell asleep. I have done it to her so often that sometimes I have to think up new ways before I get a stir out of the dragon. Sometimes, I embarrass myself with what I think up.

Well, the dragon started straining against its reins very quick last night, when the Hippwell One jumped out of the bushes down at the lake so sudden that the two swans took off, afrighted. Up on my back she jumped and wrapped her arms around my neck real tight, her legs around my belly. She hadn't a stitch on.

"Get me," she hissed in my ear. "Get me, get me, ya big-mickeyed buller, Billy Bates."

"Be God, I'll get ya, ya hure, Hippwell," says I, and I wrestled her off me, threw her down on the ground so quick on her back that the wind was knocked out of her. For a second she lay there in the moonlight, her legs splayed as wide as a turkey's wishbone, drops of wet shining in her belly hair like fresh dew in the early sun on cobwebs.

I fell on her as quick as a cock hopping up on a hen, but before I could get into her she said, "The rope, the rope, ya big-balled bastard, Billy Bates." Then she fought against the rope like a year-old bull calf getting his balls cut out by a man with a blunt penknife. Before I even had the rope around her wrists, the dragon was roaring for satisfaction, and the Hippwell One was squealing like a mare that can't stand the teasing teeth of a stallion any longer; squealing at him to do it to her; and to get her point across, whacking him in the belly with double-barrelled, rear hooves that would kill a man dead.

That was it. I didn't have to go any further, and I started heaving and shuddering like a dog shiting after a feed of hazelnuts. I pulled the shirt into place just in time.

Now, as I lay there wondering how the Hippwell One knew about the size of my balls, the dragon started coming to life again, but he slunk back into his cave when the cow in the tin shed bawled in my brain.

There's something telling about the bawl of a calving cow, and there's something more telling about the bawl of a cow that's having trouble calving. Up like a shot I got and lit the yard lamp, pulled on my trousers, and, sure enough, the minute I saw her I knew there was something wrong. One shining calf leg sticking out of a cow's arse all by itself is the same as someone holding up a sheet of galvanised iron with *Trouble* painted on with a tar brush.

"Shag," says I out loud, because I knew right away I'd have to work up the nerve to go for Johnny Glanvil, which meant Duncle would be pissed off in the morning. He doesn't want me getting anything from Johnny because he'll have to pay him back some way – like, give Johnny the loan of me for a day. Duncle Murt makes me take care of the calving cows, but when I have to get Johnny he goes mad.

But would Duncle ever get up to a calving cow in the night? The shagging old bastard! When one of his cows shows signs of calving, he makes me drive her over here and put her in the tin shed, so he won't be wakened from his beauty sleep, and he'd have to sleep for a long time before he'd even get within an ass's roar of pulchritude.

And, as well as that, it's me who has to go to Johnny and do the asking, knowing that Duncle is unfair when it comes to returning a favour. Talk about lack of perceptivity and abundance of short-sightedness! Duncle Murt's so shagging tight-fisted that one of these days the tips of his fingers are going to come out through the backs of his hands.

I'm the one standing in the middle, while Duncle's bitter shite whacks me in the middle of the back and Johnny's barely controlled sarcasm scalds me in the front. I'm forty-two, for shag's sake.

The battery was dead in my flash lamp, and I've yet to ride the bike holding the yard lamp without getting burned. There was nothing for it but carry the bike across the two fields and then ride up Derrycloney Lane in the dark for Johnny, smacking the balls off myself against the point of the saddle every time I went into a pothole. Only it was a clear night and there was a track of stars between the high hedges on each side of the lane, I'd have gone into a ditch twenty times, head first.

I hate opening the wicket door of Johnny's place, afraid his mongrel will ate me alive. But the dog must have been asleep somewhere, dreaming he was down at the lake, maybe, sniffing around, looking for a dog-version of the Hippwell One. While the hairs on my arms settled back down out of their nervousness, I heard a hen making one of those ghostly noises hens make in their sleep, as if it was yawning. Missus Brady says the worst sign of bad luck is the sound of a yawning hen in the middle of the night. Missus Brady has some very quare ideas. What, I ask you, would a hen know about luck, good or bad?

I hate waking up Johnny and Kate; it's like I'm looking in at them sleeping in the same bed. Kate's a good-looking woman, better altogether than the Hippwell One. Johnny must be always up on her.

I don't think my knuckles had even touched the bedroom window when I heard, "Who's there?" hissed, like the hisser had been doing something secret and dirty. It could have been either of them, Kate or Johnny.

"It's Billy, Johnny," I said. "There's a cow in trouble."

"I'll be out in a minute," Johnny said softly, and I heard the bed creaking.

When I was feeling my way around the water pump to go back out on to the lane, I heard the links of a chain slipping through an iron ring and the sound of a big animal moving – either getting up or lying down. Then, as my fingers touched the latch on the wicket door, I heard the sound of dung plopping into its own pancake. The animal had stood up to make a shite. Only in Johnny's barn! says I to myself. If it was Duncle's animal, it wouldn't bother to stand up; just lie there with its tail jammed up against its arse and squirt the shite all over itself, so that the next time I rubbed against it I'd get plastered.

When I found the handlebars of the bike, I stood there in the dark, ready to take off the second Johnny appeared. You can't keep that man waiting.

Everything goes perfect for Johnny, from his great catch of a wife to his gramophone and new turnip barrow, and his children and all the other things he has, all the way down to his animals standing up to shite when they're tied in for the night. The Glanvils are the only ones in Derrycloney with a back door as well as a front one. Johnny's the opposite of Job. He's like your man, Midas; everything he touches turns out well. His cattle never die – except for that one time with the calves and the paraffin oil – his spuds never rot in the drills from the wet, his wheat never lodges, his sugar beet always yields the best. Is it hard work and prayers, or is he just lucky? Of course, he has a sister a nun who's always praying for him.

But there was that once, the one time when I saw something backfiring on him; only backfiring because he was so cross with Duncle that his judgement was clouded. Duncle had sent me up to Johnny on a wet day as payback for all the times Johnny had helped us. I told Duncle that was the same as paying a man his wages with food that's rotten. Of course, when push came to shove, I had to go. But was it Duncle who nearly got killed when the bull came through that window, when Johnny's plan didn't work? No! It was me, the rain spilling on my face while I lay on my back on the dunghape.

And there I was again, standing in the middle of the night on Derrycloney Lane, waiting for Johnny to help me with a cow that was calving wrong. It's at such times I know for certain I should have gone to Anthony in Pennsylvania. If only I was younger, I'd tell Duncle to stick the farm up his arse and I'd take off, maybe whack him on the head like the Playboy of the Western World, only I'd make sure the shagger never recovered.

Johnny came silently through the wicket door, wheeling his bike. Of course, he had a flash lamp with a good battery.

"What ails the cow, Billy?" he asked, in the sound of his voice stooping down from his more-organised-than-thou heights, as if he had trained his cows never to calve in the middle of the night.

"She's calving and there's only one leg out," I said, and that was enough for Johnny.

"Are ya ready?" he asked, and he didn't wait for an answer. He threw his leg over the saddle and took off down the lane. Then, after leaving his bike in the ditch and taking the lamp off its holder, he led the way, with long steps, across the two fields to the house, I was at a half trot trying to keep up with him, stumbling over clumps of rushes in the dark.

He stood at the door, lamp in hand, lighting my kitchen, while I gathered up the necessities for the operation: bar of soap, six eggs, scissors, twine, bucket of water. I kept fretting that Johnny would go home and tell Kate about the mess he saw in my house. His sheds are cleaner and tidier than my kitchen. But what the shite! "Shag it!" says I to myself. Then we went to the harness house, where I got two bits of rope and a piece of soft sack that would do for a towel.

When we went to the tin shed, I lit the yard lamp, and the cow looked around at us, her big eyes bulging and the calf's leg still sticking out of her arse. She gave a low moan, telling us the calf was stuck, asking us to give her a hand to get it out.

The calf's chin should have been lying on the two front ankles just inside her arse, but one of the legs had fallen down and was back under the calf's belly. It was bent below the calf, bulging out the shoulder and making it too big for the calf to slip out. The calf was on its way to being born, but it would have to be pushed back in and the missing leg moved into the right position.

Johnny took off his short coat, hung it on the handle of the four-prong fork standing against the wall and, as he walked over to the cow's arse, he rolled his shirtsleeve up to his shoulder. I followed him with the yard lamp. Now that Johnny had taken over, my function had been reduced – or elevated – to that of shiner-of-the-light-on-the-right-place.

Like a surgeon who had done the same operation a million times, Johnny broke an egg in his left hand and smeared the whole thing on his right arm. He brushed off the bigger pieces of shell and slipped his hand into the cow. His elbow disappeared. Without even having to look for it with his fingertips, Johnny grasped the calf by the head and, as he pushed it back down into the cow, he moved closer to her arse. The rest of his arm disappeared up to the shoulder.

I'd swear to God, it took him no more than seven seconds to find the missing leg and pull it forward. Slowly, his arm came out, glistening in the flame of the yard lamp, and in his hand were two yellow feet.

"She's a bit dry," he said, and that's all he had to say. I handed him the rest of the eggs and, one by one, he pushed them inside the cow's arse, squeezed till they broke. While he was breaking the last one, I got the two ropes and held them in such a way that Johnny could easily take them one at a time. I was the nurse handing the instruments to the surgeon.

When each leg was looped above the hock, he moved back, gave a small pull to let the cow know it was time to push. We waited a few seconds. Then, like a runner answering a starter's command, the cow held her breath. Johnny gave another slight tug. With a sudden start, the cow moved her back legs apart and gave a low moan as she pushed. Johnny pulled and the whole thing was over in a second. Like it had gone asleep with its head lying on its ankles, the calf slipped out and violently joined the rest of us on this miserable ball of shite; it fell down out of its mother's arse on to the floor with a smack that sounded like a sopping sack falling on to a concrete floor from twenty feet up. The calf was flecked with bits of eggshell.

Johnny lifted up one back leg. "Heifer," he said.

While I cut the cord, Johnny washed up in the bucket of

cold water, and the cow tried to bend her neck to see what had come out of her. Then, in high-pitched maternal moans, she asked to be let free of her chain so she could take care of her child.

Johnny put on his short coat, and I let the cow loose. With the afterbirth slapping around her legs, she swung around and, with coarse tongue, cleaned the mucus off her shocked and shivering calf.

Even though he told me not to bother, I walked across the two fields to Derrycloney Lane with Johnny. For all the talking we did, I might as well have stayed at home and gone back to bed. When I thanked him for his help, Johnny pretended he didn't mind at all, said he didn't mind getting up in the middle of the night to help Duncle's cow to calve. His words were moist with sarcasm. I knew damn well Johnny was remembering that wet day when Duncle had sent me up to him as a payback. Johnny tries to hide the sarcasm, but it always squeezes out of the edges of his words.

So, here I am, leaning on the top bar of the gate watching the light of Johnny's flash lamp fading into the distance. I wonder will he stay up and start the day's work, or will he go back to bed. If it was me, it's to the bed I'd go, waken up that woman and tell her the dragon was roaring to get into her cave.

I can imagine Duncle asleep in his bed, undisturbed, unconscious, above it all, while Johnny and myself have been doing his work for him. The old shagger! The tight-fisted old bollicks!

Johnny's light is gone. I'd better go back and milk the beastings, feed it to the calf out of a bucket, my hand buried in it with my fingers bent up pretending they're the mother's paps, the calf sucking the hell out of them.

7. Kate Glanvil

Every time he comes into the kitchen to get the bandage changed, Benny pulls the chair as close as he can to the fire, and every time I say to him the same thing. Before he has the raggy cloth-glove pulled off the hand, the place is filled up with the smell of hot rubber, the red fire heating up his wellington boots so much that if you touched them you'd get burned.

"You'll burst into blazes one of these days, Benny," I tell him, while I take out the safety pin holding the bandage together at the back of his hand. A little rush of air through his nose is his way of smiling, his way of telling me he heard me, maybe his way of telling me he likes it that I spoke to him – like the pony snuffling when you scratch deep around the roots of her ears.

The wonder is that he feels the cold at all, that he's alive to feel it. He's so thin, not a pick of flesh on him, you'd think he should be dead. I squirm every time I feel the bones in his arms and hands. They're like slippery sticks inside a thin cloth bag sliding out from between your fingers. The shape of his skull is plain to see, his face thin like a ferret's; black hair, white skin, the sunk-in eyes like two burnt holes in a blanket. The poor teeth; brown stumps that make his jaw swell up when he gets an abscess. When he's eating, he moves the food around his mouth looking for the least painful place to chew.

"How's the hand feeling?" I ask him, and he never whines, never complains.

"All right," he says.

He wears his topcoat all the time, winter and summer, a piece of ravelled binder twine for a belt. The coat has small tears in it, as if mice were at it with tiny teeth, and it smells like the elder of a cow, and the backside of a cow too. The peak of his cap is broken in the middle.

The last layer of the bandage is stuck to the back of his hand. I cut off what I've already unwrapped and put his wounded hand into the washing-up basin of lukewarm water on the hob beside him. While the bandage is soaking loose, he holds the palm of his right hand out to the red coals.

I sit down on the other side of the fire and try to carry on a conversation. But Benny never says anything unless you ask him a question, and after a while I can't help but feel he must think I'm just a busybody. So the two of us look into the fire, the smell of the scorching rubber filling the kitchen.

It's only when I'm finished I see that my fingers, by themselves, have rolled up the dirty bandage, a strip of a flour sack, and I remind myself of Mrs Cavanagh-of-the-shop talking to me across the counter one day, fiddling with her fingers and tearing the ten-shilling note I had just paid her into little bits. Ned, the husband, must have et the face off her, if she was eegit enough to tell him about it.

He's a not-loved and lonely person, Benny. I often wonder how he feels every night when he gets up on his dreadful bike with its two wobbly wheels, no brakes, loose saddle and no light, and rides off to Drennans' out in the bog for a place to sleep; leaves his own house and faces that four-mile ride in the dark, along narrow roads with holes in them deep enough to drown a dog in. The Drennans are some sort of distant cousin of Paddy, and they're not nice to him either. It's not so much that they aren't nice, as that they're not warm people; cold as frogs.

Just because he has nothing to say for himself, the Drennans and the Burnses treat Benny like he's an eegit. But I have to agree with Missus Brady; Benny's no eegit. He just never got over the mother and father dying when he was a child, and then the Burnses came like big cuckoos – pushing him out of his own nest to make room for their own. He's still a little boy lost, going around not knowing what hit him, silent because he can't think of anything to say, not knowing his place in the world, always thinking he's in someone's way. What is there to say, I ask you, when your father and mother die, and you're still a child?

"Always pray yeer father and mother won't die till yeer grown up." That's what Sister Gerard used to say in fifth class. I have often wondered why she said it so often. Maybe her own father and mother died when she was a child, and no one loved her after that. Or maybe going into the convent is the same as parents dying, and of course there's no love in a convent at all, only politeness. One way or the other, I can understand now what she was talking about when I look at poor Benny dragging himself around Derrycloney. Benny at almost twenty-one doesn't talk to anyone, he's as thin as a whip, he's so badly fed that his flesh won't heal, and he has no relative with an interest in him.

The Drennans think they're telling funny stories when they talk about the lads out there putting nettles and briars in Benny's bed, or tying a rope across their lane to knock him off his bike in the dark. There's nothing funny about that at all. They're cruel things to do, and the lads wouldn't be able to put the nettles in Benny's bed unless the Drennans let them into the house to do it. For all I know, it's the Drennans themselves who torment him, hope he'll not come any more.

It's always a wonder, the great rounds people will go to tell someone something. And because they go the long way around, they do it secretly, and when they do it secretly, they do it cruelly.

It was the same story for Benny when he was a chap going to school. He was one of those children all the other children picked on. I read in the *Woman's Weekly* that when a parrot escapes and flies out into the wild, all the other birds attack it because it's so different from them, all that colour and everything. Benny was the same, only he was far from colourful. He was dull. He was quiet. The seat was out of his trousers. He smelled like sour milk. There was solid dirt at the back of his ears. He was delicate looking. He looked at the ground all the time. He never knew his lessons, would just stand there and say nothing when he was asked a question. The teachers picked on him in front of the other children and made a laugh of him. There was no one at home, father nor mother, Paddy nor Lizzie Burns, to give him encouragement, to help him with his homework. It was only for the few months that he lived with Missus Brady after the mother died that he got any nourishment of that nature. It was in her house he learned to write his name, and after that he can't write anything, or read anything, for that matter. He never went to school after his twelfth birthday.

What's going through his head now, one hand in the basin on the hob, the other nearly in the fire, the boots melting off him? I wonder does he know what's going on about his twenty-first birthday between Paddy Burns and Missus Brady.

"How's the bandage doing, Benny?" I ask him. He lifts the hand out of the water and gingerly tugs at the flour sack.

"Still stuck," he says, with the back of his head towards me, and he lowers the hand back into the basin, settles back into his perch.

He was working with Johnny when he hurt the hand; caught it between the shaft of the horse's cart and the wall when they were backing a load of turnips into the boiler house. Doctor Mansfield said there's no bones broke, that a bandage with goosegrease is the best thing for it. But the crushed flesh hasn't changed much in colour or size since the day he got it caught.

"Are y'able to move yer fingers, Benny?" I ask him, and the poor devil moves the fingers of his good hand, the one he's holding out to the fire. I'm afraid I'll only embarrass him if I tell him I meant the fingers of the injured hand. After a while, I say, "Now see will the fingers on the sore hand move as good as the ones on the good hand."

He lifts the dripping hand out of the basin, the fingers slightly bend at the middle knuckles.

"Is it hurting ya, Benny?"

He drops the hand into the basin. "A bit," he says, and he settles back into his position on the chair.

When Paddy Burns and Benny have their own farm work done, Johnny hires the two of them to work by the day; three meals and ten shillings for Paddy, five shillings and meals for Benny. Johnny gets Benny to work around the yard, because he would never send him across the fields with Paddy to cut the hedges. Johnny thinks Paddy jeers at Benny, is always belittling him, always telling him how useless he is. Johnny, despite always demanding hard work out of everyone, feels bad for Benny, knows he isn't strong, remembers how he sort of closed down when the mother and father died. "He pulled down his blinds the way people pull down the blinds when there's a death in the house, only Benny never let them up again," is what Johnny says. He doesn't get cross at Benny when he finds him standing there waiting to be told what to do next, when he should know what to do because he's done it so often before. I don't know how he's going to manage when Paddy and Lizzie move out, but at least he'll be able to sleep in his own house, in his own bed that Lizzie took from him the day she and Paddy moved in, took and gave to their own child while Benny had to sleep on a sack of straw in a corner of the kitchen with nothing only his overcoat on him for a blanket.

Johnny thinks Lizzie makes Benny hand over the five shillings he earns here. He says it wouldn't surprise him if she doesn't even leave him a few pennies to spend on himself. Johnny never liked Lizzie, thinks the way she throws the food on the table means she doesn't care about her family. He likes Paddy, thinks Paddy is a great worker, that only for Lizzie he'd be nicer to Benny.

But I don't dislike Lizzie Burns. I know she hasn't been too nice to Benny, but she has fed him the way she knows how to feed anyone. The one thing I would say is that she shouldn't make Benny ride off out to Drennans' every night. I know the house is too small for them all, four Burnses and Benny and three rooms including the kitchen, but Paddy could have made a warm place for Benny to sleep out in the barn. Even sleeping on a sack in the hay would be better than facing that ride out to Drennans' every night – hail, rain, frost or snow – and the same ride back in the morning. At least, if I were Benny, that's what I'd rather do. Of course, Johnny says sending him off to Drennans' is Lizzie's way of not having to feed him his breakfast on the days he doesn't work here. I wonder what the Drennans give him to eat; do they give him anything?

"Try the bandage again, Benny," I say.

This time the bandage stays in the water when he lifts up his hand. The purple and blue and yellow and swelled-up hand hangs over the basin like an egg of pain.

"Give it here to me," I say. I reach up behind me and take the drying cloth for the delft off its nail. When he sails the hand over, I take it in the towel and pat it dry. Now that I see it up close, there's little or no improvement. His hand is so relaxed it feels like a day-old chicken in my hands. I think Benny could sit there for ever with me holding his hand and he wouldn't move, his eyes on the fire or else closed. For a while I hold the wounded hand, the wounded Benny, and I feel very sad for him. I have to make an effort to keep from crying. The poor lonely child.

The smell of hot rubber breaks the spell, and I tell him to pull back from the grate before he goes up in flames. He pushes the chair back less than an inch with his backside. I give him back his hand, and take the jar of goosegrease off the big hob beside me. While he gently rubs the grease over the coloured wound, I take the ever-boiling kettle off its hook on the crane, the corner of my apron between myself and the hot handle.

While the teapot is drawing on a coal on the hearth, I wrap a clean bandage around the damaged flesh; have to take it off nearly all the way again when I ask him is it too tight. He wouldn't have said anything only I asked him.

While he tenderly pulls the raggy glove over the bandage, I pour a mug of strong tea. When I put the mug and the small plate with the two cuts of currant cake on a chair beside him, I say, "You can dip the cake in the tea, Benny, and it'll be nice and soft to eat."

He says it so low, I hardly hear him saying, "Thanks."

Then I tell him I'm going to make the beds, because I know if I stay in the kitchen he'll be too shy to dip the cake in the mug.

Benny's gone when I come back after doing the beds. There's drops of tea on the chair where they fell off the cake on its way to his mouth from the mug. The smell of the melting wellingtons will be in the kitchen all day, and when the children come home from school they'll all say, "Benny was here to get his bandage changed." They're still too young to see far enough beyond themselves to ask how his hand is mending.

8. Liam Glanvil

Dear Sister de Monfort,
   Thanks for *Kidnapped*. I read it in nine days. I learned about ships and geography.
   The name of the composition is "Our Road".

I remain, Your nephew, Liam

OUR ROAD

Our road starts at Wolfe Tone Street between the maltings and Miss Moran's house. One and a quarter miles later it ends at Murt McHugh's front door. The last mile is shaped like a Red Indian's bow just before he lets the arrow fly, but there are three bends on the first part.

The first bend is on the Fiery Hill. One of the fields beside the road at this spot is covered with furze bushes. The furze turn yellow when the flowers blossom, and they look like a fire with no smoke when the sun shines on them.

The Tober is another bend, but nearer to the town. There is a well in Paddy Burns's field beside the road, and *tober* is the Irish for well. The water from the well runs away in a deep drain called Cosgroves' Ditch. One time an ass was down in the ditch eating the sweet grass that grows near the water when it got stuck in the muck. It was dead for a long time before anyone knew it was stuck. No one could take the ass out because the smell was so bad. Whenever anyone went by on the lane, they tried not to breathe and not to look at the place where the ass was going bad. Then the grey crows started to eat it. Paddy Burns said the first thing the grey crows go for is the eyes.

One day, Paddy Burns and Benny Cosgrove put a whole jar of Vicks on rags and wrapped them around their faces. They dug a new piece of drain beside the ass. At the same time they covered the ass in the old drain with what they were digging out of the new one, and my father said that's what killing two birds with one stone means. The Vicks was to keep the dead-ass smell away. Paddy Burns said everything in the world smelled like Vicks for a year after.

The last bend is called Morans' Bend because it is near Miss Moran's house. Nothing ever happened there, except that Miss Moran is a dressmaker and she made my First Communion suit with a peaked cap and a button in the middle on top. The suit and the cap were brown. The first time I fitted on the suit, it was held together with straight pins, and Miss Moran drew lines on the cloth with a piece of chalk shaped like a flat stone.

When you are going down our lane, Missus Brady and Jim live on the left just pass the Fiery Hill. Jim is a stonemason and he is always cross. Missus Brady grows onions in her back garden and flowers in her front one. Paddy Burns's cow broke into the front garden one time and ate her flowers. Missus Brady broke the handle of her kitchen brush on the cow's back. She broke her hip when she fell off her bike after riding over a Protestant's dog on a Friday. Now she has to walk everywhere with a limp. The dog that knocked her down was a brown-and-white setter called Shep.

Crissy the widow lives on the same side of the lane just past the Bradys. When the whitewash flaked off the walls in patches, she covered the bare spots with yellowwash and now her house looks like a man with scabs on his face. Her garden is full of nettles and thistles, but my father says there are nice beds of flowers gone mad in there too. Crissy has a small hump and she is older than Missus Brady. She is always looking at her watch and listening to it ticking. She has four beehives, and my father says if she stopped annoying the bees every day she would have twice as much honey. Whenever she gets stung badly, she stays in the house and knits. Missus Brady says everything Crissy knits looks like a patch for something else. All the people who live on the lane try not to meet Crissy, because she talks about her bees and her dead husband in Africa and her knitting and her watch and Lieutenant Colonel Edwin Pickwoad all the time. Sometimes it is hard to know which one she is talking about.

Our house is on the right, about five hundred yards from Crissy's. My father is a farmer and my mother is a farmer's wife, but she does not milk cows. My father says that anyone who milks cows smells like a cow's elder all the time. I have one brother and two sisters – Jayjay, Becky and Ruthie. My father has eighty-two acres, and my mother has eighty-four turkeys. My father will tie the turkeys' legs together and bring them to the last market before Christmas in the horse's cart, with the wingboards off so people can feel the turkeys they want to buy. My mother told us there is a woman who sells fish in the market, and if she sees someone feeling her fish, she shouts out in a Dublin accent, "If ya don't want the fish, don't maul them." My father does not mind if people feel the turkeys to see how fat they are. When the county doctor examines me in the school with my shirt off, I feel how I think a turkey must feel when it's poked.

Our nearest neighbours are the Burnses and they live on the right side, too. Paddy Burns can take a piece of burning turf out of the fire with his fingers to light the tobacco in his pipe. "Another match saved," he says every time he does it, and he rubs the tips of his fingers on the leg of his trousers. There is always a rabbit skin hanging in the chimney drying out. One time Paddy made a little wooden man that danced on a board when he whistled. There's Tara Burns and Colleen Burns, but they don't play with us because they're older than we are. The Burnses eat black pudding on Sunday mornings with big pieces of gristle in it. Missus Burns cuts the bought bread too thick, and she puts a dollop of butter in the middle of the slice instead of spreading it. She never bakes her own bread. Benny Cosgrove lives with the Burnses, but every night he rides off to the Drennans to sleep. Paddy Burns has such a long moustache that he can whistle without anyone seeing him.

Crip Quigley lives by himself on the opposite side of the lane, about one hundred yards away from the Burnses. Crip's thatch is black and a part of the roof fell into his bedroom. When Crip had hens, they picked at the whitewash on the walls because they needed the lime to make their eggshells. Where the whitewash was gone, the rain ravelled the yellow mud that the walls are built with, and it ran down the front of the house like stuff out of sores on Peetie Gahan's face. Crip has no more hens. When he cut their beaks off to stop them from eating the whitewash, they couldn't eat anything else either and they died of the hunger. I have never seen Crip not wearing his cap.

You can't see Cha Finley's house from the road because he lives off in the fields on the left, and you have to go down a dark lane to get to it. His sister used to live with him, but she died all of a sudden just before the threshing one year.

Cha smokes a pipe and, when he's finished with a matchbox, he throws it in the kitchen window. There were twelve boxes in the window one time after only a week. I help Benny Cosgrove with the Sunday-morning jobs at Cha's house and I gather up the matchboxes and bring them to Sister Claire on Monday mornings. She makes them into little cars for prizes. The cars, except for the wheels, she covers with shiny, bright red paper that is the slipperiest thing I ever felt. It is as slippery as ice in the winter on the loughs of water on the lane. I won a car once, and it is still in the wall cupboard on the shelf over the flour sack. Paddy Burns says Cha Finley smokes more matches than tobacco. I was taller than Cha when I was eight. Billy Bates calls him Little Cha Horner, but not to his face. My father said that if he ever hears one of us calling Cha Finley that name, he will flail us alive. We are not even allowed to say the nursery rhyme.

You can't see the next house from the road either. Murt McHugh owns it, but his nephew, Bigword Billy Bates, lives in it by himself. When Murt McHugh dies, Bigword Billy will own the big house and the farm. He swims in the lake with nothing on, but he waits until all the people from the town are gone home. One time he swam with a whole crowd of tinkers. Billy Bates is his real name, but everyone calls him Bigword Billy, but not to his face. He uses big words that no one can understand. One day he said "negotiating", and he was talking about someone walking: "Crip Quigley was negotiating his way along the lane between the loughs of water," he said. Missus Brady said that, for all the big books he reads, Bigword Billy is a bit of an eegit, and that he got that way from living by himself out in the middle of nowhere in the silence.

Murt McHugh lives by himself in the big house at the

very end of the road. He is a very old man who is always dressed in a dirty gabardine coat with patches he sewed on himself. But his hat is always new. My father says Murt McHugh has done everything that can be done and that he knows everything that can be known. Murt used to hunt otters on a river in a flat-bottomed boat. When an otter bites something, it won't let go until it hears a bone cracking. Murt McHugh used to fill his wellington boots with coal cinders when he went hunting in case an otter got him by the leg. The cinder would crack and the otter would let go. Murt McHugh got the cinders from the furnace in the Convent School. My father said that Murt should have put cinders in his hat and then he wouldn't have got brain damage from the bite of an otter. I don't think an otter could put a man's head in its mouth. I saw a man in Duffys' Circus putting his head in a lion's mouth.

The last people on the lane are not people at all, and they don't live on the lane either. The lake is not far across the fields from our house, and two swans live on it. Missus Brady says the queen of England owns all the swans in the world. Everyone in Derrycloney likes to look at the swans gliding around in the water, especially after the young ones are hatched. No one would ever kill a swan, because it might be one of the Children of Lir. Swans always look sad.

Our road is a lane. In the summer it is dusty and in the winter it is mucky. When it rains, all the holes fill up with water. We can't whip tops because the lane is not smooth, and when we ride our bikes we get splashed and mucky. I wish our road was tarred like Wolfe Tone Street, where you could throw out buckets of water on a winter's night and have smooth ice to slide on the next morning. I could lie down all day on a tarred road, it would be so smooth and clean, and there would never be loughs of water on it, nor muck. I could ride my bike all day and not feel one bone-shaker, like when you ride into a pothole.

Our lane is the width of one horse's cart. There are two lines of grass between the three tracks made by the two wheels of the carts and the one made by the hooves of the horses and ponies and asses. There is a high hedge on each side. We can't play with a ball on the lane because the ball always gets lost. My father tells us to play ball in the fields, but then we get covered with cow dung. People in the town think people who live on lanes are dirty and smelly and thick.

I wish we had the electric light.

9. Paddy Burns

Ah, Jazus, Jazus, Jazus.

Fecking balls. And I just peeped out around the henhouse to make sure the road was clear before I drove out on the lane in d'ass-and-cart.

Can I not go up the fecking lane once in my life without meeting Missus Bloody Bitchy Brady?

Jazus fecking Jazus.

She must watch to see me driving out of the yard, and then grabs the bucket and the jug. I've a good mind to turn d'ass-and-cart around and go back, but then she'd be able to say I was afraid to face her, and Lizzie would ate d'arse offa me. I could stop d'ass and stand up in the cart and go through the motions of looking for something in my pockets, and then go back. Lizzie would still ate d'arse off me, and Missus Brady would still talk about it, say I was pretending even if I wasn't. I'll just put my head down and let d'ass jog past her, and if she says anything about Benny, I'll let her have it right, left and centre, and she won't know what hit her.

I hate her. I hate meeting her. You'd think Benny's fecking birthday was next week. She's a terrible badgering bitch of a woman. It's bad enough having my own Missus at me. Lizzie's worse than a badger trying to get a hen off a nest of eggs.

"Go up!"

It wasn't as if I wanted to come to Derrycloney in the first place, when Mick Cosgrove decided to die all of a sudden and leave Benny to fend for himself. What choice did we have, what with the Missus being the only aunt? If we hadn't come to take care of Benny, then everyone would have said what kind of people are we at all.

We've spent fifteen years slaving a living out of the forty-one acres for Benny Cosgrove; forty-one acres that grow nothing but buchalawns and rushes and thistles and buttercups and sedge grass a hacksaw wouldn't cut. And what's Missus Brady telling us after the years of living in muck and shite? Reminding me and the Missus every chance she gets that Benny's twenty-first birthday is on the twelfth of November, that we'll have to get up and go. Go where? Go where, I fecking well ask you?

We gave up our council house to rear Mick Cosgrove's child, and now that Benny's going to be old enough, we're to be left with nothing. I slaved for Benny as much as I worked for my own; slaved, and he only related on Lizzie's side. And when I'd be finished with my own work, I'd hire myself out like a fecking spalpeen to Johnny Glanvil to make a few miserable bob cutting his fecking hedges and stubbing his fecking furze.

"Ya'll have to do something about staying here," Lizzie keeps saying. "And what can I do?" I say to her. "Shoot Benny with Mick Cosgrove's oul shotgun and pretend he just died all of a sudden?"

"Go on up out of that!"

Missus Brady knows as well as anyone how much Lizzie and me worked for Mick Cosgrove's child. But she never lets a chance go by but she reminds me who the fecking oul land and the fecking oul house belong to. "Aye, Missus

Brady," says I to her, "it might belong to Benny, but not till the day he's fecking oul twenty-one."

Anyhow, anyone as thick as Benny isn't entitled to own a farm. He's the thickest child I ever met; never has anything to say. He just looks at you with those stupid brown eyes and says nothing. A bloody bullock after getting hit between the ears with a sledgehammer is what he looks like.

"Get to feck up out of that."

Missus Brady just never forgave me for the time the cow broke into her front garden. She was livid. She et the face offa me, and the whole time she murdering the cow with her kitchen brush. I never saw anyone in such a rage, and the cow ploughing around through her flower beds with her big hooves, walking down anything she hadn't eaten already. Missus Brady cursed me and cursed the cow. She only got worse when I toult her it was her own fault for not having a better fence around the garden. She followed me up the lane when I turned the cow out, and she screeching like a hen facing a rat. I got fed up with her. "They were only fecking oul flowers," I shouted at her. That made her worse than ever. "Fecking oul flowers!" she screamed. "Fecking oul flowers!" She followed me the whole way up to the tober field, lashing me with her tongue all the time. Ever since then she says "fecking oul" as often as she can when she sees me. "Yer fecking oul cow was on the lane by herself this morning," she says. "Did ya get in yer fecking oul turnips yet?" she'll ask me. It's your fecking oul ass and your fecking oul this and your fecking oul that. Everything belonging to me is a fecking oul something. She's like a dog with the same oul bone it's been chewing on for years. There's the swans flying.

"Go up!"

You'd think she was as pure as the driven snow herself;

thinks she's a fecking martyr for taking care of Benny when the mother died the year before the father. Well, charity begins at home, Missus Martyr Brady, and you ran out on your own when they needed you; waltzed out and left your oul father and mother and married a man whose first wife wasn't coult yet.

"Go up to hell out of that!"

She didn't so much marry Jim as leave her father and mother to fend for themselves, and neither of them able to walk with rheumatism and old age. But she'd never let on about that, never say she married Jim just to escape the Irish Slavery. Well, Missus Perfect Brady, you escaped your father's and mother's old age and rheumatism all right, but you jumped right into Jim Brady's frying pan, sizzling with bitterness and crossness and coarseness. Jim's so coarse he'd strip a winter's coating of shite off a cowhouse wall with one blow of his breath.

I hate facing her. If it's not her, it's Lizzie. Neither of them will leave me alone. If Missus Brady starts anything I'll let her have it straight between the eyes. I've a good mind to call in to Jim-the-husband, the dirty oul shite, and tell him to keep a tighter rein on his Missus, stop her from going around the country talking about people. But I'd be only pissing into the wind. "Stick it up the hair of yer arse," he'd say, like he says about everything.

God! Will you listen to Quigley's cow bawling to be milked! Someone should tie a bit of twine around Crip's mickey and let him see what it feels like.

The oul cow! Her skin is the colour of ashes off bad turf, and it wrinkled worse than a bull's ball-bag on a coult day; her grey hair all tied up in a pile, ready to fall down and make her into a witch at a second's notice; the snuff rag always in her hand, and she pretending for years it's her handkerchief. She's been on the snuff since she came to Derrycloney, but she'd never admit that either; as thin as a snipe, but she spends her pennies on snuff. She calls it white pepper: "I have to go up town for me white pepper," she says, as if she was the head cook in Buckingham Palace, and she with nothing but spuds and onions to put in her pot.

"Go up, ya fecking lazy ass! Go up!"

Just because she took care of Benny for a few months after the mother died in childbirth, she thinks she's his fecking guardian angel. Well, I'll tatter her tail feathers if she says as much as one word to me. Twenty more yards to go, and she's stopped walking, thinks she's going to make me stop to talk, to listen to her fecking oul shite, that ugly Irish terrier at her feet looking like he had the mange, his balls hanging out real impudent-like, as if he was the only one in the universe with a pair. If Missus Saint Brady only knew what Lizzie did last night, and what I have in my pocket this very minute, and where I'm going with it, she'd flail Lizzie and me alive. It sounded like a good idea in the dark, but in the light of morning it didn't sound so good at all. But once Lizzie gets a notion into her head! She'd nag the shite out of a bound-up bishop.

"Go up! Go on!"

Jazus, she's limping out into the middle of the road, her hand up like a guard stopping traffic in Dublin. She's saying something that's drowning in the sounds of the wheels, and the draughts and the tacklings and the crossness that's in me. She's behind that wall of water again.

"Go on up out of that!"

She's still trying to get into my way. I'll pretend to go right at her and then I'll swerve around behind her, go between her and the ditch, and feck the dog if he gets in the way.

"Go up! Go up!"

Feck. I'm going to hit her with the wheel. Will you get out of my way, you fecking oul bitch! She's still talking to me, still holding up the hand.

"Go on!"

As I swerve around Missus Brady, the dog yelps and jumps into the ditch, falls down through the briars and long grass, disappears. Something comes out of me, but the rage at her is so pent up in me, like a held-in shite, that I don't know what I'm shouting. All that counts is I didn't hit her. But I left the oul bitch tottering, nearly falling into the ditch on the other side of the road. Feck her, and feck her dog, too. Jazus!

10. Missus Brady

Suffering duck! Here's Paddy Burns.

I can never go up or down the lane but I run into him. He does it on purpose: sees me going for the water and then sets out to make me nervous, makes me move over on the lane, get out of his way. He has to show me he has more of a right to the lane than I do. He's like all men, the way they wish they could go around peeing like a dog on bushes and clumps of tall grass. Well, maybe I wasn't born near this place, and maybe I'm only living on the lane for nineteen years, and maybe I'm not related to Benny Cosgrove, and maybe I don't stand to pee, but I'll stand up to anyone who's mistreating Benny, and that includes fecking oul Paddy Burns and his fecking oul Lizzie, that thrower of gristle on other people's plates, that dolloper of butter on thick cuts of bread.

Benny was my child for a while, and only for his father's stubbornness he could still be mine, instead of having Paddy and Lizzie Burns bossing him around and kicking him out of the house when it's time to go to bed.

Paddy and Lizzie – they never gave Benny half a chance. When they moved into the house they treated him like he wasn't there. They think he's thick. He's not thick at all, but I won't say he's normal. But how could he be normal?

When the mother died giving birth to a stillborn, Benny was barely five, and less than a year after that his father was dead.

The Burnses were like two big icebergs moving in and, as far as I can tell, Benny has just bobbed around in their coldness ever since like a cork in the water. All he was to them was a snot-nosed child who stood in the dark corner of the kitchen not talking. The Burnses' own two girls aren't the warmest of things in the universe either. Every time I meet them I think I hear ice cracking.

If Paddy and Lizzie had only thought about it! Here was Benny, his mother and father dead and buried in a year, with four strangers moving into his house. Even his own bed was taken away and given to his cousin. A sack of straw in the corner of the kitchen and an oul topcoat for a blanket was what he got. No wonder he hardly talked: still doesn't and he almost twenty-one.

Where could Paddy be going at this time of day in the ass-and-cart? I thought he was cutting Johnny's hedges, and he only goes to town on Fridays for the messages. I'd swear he had the ass yoked to the cart for hours, was peeping around the corner of the henhouse waiting for me to step out on the lane. For a man who shows signs of being clever, sometimes Paddy does terrible eegity things.

Since I started talking to him about Benny's twenty-first birthday, Paddy's been nudging me, poking at me in such a sly way that, if I stood up to him, he'd drop his jaw all innocent-like and ask me what I was talking about. I hate it when someone won't come out and fight in the open. I hate a sniper going around sniping at you all the time until you want to wring his neck. Fecking oul flowers! I'll give him fecking oul till the day he moves out of Derrycloney, and there's no doubt in my mind but that he and Lizzie and their two stuck-up girls will move out of Derrycloney on the day Benny is twenty-one.

The only thing the daughters have to be stuck up about is the dunghape out in the haggard, and it's not even a big one at that.

There's the sound of the swans flying. And there they go, swooping over Crip's house on their way to the lake.

I'll never forget the day poor Kitty Cosgrove died. The father sent Benny up the lane to get me, and I ran down all the way, because that was before I broke my hip. But when I stepped around the windbreaker wall, the excitement was knocked out of me by the sight of Benny's father sitting over at the fire that wasn't going. It took everything I had to make myself turn right and take the few steps to the bedroom door.

There's something terribly ghosty about a room where there's a dead woman in a bloody bed and a dead infant beside her lying like a just-born piglet, that terrible purple ropey thing coming out of its belly. That's what I walked in on years ago in Mick Cosgrove's house. Kitty was as white as flour before the War. I didn't know whether to look at Lizzy or the child, and the last thing I wanted to do in the world was look at either of them.

That's the kind of hatchet blow to the skull that anyone should get only once in a lifetime. It staggered me. I can't imagine what it did to Benny! Poor Benny! the way he looked up at me when I came out of the room into the kitchen. I thought it would be easier to stick a knife in his heart than have to tell him his mother was dead, the father with his back to us, sitting and leaning in over the cold fire, his head in his hands.

In the cemetery at the funeral, Benny held on to my hand the whole time and, even though he wouldn't have been near me if we hadn't been standing at the edge of his mother's grave, I have to admit that the child's hand in mine gave me such a feeling that I was almost – almost, mind you – I was almost glad that Kitty had died. Even though the five-year-oul child was broken-hearted and whimpering beside me, I was almost glad that he was, because if he wasn't I would never have felt the feeling I got from his little hand in mine; it was so soft and small, so trusting.

Mick, the father, was drunk; wife dead and a young son depending on him who couldn't be depended on for anything. He was across the grave from us doing everything he could to look sober. But the harder he tried the more plastered he looked, weaving about at the hips like he was trying to keep the top part of his body from falling off the bottom part, like a circus clown balancing spinning plates on top of a pole sitting on his chin.

The poor child – Benny – kept pulling me nearer the grave as the coffin was lowered. The noise the men made when they pulled out the lowering ropes didn't break his stare, and he never even noticed them picking up their shovels and stabbing at the mound of clay. Maybe he didn't even see the first shovelful going down until it exploded on top of his mother. He nearly left the ground with the fright, and at the same time a wail came out of him that curled the hair on the back of my neck. That cry at his mother's grave was the cry of a child who knows the protecting hand is gone, that there is nothing between him and the pain of the world.

There's Crip's cow bawling from the pain in her elder to be milked.

After the mother was buried, I took in Benny. I can't say it was Jim and myself who took in the child, because it was from Jim's twisted tongue that I had to protect Benny. He tormented the child non-stop; when he'd be finished lighting his pipe, holding the lighted match out to Benny and telling him to stick that into the hair in his arse – a five-year-old child. And then that terrible two-line song he used to sing at him:

> I stuck my nose up a nanny-goat's hole,
> And the stink, it nearly blinded me.

The dirty oul bugger. Jeering at me, too, whenever he saw me mothering the child; asking if I could feel the milk flowing.

I had Benny for nearly a year. I could still ride the bike then, and every morning I'd take him to school on the carrier over the back wheel. The feeling I used to get when he'd wrap his arms around my waist so he wouldn't fall off! It was like the feeling in the cemetery. It was the best feeling I ever had in my life. And then there were the little things he started doing that made the feeling stronger; he'd run to me with his arms out, wanting me to take him in my arms and squeeze him, his arms around my neck like he was holding on to something solid in teeming water. He'd snuggle up to me on the form against the windbreaker wall when we'd be sitting at the kitchen fire after supper. The feeling I used to get! It was like he loved me. It was the greatest feeling I ever felt. It's the only time in my life I felt entirely loved.

Suffering duck! Paddy's galloping the ass, beating it with the reins. He looks like he's in a terrible hurry and he's a lot closer than . . . Bloody into it! He's going to run over me. I'll get over to this side of the road.

"Cinders. Come over here, ya stupid eegit of a dog. Paddy, will ya slow down and let me get out of yer way. Yer ass-and-cart is going to knock me down. Me hip, me hip!"

As he's going by, I shout out to him, "What's wrong with

ya at all, Paddy?" and I declare to God he cursed at me. He called me an oul cunt. I'd swear to God that's what he shouted at me. "Get out of me way, y'oul cunt." Sweet Jesus tonight, and no one has ever used that word to me before, not even Jim. What's wrong with Paddy at all?

"Cinders, Cinders, where are you? Where did ya . . ?" Y'oul cunt! Holy mother of God.

11. Billy Bates

Will you look at Johnny looking through the far hedge at Missus Brady negotiating her way down the lane between the loughs of water, like she was the *Titanic* dodging icebergs. Even though I can only see her grey head, I can see her limping from here, the way the head snaps to one side then to the other, limping down to Johnny's for the water and the milk and the chat on the little hob. I'd swear Kate uses boot polish on that hob, always shining.

Will you look at Johnny hiding behind the whitethorns, and one of the children with him? He's always hiding somewhere. It's a fact beyond a doubt that I can never go up or down the lane without Johnny seeing me and with me never seeing Johnny. He's like a corncrake that way; you know he's out there somewhere, but you can never see him. But it's not only Johnny! Someone is watching me the whole length of the lane when I'm on it. First, it's Quigley if he's up, from behind the hedge in his haggard or from under his pissing bush in the yard or from behind his webby kitchen window; and then Lizzie or Paddy Burns from behind the curtain on their kitchen window, or through the barn door open a crack at the end of the yard; and then Kate or Johnny from a hundred places, pighouse windows, behind bushes, over walls, through the crack where the two big gates meet in the middle, from behind an apple tree in the garden; and then Crissy, although I wouldn't give a standing fart about Crissy; she's as thick as a double ditch, and it's a long time since any sunlight got through to her. And then Missus Brady always at her door or in her flower garden, or coming down the lane to chat with Kate, or home from her job in Doctor Mansfield's clinic.

The only one who doesn't see me on the lane is Cha Finley down in the fields. Alias Little Cha Horner.

> Little Cha Horner
> Sat in his corner,
> While his sister counted the sheep.
> His eyes he did wipe,
> Put his thumb on her pipe,
> And sent her for ever to sleep.

They all hate it when I recite my rhyme, afraid someone will understand and tell the guards and get poor Cha hung.

Duncle Murt at the end of the lane seldom if ever sees me on the lane, but he knows every shagging move I make because he's in charge of the purse. I can't buy a loaf of bread without asking him for the money, and then he knows I'm going up town, knows I'm going as far as Eamon's Emporium, knows who I'll see on the way, and knows I won't go any farther than Eamon's because I have no reason to go any farther, because I have no money left out of the price of the loaf. He gives me the exact thing; no change left over to be saved. He even knows the price of a jar of Bovril, the smallest one; he'd never lay out the price of a big jar – wouldn't have someone else using his money while all that Bovril is sitting in the dark in the cupboard doing nothing. "Big jar, me arse," he said to me once. "All them oul rich ones in England at the opera with me money in their pockets and their Bovril sitting in the dark . . ." and on and on he goes *ad nauseam, ad infinitum, in aeternum, in perpetua,* while I'm standing there with my hand out like I'm a frigging tinker begging. *In manus tuas, Domine,* and I'm forty-shagging-two.

I nearly forgot Jim Brady, but he doesn't count, the contrary old bollicks.

There's Crip's cow bawling. Still in bed *post meridian,* the lazy hure. No wonder the country's broke, with farmers like him around. But he's never this late. Maybe the cow's bulling. Another two and six for the use of Johnny's bull. I'd love to be that bull, with all the cows and heifers coming to me. I'd bull their brains out. The size of its balls, the length of its mickey, red and glistening. Sometimes, when I see it plunging into the cow, I get all excited myself, and I think of doing it to the Hippwell One. Better stop that. Can't piss and be hard at the same time.

This is the first chance I ever got to watch Johnny watching someone else. This is how he looks when he's looking at me. Look at him now, and he pulling the child down so Missus Brady won't see them when she comes to the low spot in the hedge. Will you look at them, almost bent double!

Aye, she has the bucket with her; everyone knows Missus Brady's white enamel bucket as well as they know Cinders. The first thing she'll do when she gets to Glanvils' is fill the bucket at the pump and put it on the road outside the wicket door. It's grand water. Clear as diamonds. Then she'll go in to have the chinwag with Kate – talk about other people – laugh at them is more like it. She's a great laugher at other people, Missus Brady. If she laughs at other people to me, then I know she laughs about me to other people. So I try not to say anything too thick in front of her. Whenever I'm talking to her I feel like I felt when I was a chap talking to a strict nun. She thinks the little job she has cleaning Mansfield's clinic once a week makes her important; calls herself Doctor Mansfield's housekeeper. She likes to make things about herself sound very grand. Veritably pavonine she is as she goes up to clean the doctor's furniture and floors, all bedighted in her mangy fox-collared coat she bought at a *marché aux puces*. But, if you ask me, she's one sixteenth of an inch above scullery maid. Anything I ever read about a scullery maid had her with a red and runny nose, red and cracked hands, buck teeth and red hair – "While greasy Joan doth keel the pot" – maybe cockeyed, too. Ugly as a mushroom growing in a tree. Missus Brady would blow you to hell altogether about de Lacy Hall. She didn't *work* in de Lacy Hall – she was *employed* in the kitchen of de Lacy Hall before she got married. She has never come out and said she was or wasn't the cook, but how many times has she told us all about the lobsters crying when they were dropped alive into the scalding water to be boiled for the big nobs? de Lacy Hall! I'd swear her accent changes when she talks about it. She gets a bit English. And we all think she only peeled potatoes and washed the plates in the kitchen. "When I was employed in de Lacy Hall. The crying lobsters of de Lacy Hall. The gardeners in de Lacy Hall." And then, "Mister de Lacy of de Lacy Hall," she almost whispers, as if he were God. There's her story about the time the electric was put into de Lacy Hall, how all the people in the village climbed up Begses' Hill to look down on the illumination, and everyone said de Lacy Hall was like a big ship out on the sea in the dark, and not one of them would know a ship if it fell on them.

There's the swans wheeling in towards the lake after their daily fly, exercising the wings. I'd love to be able to fly like a swan.

I asked Missus Brady one time why she fills the bucket first thing and puts it outside the wicket door before she goes in to the hob. "Himself can be gruff at times," says she, meaning Johnny of course, "and I like to get away quick when he comes into the kitchen."

Everyone knows Cinders pisses in the white enamel bucket, three or four real quick shots, but nobody will ever tell Missus Brady. It's everyone's way of getting a laugh at her. I saw the young Glanvil lads laughing at him colouring her tea water one day with a couple of good yellow squirts, his stub tail up in the air and his balls hanging out, like he was daring all the fuckers in the world to do anything about it.

She has to leave Cinders on the lane because he runs after Kate's hens, pulls the feathers out of their tails and the hens gone mad; you'd hear them cackling in Timbuktu, and Cinder's mouth full of red feathers – Rhode Island Reds.

By God, I nearly missed that; look at Paddy Burns passing the field gate and he beating the shite out of d'ass with the end of the reins. I heard the cart before I saw it and knew it was Paddy. D'ass is in a gallop, but she won't keep that up for long; short and sweet like an ass's gallop, like they say. The best way to keep an ass galloping is to yank up her tail and stick a bunch of nettles under it. The more she squeezes her tail against the stinging, the more she keeps the nettles from falling out. We did that when we were young; you do cruel things when you're a lad; blew up frogs with a straw up their holes, too. Paddy should know better. D'ass'll stop galloping in a minute and Paddy can beat her to death with the reins and the most he'll get out of her is a trot. They say an ass has more brains than a horse because a horse will run till it drops dead; an ass will lie down in the road – still in the shafts of the cart – if it can't go any farther. It happened to me once coming home from the bog. Paddy's gone behind the hedge again, and now all I can hear is the jangling of the wheels and the tacklings and the draughts.

Ah, Johnny has heard Paddy, too. He won't have to look to know whose cart it is. Everyone knows the sound of everyone else's chains, but look at him easing up to peep out again. He's keeping the child out of sight while he watches.

Someone shouted something and Johnny ducks back down real quick. You'd swear he was playing cowboys and Indians and that he just saw an Indian. It must have been Paddy shouting at Missus Brady, but what the shag did he say? I didn't hear her saying anything. But maybe she started at him about Benny's birthday again. She's been needling him all year about it, even in front of other people, telling him the house isn't his, that the day Benny turns twenty-one the good times will be over.

Missus Brady's head has stopped moving and she's looking up the road after Paddy. The sounds of d'ass-and-cart are gone before she turns around and heads off for Glanvils' again. God, I'm getting cramps in my shagging knees.

Missus Brady goes about fifty yards before Johnny stands up again and starts swinging the billhook at the whitethorns, the child picking up the bushes and throwing them on the pile. He's a terrible man to work, always at it, and he has the children working since they could drag a bucket after them. He can't stand to see someone doing nothing.

Last spring, on the Saturday night de Valera came to make a speech for the elections, Johnny was sowing turnips with his new turnip barrow – still all yellow and green with newness and he as proud as Punch – off over at the Commons Road and the oldest lad, Liam, with him driving the horse. He didn't need the child at all – it's more a hindrance than a help to divide up the driving of the horse and the steering of an implement. Everyone in the country was in the town to see Dev, whether they agreed with him or not, just because he's so famous and escaped from an English jail. I was there myself without a penny in my pocket because Duncle said, "Ya don't have to have money in yer pocket to look at a man." I'll never forget it, and all the lads going in for a pint when it was all over, and I had to come home feeling like a shagging eegit. Johnny and Liam could hear the speechification in the loudspeakers, and the child kept asking to be let go up town to see Dev. In the end, Johnny got so fed up of hearing the child whining that he shouted, "Dev Alera won't sow our turnips." And the poor child had to work till ten with the sounds in the sky reminding him that every child in his school except himself was seeing Dev.

I'd swear Johnny runs Missus Brady off the little hob because he can't bear to see her sitting down talking and keeping Kate from doing her work.

That's the oldest one he has with him, Becky or Ruthie — why they gave their girls Protestant names is beyond me — I can never remember which is which. She's a quare one, the oldest daughter. At the end of last spring I came across her up the lane the far side of Missus Brady's with her bike lying in the middle of the road. She was kneeling in the muck beside a lough and she holding a hen's head in the water. The rest of the hen was in a sack. When she saw me, she let such a shriek out of her that I could feel it in my balls. Into the basket on the front of her bike she threw the bag with the hen, and off home she took like a squirt out of a duck. Maybe there's something wrong with her, but I'll tell you one thing, she can throw bushes. That pile must be six feet high and she's still throwing them up. But she'll soon have to leave them beside the pile and let Johnny finish the job for her. There's nothing worse than a big spread-out pile of bushes when you go to burn them in the spring. You spend all your time throwing bushes in on the fire, and you end up with all kinds of aches and pains from the heat of the fire and the cold of the air. I've often paid for it for standing too long at a big fire in a field in the cold weather. It nearly killed Duncle one time. Pity it didn't, the tight shagger – tight as a bull's hole in August.

I can hear the twack of Johnny's billhook a second after he hits the whitethorns. That means there's no wetness in the air. I'd say I'll hear the train tonight off out at Derlamogue Bridge. I love hearing it in the middle of the night. It's a grand sound, the train off out there in the cold of the night and me snug in the bed in the dark by myself; snug as a bug in a rug, as they say. I wonder what it's like to be snuggled up to a woman. I'd be sticking out the whole time. I'd have to keep turned away from her so she wouldn't feel it in her back like a stick. "What are ya poking me with a stick in bed for?" she'd say, and I'd have to explain to her it wasn't a stick at all.

There's Missus Brady passing the field gate – thin as a rake handle – and she must hear the sound of Johnny's twacks too. She's not an eegit; she has to know now he was behind the hedge the whole time, but Johnny couldn't waste any more time waiting for her to get out of earshot.

Johnny and the daughter watched her, and now I'm watching her. If someone's not watching me, I'm watching them. If I'm not watching anyone, then someone is watching me. That's why I'm always careful about where I take a shite.

There goes the hand with the bit of a flour sack to the nose – a good snort of the snuff before she goes into Kate's kitchen. How many times has she gone up and down the road for the water, hiding that snuff rag in her hand, taking a snort at the last minute? A thousand times, or two thousand? More altogether! Say she's here with Jim-the-husband for twenty years. That's ten times three-hundred-and-sixty-five, and two times that is two times nought is nought, and dum dum and hum and that's seven thousand three hundred. Seven thousand three hundred times! And that's only one way. Counting up and down the road, it's nought nought six fourteen thousand. Fourteen thousand six hundred times. It's a good job she doesn't walk in the same place every day or she'd have a path two feet deep worn into the road.

It's a wonder people don't wear their legs down to stumps from walking.

There she goes, behind the far side of the house. I'd better get going. God! My knees are killing me, but at least there's still enough soft grass around to clean my arse with. There's a good piece over there. I hate having to waddle like a dwarf duck on my hunkers with my arse hanging out to get a piece of good grass. It's only when I wait too long to have a shite that I forget to get a handful of grass first. Grass or no grass, there's nothing like a good shite. That's what I always say; nothing like a good shite. A man could have all the money in the world and not be able to make a good shite and then what good would it do him? But if he had a lot of money he could buy fruit. They say fruit keeps you regular. Nothing like a good shite, fruit or no fruit. Cha Finley should eat an apple now and then and he wouldn't be passing out on his dunghape from forcing. They say a man could blow a blood vessel in his brain from forcing, and kill himself. "Died from Forcing", the paper would say.

I wish I had someone, even if it was only a child, to be out in the fields with me. It gets terrible lonely out here betimes.

12. *Johnny Glanvil*

How many times has Kate asked me why I hide when I see someone coming?

"It's not right to be always hiding like that," she says. "Every time the children see ya doing it, yer teaching them to do it too. And as well as that, I don't know how ya ever got married if ya were always hiding behind a bush."

"It was pure love that made me come out from behind the bush to ask ya, as well as them legs of yours," I tell her, and that wobbles her train of thought around the tracks, makes her blush, and she tells me to stop it – "The children will hear ya," she says.

I'm never sure what to say when someone talks to me; that's why I hide. And whenever I do talk to someone, I spend the rest of the day thinking about what I said, wondering did they take what I said the wrong way, or if I gave away too much, or if the person thought I was trying to hide something, or if I said something that could be turned into gossip with my name attached to it: "Johnny Glanvil said this about ya."

I'm not quick with a clever lie when I don't want to give the right answer, like when Bigword asks me the price I got for a bullock or a cow. That fellow's always rushing in where angels fear to tread, as they say. You'd think from the education he has and from all the reading he does he would have come across people who were tactful, would have learned something from them. The few years he was in the seminary did him more harm than good. He'd blow your cap off with his jawbreakers that no one understands. He must have a great dictionary, a bigger one than the one we got from Sister de Monfort, I'm sure. There's Crip's cow bawling.

It's when Bigword asks something he shouldn't that I feel at a loss for words altogether. But when Becky asked me just now why are we hiding, I was able to come up with a quick one: "If Missus Brady stops to talk we'd have to stop working to listen to her and we'd never get the hedge breasted." It's easier to cod a child with a lie. But you'd think I'd be used to Missus Brady by now, know how to talk to her.

I never even stopped to think when I saw her coming; I just hid like I always do, like a rabbit running for cover when it hears footsteps. I should have kept cutting away and said hello to her; it'll take her ages to pass by and walk out of earshot of the billhook.

Missus Brady is a real odd one, so nice one minute and like a scalded cat the next. I don't know what I'd do if she ever talked to me the way she talks to Paddy Burns. She's been throwing mouthfuls of broken glass and rusty fishhooks at Paddy for nearly a year now. Whenever she hears him coming in d'ass-and-cart she must sharpen her tongue like Jack the Giant Killer with his hatchet before he went out to kill the giant. But then, the miserableness of Jim-the-husband is a grindstone always spinning around, for ever keeping a fine edge on her tongue. Maybe when she leaves the house she's always trying to stop her tongue from cutting people, always trying but not able to do it, like

when she sees Paddy Burns. I'd hate to have her splitting
the air around my head with her pointed comments and
the slashing tones of her voice. She's the quickest one I ever
knew with such a cutting tongue and with such quickness
to use it.

I wonder what her jabs about Benny's birthday are doing
to Paddy and the missus, reminding them they all have to
move out of the house when Benny turns twenty-one;
asking Paddy where he's going to live when Benny comes
of age. She's not showing any mercy for Paddy's Lizzie
either, asking her the same questions, and everyone knowing
they're not questions at all.

I feel bad for poor oul Paddy. He only has seven weeks
left. When they came to live there, fifteen years ago, it
looked as if 1947 would never come. It was like Hong
Kong; 1997 is so far away no one thinks it will ever come;
they think that the English will be there for ever. That's how
Paddy and Lizzie must have thought when they moved in
to take care of Mick Cosgrove's child; they'd be there for
ever.

There's the sound of the swans flying, but I can't see them
from here. The one note they make with their wings is like
a child blowing the same sound over and over on a tin
whistle.

Everyone, not just me, liked Paddy before he ever moved
into Derrycloney. Everyone in the town and countryside
knows him, and he must have worked for anyone who ever
needed a man for a few days. He could, and would, work
at anything. He'd be a slanesman on the bog one day, and
the next be on his knees weeding a drill of potatoes in
someone's field; from tradesman to labourer and he never
cared. I've seen him making chairs and tables and even an
ass's cart, and I've seen him up to his knees in muck cleaning

out a drain. He even made a yoke for making ropes out of binder twine — all moving parts and handles; sent away for a government leaflet and made it from the plan. He's a great worker and a nice man. But Lizzie-the-wife is a different story.

Lizzie's cruel. Even the way she treats d'ass when she thinks no one is looking; beating it on the head with the knobby end of an ash plant. I saw her giving Benny such a beating one time out at the back of the house that I had to make a loud cough to let her know someone was going to see her. Even the way she throws the food on the table for her family, big thick slices of bread with a lump of pale country butter that's too salty stuck to the middle, as if to say, "Spread your own bloody butter." Mugs of tea with too little milk that would burn the lips off you. And the black puddings with pieces of gristle in them big enough to choke a cat! Where does she buy the stuff? Why doesn't she poke the gristle out with a fork and throw it on the fire before she puts the pudding on the table?

Jakers! Here's Paddy's ass-and-cart on the road, the chains jangling like the ass was galloping. I'd hate it if he saw me hiding from Missus Brady. He'd be bound to say something.

"Becky, sit on yer hunkers and don't say one word till Paddy goes by."

I should have told her to put her fingers in her ears, too. Jakers! I hope she didn't hear what Paddy shouted at Missus Brady. He must be terrible cross with her altogether.

"Get out of me way, y'oul cunt."

That's terrible. I never heard Paddy using a bad word like that before. He must be completely fed up with Missus Brady going on about Benny's birthday. Wait till I tell Kate. She won't believe it. I wonder will Missus Brady tell her.

I don't think Kate knows what "cunt" means.

13. Crip Quigley

There's the swans up in the sky somewhere, but I don't even look up to find them. The eyes are gone to hell.

I can hear Paddy Burns's ass-and-cart up the lane, but I can't see sight nor light of it. That's another thing Bride bothers me with, the eyes. She must have seen me squinting, when squinting was a help.

"Ye'll have to get glasses," says she.

"Glasses?" says I. "Glasses! And what would I be doing under a cow milking and wearing glasses. For God's sake, woman," says I, "everyone would be calling me professor and laughing their heads off at me. Glasses me arse!"

Will you listen to that frigging cow. She'd waken the dead. You'd think she'd be used to a full bag by now.

Since I started not being able to see very far, my hearing has got very keen. I haven't told anyone about what I do be hearing in the sky since the eyes got weak or they'd think I was mad. Nobody else must hear it or I'd have heard them talking about it.

I know Paddy's galloping d'ass, because I can hear her hooves on the lane and from the jangling. The gallop won't last long, though, because, like they say: short and sweet like an ass's gallop. It's an ill wind that blows no one good. See! I remembered it. That happens to me sometimes; I won't be able to remember something and then it's suddenly in my head hopping to get out. It's an ill wind that blows no one good. Oul Mangan taught us that one in the Boys' School and, when no one in the class could tell him what it meant, he told us we were all thick.

"Yee crowd of thick eegits," says he, and he red in the face. Then he told us our fathers and mothers were thick, too. "That's why yeer all so thick," says he. And then he told us to ask our fathers and mothers what it meant – it's an ill wind that blows no one good – "And that'll prove they're thick, when none of yee can tell me the answer in the morning," he says. He was from Cork or from somewhere where they talk funny.

The next morning we all knew what it meant. And when oul Mangan had finished examining us, Gussie McNee put up his hand and said, "Sir, sir."

"Yee can go, McNee," says Mangan without looking up, meaning Gussie could go outside and do his water in the hedge.

"I don't want to go, sir," says Gussie.

"Then what do yee want?" says oul Mangan.

"Me father told me to tell ya, sir, that if ya call him or me mudder thick again, that he'll kick the jow out of ya."

Gussie McNee's father would put his left arm under the belly of a twenty-stone pig and grab its tail with his right hand. Then he'd throw it up into the back of a horse's cart, four feet off the ground. That was his job. He'd go with the jobber from Shamrock Meats and, when the jobber bought a pig from a farmer, Gussie's father collected the pigs. He was as well put together as a pair of pliers and every bit as vicious. Everyone who knew McNee's father said he et a plateful of six-inch nails for his breakfast every day.

When Gussie made his speech, everyone in the class

laughed behind their hands. Oul Mangan got all red and said nothing. He never called us thick eegits again, never mind our fathers and mothers. It's an ill wind that blows no one good. Another one about the wind was, no weather is ill when the winds are still; but that's not right if the rain is coming straight down for a month, not a slant on it.

This is the longest water I ever took in my life. But, then again, I always make a water as long as a bullock's in winter when I get up, that's if I haven't done it in the mattress in the middle of the night. The good thing about watering here under the elder bush is that I can see what's happening on the lane at the same time; well, not see too far. But at least I can have a good listen while I water. I save time that way. Kill two birds with one stone, is what oul Mangan would call this, watering and listening; killing two birds. I wonder do they teach those old sayings any more in the school. I'd say everyone must have forgotten them, everyone except myself and all the lads in oul Mangan's class. Other ones with birds in them were: a bird in the hand is worth two in the bush; birds of a feather flock together; one swallow does not a summer make; the early bird catches the worm; when the north wind doth blow and we shall have snow, then what shall the robin do then, poor thing; but that's not an old saying. That's a . . .

Good Christ! There's Paddy shouting. Jow! and I can't see a frigging thing. What did he shout? Who did he shout at? Maybe d'ass shied and nearly went into the ditch. I never heard him shouting in my life before.

Whist! All I hear is the trot of the ass, so she's not in the ditch with Paddy and the cart on top of her. But she's not galloping any more. Under the elder bush I'm listening, and I don't even know yet that I've stopped watering so I can hear better – just goes to show you that you can't hold two turnips in one hand or you can't whistle and chew oats at the same time. The sound of Paddy's ass-and-cart goes off into the distance and I can't hear anything up the road at all.

I like that feeling I get all over after a great relief, after I finish watering. I feel like my bladder has shrunk and that a big part of my guts has slipped back into its real place. Still and all, despite the nice feeling, I'm cagey enough to glance over my shoulder, to look down the lane, to make sure that old bollicks, Murt McHugh, isn't sloping along the grass verge beside the hedge. He caught me once, a few years ago, but, as they say, once bitten twice shy. Oul Mangan again.

The time he did snake up on me, Murt nearly frightened the jow out of me. He thought he was being real smart and funny, like he always thinks he is. There I was, watering away, in amaze like a pig pissing, as Mangan would have said if he could say that word, and I thinking of nothing, when Murt suddenly started talking beside my ear. I watered all over my front and inside my trousers, because I stuffed my mickey back in before I could stop. My two hands were drenched. "Yel have great berries on that elder bush next year," says he. "Yel be able to make great elderberry wine, Crip. Elderberry wine, with a taste of urine," says he, and he laughing like a jackass, laughing at me wetting myself with my own water, rubbing my hands in d'arse of my trousers. "Jazus, Crip, ya could join the fire brigade with a mickey like that," says he, and he looked like a jackass again. His laugh is more like a jeering snigger than anything else – it comes out through his nose like a goose hissing.

I'll never forgive the old bollicks for that time they all came to help me with the mare, to get her up off the stable floor. She'd been lying down for three days. Johnny made a big sling out of sacks and ropes, and pushed it under the mare. Then he tied the four pulley wheels he borrowed from the maltings to the poles in the roof. Of course, all Murt did was give directions to everyone else. When we hoisted the mare up on her feet, the first thing she did was the biggest water I've ever seen an animal doing in my life. It was like it was pouring out of a bucket that was tipped over. And the colour of it! It was so yellow it was almost green. Everyone jumped back out of the splashes, and then Murt says in that know-it-all voice of his, "Stick yer lip under that, Crip, and get a good dose of vitriol for yer consumption." He only said it to make a laugh of me, to show how smart he was, and I could hear the others sniggering behind my back, too. The old bollicks! No one in my family ever had consumption.

I try never to say much to Murt McHugh. He knows everything, and nobody else knows anything. But he's not as smart as he thinks he is, and the rest of us do a bit of jeering up our sleeves at him. There was that time he was up in Nelligan's Pub after closing time when the guards raided the place. Murt was sitting up on a high stool at the bar, and he thought he was different from everyone else because himself and the sergeant always went duck hunting in the winter down at the lake, hiding for hours in the bushes, frightening the swans to death; a terrible cold way to spend your time, if you ask me, ducks or no ducks.

When the sergeant appeared in Nelligan's front doorway and the two guards came in through the back, Murt said in that real slow and loud way he has of talking that makes you think he is always right, "What will ya be having, Sarge?" And the sergeant said right back, "Yer name and address, sir." And the guards took down everyone's name and address and they all got summonses, including the bold

Murt. Every one of them got fined half a crown and their names in the paper.

If you say to anyone in the town, "What will ya be having, Sarge?" they know what you're talking about. They laugh all the harder because they know they're laughing at Murt, the old bollicks.

There's a bit of the land-grabber in the cagey old jow, too, but I put a quick stop to that, even though I would never get into an argument with him.

Down below, where I have a right-of-way through Murt's field to get into my acre and a half, he ploughed an extra sod off the six-foot-wide pass that was there before my father's time. While he was still in his field with the horses, I went and got down on my hands and knees and turned the extra sod back into its place, all one hundred and twenty-two yards of it. When I was finished, I stood on the right-of-way and kept looking over at Murt ploughing behind his horses until he looked over at me. I just looked back at him and said nothing, but he never tried to move in on my right-of-way again, and he never even mentioned anything about it to me. The stingy old bollicks. He would never have tried that in Pop's time. My father would have taken the head off him with a blow of a billhook, and Mick Cosgrove would have helped him, because that was a right of way to Mick's three roods, too.

I always give a great shake. I hate it when the water runs down my leg to my knees when I don't give a good shake. Paddy Burns was telling me the other day that Johnny won't be watering in the bushes any more, that he built a jowhouse out in the garden where he can water and jow at the same time. I wouldn't please Paddy to ask him what's inside the jowhouse in case he'd think I was a real eegit altogether. But why would you build a special house for it?

It must be the devil entirely having to jow in a pile of everyone else's jow. I'd rather do it on the dunghape or under a hedge, where you can kick up something to cover it when you stand up. The only thing that's better than making a good water under a bush is making a good water and a good jow under a bush.

14. Kate Glanvil

There's Missus Brady's latch-rattle at the wicket door, but it's too early for her today; only half-past two. Mother of God! I hope it's not Crissy the Widda. Please God, don't let it be Crissy. I haven't the patience to deal with her now; the dinner plates just washed and dried and my first sit-down at the fire since seven, my only chance to read the paper all day to see who died.

The pump will start hacking in a minute if it's Missus Brady. But I'd better be ready to pretend I'm on my way out in case it's Crissy. May God forgive me, but I can't stand her and her bees and her husband dead on Telana Hill nearly fifty years ago. I told Father O'Shea about her in confession a couple of years ago – how I feel guilty about avoiding her. "Yer not a keeper of a lunatic asylum," he said. "There's people who get paid good money for doing that." But I still feel guilty.

Crissy the Widda a lunatic! A lunatic is someone mad like Shem Woods was mad, that time he went out to his cowhouse in the middle of the night with nothing on and hung himself from a rafter, and he after trying to kill himself in different ways a couple of times before.

Crissy's a harmless lunatic, but it's like having a fat slug in the kitchen looking at you when she comes in with her terrible black dyed hair, her bee stings and her hump.

From what Johnny's mother told me, Crissy's madness probably began the day she got the famous Pickwoad letter from South Africa telling her how valiant her husband, Poor Ned, had died in the first hour of the first battle of the Boer War. And the thing that played most on her mind was that Poor Ned had been dead for almost four months and she hadn't known; dead and buried along with thirty other enlisted men of the Irish Fusiliers in a small place called Dundee.

Over the years, as she slowly sank into her own ever-shrinking world, Crissy has jumbled up everything she knew about South Africa to the point where no one can figure out how one thing relates to another any more. But everyone in Derrycloney knows the name Lieutenant Colonel Edwin Pickwoad as well as they know any nursery-rhyme name – Puss in Boots, Little Boy Blue, Mary, Mary Quite Contrary, Lieutenant Colonel Edwin Pickwoad.

In Crissy's sudsy mind, Lieutenant Colonel Edwin Pickwoad suddenly appears among the stitches of her knitting or on the streams of honey flowing from her hives. The Battle of Telana Hill tumbles out of her mouth at the most unexpected times. Shrapnel has become Sharp Nell, and it was Uncle Paul Kruger himself, sitting on top of Telana, who had set Sharp Nell on Poor Ned and the other men as they fought their way up against the Boers. Sometimes Dundee is in Scotland, sometimes in Zululand, sometimes in Swaziland. Sometimes Poor Ned has choked on a bit of biltong; sometimes he's fallen down Telana and drowned in a shallow river that Crissy could have waded into to save him if she'd only been there.

I have often thought how better it might have been for everyone if Poor Ned and Crissy had had a child. She'd have been all right for money with her British army pension, and I'd say she wouldn't be half as mad. At least she'd have had someone to talk to during all those terrible nights after getting the letter from Lieutenant Colonel Edwin Pickwoad.

I don't know whether I feel guilty about dodging Crissy, or whether I'm afraid she's aware that I'm always backing away from her like everyone else. Maybe she doesn't realise how people avoid her; everyone, me included. I hope she doesn't. It would be terrible if she felt as bad as I'd feel if I were treated the way she is. She can't know, or else she wouldn't keep putting herself in places where she's ignored or laughed at.

Whether it was Poor Ned's death or the fact that he'd been dead four months before she knew about it, one thing is for certain: she was bound to go entirely mad from living up there in that damp cottage by herself, every one of her brothers and sisters living in England and her father and mother dead. Crissy's one of those unfortunates who was left behind by herself to spend the rest of her life going around in ever-smaller circles and getting nowhere, just like Crip below and Bigword and Murt McHugh and Cha Finley. Cha Finley – talk about lunatics! – and he making sure the timing of his own sister's death wouldn't interfere with the threshing, and he thinking it was the right thing to do. And that latest one Missus Brady told about Cha! I still don't know whether it's funny or embarrassing; Murt McHugh going down to see him about buying a new calf off him, and he finding Cha unconscious on top of his dunghape with his trousers down around his ankles. The thoughts of it! Thanks be to God it wasn't me who found him. I'd have turned around and pretended I never saw him; Cha with his bare bum in the cow dung and his things to the sky, and then what he said to the doctor! Cha's like

Crissy and the rest of them – he's been living by himself too long. And I can't figure Bigword out at all; he's every bit as mad as the rest of them. You'd think that with all the reading he does he'd be a bit saner, but I'm beginning to think that the more he reads the worse he gets, or is it the loneliness that's driving him bonkers – that and Dunkle.

Out of the eight houses on Derrycloney Lane, in five of them there's odd people living, counting Crissy. She gets worse every year. Her bees, Poor Ned, her watch and her knitting. Her knitting is unending scarves full of dropped and pulled stitches, and if she runs out of wool halfway through one of her crooked creations, she finishes it with whatever colour she happens to pick up. She used to bring the knitting with her to show it off, stand there and rattle the needles at me, no rhythm, the uneven beat of the needles poking me in the nerves like thorns in the eyes.

I wonder what'll be the end of her. She'll be found dead in bed some day, or stung to death at one of her hives, and everyone will say, "We should have done more for Crissy." But what can we do? She'd drive you to distraction and, no matter how hard I try, I can't make myself welcome her. Every time I hear her coming I let her think I'm on the way out to do the jobs. She used to traipse around after me outside, but then she got hen dung on a shoe one day and that was the end of that. It's funny! You spend all this time planning out ways to get rid of her, and there's the answer lying on the ground the whole time in little piles.

The pump didn't start wheezing yet. It was definitely Missus Brady's latch-rattle, but she should be at the pump by now. I'll go on out, and if it's Crissy the Widda I'll keep going. I can't stand it any longer.

Just as I'm taking a step towards the kitchen door doesn't the latch go up all of a sudden and frighten the life out of me. But it's Missus Brady and in my head I'm saying, Thank God it's not Crissy, and I'm thanking God so much that it's a few seconds after she says it that I hear what Missus Brady is saying. She has the white enamel bucket in her hand, the first time she ever brought it into the kitchen.

"Paddy Burns just called me a terrible thing, Kate," she says. "I was trying to dry my eyes before I came in, but I couldn't." There are tears running down Missus Brady's face and, I declare to God, it's the last thing I thought I'd ever see in my life: Missus Brady crying. I always thought she was as tough as nettles.

15. Liam Glanvil

Dear Sister de Monfort,

Thanks for *The Nine Tailors*. I read it in eleven days, and Daddy is reading it now. I learned about England and church bells.

The name of the composition is "Threshing Day".

I remain, Your nephew, Liam

THRESHING DAY

There is so much excitement at threshing time that it's nearly too much to bear.

The excitement begins many days before Mick Dunphy's steam engine comes puffing down the lane, as slow as Missus Brady limping, pulling the thresher and the straw carrier, twelve iron wheels crunching the gravel of the lane, six on each side clanking into the same potholes one after the other like big, slow monsters that will keep coming and coming and get you in the end no matter how far away you try to get.

Once the day of the threshing is set between my father and Mick Dunphy, everything changes. That very night we all pray that the weather will stay fine for the people who will do their threshing before us. If it rains on other peoples' threshing days, then our threshing will have to be put off, and all the preparations will have to be changed, too. And then the Burnses and Crip Quigley and Cha Finley and Murt McHugh will have to change all their preparations, too, and all the people after them. Everyone prays, too, that there won't be any funerals at threshing time. Ten years ago, Cha Finley's sister died on a Friday night at threshing time, and was buried on Sunday. If she'd had to be buried on a workday, everyone's threshing would have been upset.

The worse part of postponing a threshing day is that the children will have to wait longer for their day off from school. One of the good parts about threshing day is that the children who live in the town never get time off for a threshing, and for one day in the year the country children have something the townies don't have. One of the bad parts about threshing day is that the jealous townie boys beat up the country boys every day for about a week before their threshing day, and they call the country boys smelly oul farmers.

The excitement rises when the men drive the horses' carts into the field and break the straw rope that holds each stack of wheat together against the rain and the wind. Stacks are taller than a tall man and are shaped like fat bottles with thick, short necks. Each stack holds eighty sheaves.

The children, except for my oldest sister, stand around the stack in a circle with sticks in their hands. We wait while the men on the ground with pitchforks throw the sheaves up to the man in the cart, building the load like a bricklayer building a house, only a lot quicker. When the last layer of sheaves in the stack is lifted up, the mice dash out and run through the stubbles like little brown engines whizzing through trees in a forest. The shrieking children run after them, trying to kill them with their sticks.

Three stacks are built on to each cart, then the ropes are

tied. The children are lifted up, and the man on top pulls them the rest of the way. When the tall load sways, the children hold on to the ropes with two hands and, no matter how much they pretend not to be afraid, their eyes give them away. Everything looks different from up in the sky on top of the wheat, and the driver shouts at everyone to duck when we go under trees.

In the haggard, the man on the load throws the sheaves to the men who are building the reeks, drops every sheaf at the men's feet so they won't have to stretch. There are two reeks – one of wheat, the other of barley – only far enough apart for the width of the thresher. The shape of the haggard changes as the two long reeks start to go up in the sky. Near the end of the day, the man on the cart has to throw the sheaves up to another man on a platform, and that man throws them up higher to the men on the reeks. When they are finished, and when you are standing between them on the ground in the nice smell of ripe wheaten and barley straw, the reeks look like two golden ships that could sail away to the land of Chimborazo and Cotopaxi where the sun shines all the time. All the men are in good humour when the wheat is being drawn in, even my father.

The barn is the place where the sacks of wheat will be brought on threshing day on a hand truck – one man pulling, one man pushing and a child sitting on the sack laughing. But, before the threshing, the dried animal dung has to be scraped off the barn floor. My father uses the spade and we sweep with the yard brush. Then you can see that the cement floor is as smooth as a tarred road. Shallow tracks spread out from a hole in the bottom of the wall, like rays of the sun in a picture. In the winter, when the animals are in the barn, the rays become little rivers, and they flow out through the hole in the wall to the dungheap.

On the days between the cleaning of the barn and the threshing of the wheat, we whip our tops on the barn floor, jump the spinning tops across the pee tracks. Our neighbour, Paddy Burns, made our tops. He painted them in such a way that you always think something is moving up the tops when they are spinning. I wish the barn was empty and clean all the time. It's the best place in the world to play; dry, warm and musty.

But on threshing day it will fill up with the full sacks, all standing up in straight lines looking like fat, brown animals with no heads, their necks tied off with new binder twine to keep them from bleeding.

Then, one day my father comes home from town in the pony-and-cart with the barrel of porter, the lemonade, the orangeade and one-hundred-and-twenty sacks. Each sack holds twenty stones, which is the same as two-and-a-half hundredweight, which is the same as one-eighth of a ton. The sacks belong to the flour company and the porter company. The ones for the wheat, with the red writing, say W.P. & R. ODLUM. The ones for the barley, with the black writing, say ARTHUR GUINNESS. The sacks smell like new ropes.

The children fight for a place at the barrel of Guinness when it is rolled into the kitchen, and then out into the hallway where no one can see it. My father puts the tap on top of the barrel and says, "No one's to touch that."

On the morning of the threshing, Paddy Burns will tap the barrel and taste the porter to make sure it isn't sour. My father said the porter has never been sour in twenty years.

The crates of lemonade and orangeade are for the Pioneers who will work at our threshing. I love the smell of the lemonade, and the little bubbles jumping up into your face so hard you have to shut your eyes when you drink.

The kitchen walls are whitewashed and the floor scrubbed, my mother on her knees with the scrubbing brush, my oldest sister putting down sheets of newspaper that look like stepping stones across a river. "No one can walk on the floor until it dries," my sister says very importantly. The smell of the distemper goes into all the other rooms, and the whole house smells new.

On the day before the threshing, the other women bring their pots and plates and knives and forks and tablecloths from their houses. There's a dozen sliced loaves in the kitchen window, and all the women make sandwiches with butter and ham. My father makes an extra table out of two doors and four sawhorses. He uses the doors off the cowhouse and the stable, but if there is any dung on them he always makes sure to scrape it off. "We can't have Crip Quigley telling everyone there was horse dung on the underside of his eating table," he said last year.

On the red-handled sandstone, my father sharpens the two broken kitchen knives for the sheaf cutters, and ties rags around the white handles to make them comfortable for the cutters.

It's harder to fall asleep on the night before the threshing than it is on Christmas Eve.

"Make sure you don't get in the way," is what my father says when the children set out in the morning, at a quarter to seven, for the maltings, to wait for Mick Dunphy's steam engine. My father said, "If Mick Dunphy says he'll be passing the maltings at seven, then that's what he'll be doing."

Standing in the high doorway of the maltings, with all those blind windows looking down on us, makes the hair stand up on the back of our necks, and we all hold each others' hands. But in a few minutes we hear them coming, then we see the front wheels of the steam engine, see the high chimney with the smoke getting left behind in the air like a thin, blue ribbon. Just as everything passes the maltings, Teddy Short rings the seven o'clock Angelus in the church.

Mick Dunphy and his helper are too busy to wave back to us. They have to steer the steam engine, and move its levers, and keep an eye bent back at the thresher and the straw carrier behind. We wait for the steam engine and the thresher to go by, and then, after the blue straw carrier clanks on to Derrycloney Lane, we walk behind it. It's like walking behind a train, the three machines are so long. We wish Derrycloney Lane would go on for ever and that we could walk behind all the iron wheels till the end of the world.

Mick Dunphy and the man who works for him are very important. They smell like the steam engine, and their clothes are oily and shiny. They seem to be cross with each other all the time, and sometimes they shout at each other crossly.

Everyone has to do what they say when the engine stops outside our yard. The machines are unhooked from each other, and the steam engine is moved out of the way. Then the thresher is pushed forward and backward until it's got around all the sharp corners made by the farmyard houses, Mick Dunphy and his workman shouting out, "Hup!" "Now!" "Back!" "*Back! I said. Bloody into it. Back!*" "Stop!' "Get that child out of the way!" One of them frightens the children when he shouts out all of a sudden like something very bad is going to happen, "*Will you mind the corner of the house! Are you blind or what?*"

When the machines are in place between the two reeks in the haggard, when the big driving belt is put on the small pulley wheel of the thresher and the big wheel of the steam engine, Mick Dunphy goes up on the engine's platform like a priest going into a pulpit to give a sermon. "In the name of God," he says to no one, "it's eight o'clock in the morning and there's not a child in the house washed," and he pulls the chain of the brass steam whistle to let all the neighbours know we are ready to start.

The sound of the whistle is sweeter than the sound of a spinning, humming top. It is so even; so smooth; so full; so pure. There is such little noise in it that it is the music I imagine an angel makes on a golden trumpet. The sound spreads out like a silent ring on water after a dropped stone on a calm day. All over the countryside it goes, one wave following when the first wave is just beginning to get lost in the mountain. The note goes into all the places where the cuckoo's call goes, into every clump of bushes, every bunch of long grass; into every abandoned bird's nest, every shining drop of dew; across every cobweb and into the sour haws the birds have left on the whitethorn bushes; into every ditch and drain; across the lake to the swans and into every hare's form; into every rabbit and badger burrow. I can even see the sweet, brass sound as it spreads across the fields, hanging like a huge, quivering cymbal from an invisible rope in the sky, and I wish the whole country could be covered with the sound for ever, to protect it from rain and the cold, wet wind. I wish I was the one pulling the whistle's chain, sending its sound out to change the dewy world.

The men arrive, each with a pitchfork on his shoulder, his cap to one side of his head, telling the world that the hard work he is going to do today is happy work. Everyone knows what he is good at doing, and he goes to the place where he can do it. When the men spit into their big hands and grasp the handles of their forks, they are giants ready to clean out the Augean stables the hard way.

The men on the wheat reek drop sheaves at the feet of the sheaf cutters on top of the thresher. The blades of the broken knives flash across the binder twine, and the sheaves unfold at the feet of the man who feeds the wheat into the whirring drum. The threshing machine purrs like a fed monster when the wheat slams against its breast and slides down its throat.

The grains of wheat come out at one end of the thresher, and a man kicks at the hanging sacks to make sure the corners will be filled. The golden straw, now broken and bent and soft and tangled, comes belching out of a laughing mouth at the other end, falls into the straw carrier, and goes up to the men building the straw reek. Out of the belly of the thresher the chaff is shaken and the chaffman, a rag tied around his neck, pulls out the chaff with a rake. He uses a beet fork to throw the chaff in a pile that will grow into a small mountain by the end of the day. The seeds of weeds are caught on screens inside the thresher and go into their own bag.

The golden grains of wheat swoosh down the spouts, the yellow straw spews out, the chaff falls down, and there are clouds of dust in the sunshine, moths of all sizes fluttering out of their disturbed hiding places, the children screeching when one lands on them and pinches their skin with its little claws. There's different noises in different parts of the haggard. There's happy talking and shouting. Above all is the purring of the spinning drum and the chum-chum of Mick Dunphy's steam engine, rocking gently on its big iron wheels, like a black-dressed granny in a dark corner in a rocking chair.

And, like God, Mick Dunphy and his helper are

everywhere at once, being important; checking belts and wheels, and squirting oil on axles; changing the screens for the barley seeds when all the wheat is finished; feeding turf into the belly of the engine and pouring water into its boiler; each trying to be more important than the other. Their jobs are so important they don't have time to talk to anyone, to even stop for the eleven o'clock tea; chewing a bite of ham sandwich as they go from one job to the next, as if they ate ham every day; when they get the chance, taking a mouthful of tea out of the mugs they have left on one of the steam engine's steps, little waves on the trembling tea like on the lake when it's pouring rain. Billy Bates said one time that Mick Dunphy and his helper only try to look busy in case they would be expected to work at an unimportant job, like taking out the chaff or pitching straw.

The corn reeks sink down, and the straw reeks rise up until they are level with each other. The men on the reeks shout at each other about how lazy the others are, and they laugh. Some of the younger men point at Crip Quigley covered in dust where he is taking out the chaff, sneezing and red-eyed, and they poke each other in the ribs with their eyes and snigger. But all the time the pitchforks are being handled as if they were batons, like the one the leader of the pipe band uses, twirling and stabbing and lifting and throwing, so that everyone else can admire the strength and the muscles.

The first shift of dinner-eaters goes into the house to be fed by the women. The men who are left working spend all their time watching the haggard gate, waiting for the first shift to come back. There are loud laughs about the glasses of porter on the dinner table. When all the eating is done, the steam engine goes back to full fire, and the cloud of dust rises back into the sky.

Mick Dunphy and his helper stand on the engine's platform to eat their dinners, keeping their eyes on every moving part of the machines, their heads jerking around like the heads of nervous hens, now and then dashing down the iron steps to fix something.

When the last sheaf has been thrown to the cutters, when the last sack of barley has been pulled into the barn, when the straw reeks have been headed and tied down with ropes and weights, when the steam engine, thresher and straw carrier have been pulled and pushed and shoved out to the Burnses' haggard, all the tired men sit on the ground, their backs against the new straw reeks. For a while there is very little talk. But when the women come out with thick, sugary, juicy apple cakes and jugs of custard, everything changes. The children bring out the cans of tea and the mugs.

Mick Dunphy and his helper can only have one piece of apple cake; they have to get up early to get the steam engine going for tomorrow's threshing. Everyone speaks to the two engine-men the way children talk to teachers and priests.

When the apple cakes and the custard are gone, the children help to carry everything back into the kitchen. They don't go out again, and before the last man has left for home all the children are in bed asleep, all full of apple cake and custard, all covered in dust – too tired to wash.

16. Billy Bates

There's the goods train at Derlamogue Bridge on its way to Dublin; half-past two on the dot.

I'd love to be the train driver going through the night when everyone's asleep, starting out in Cork or Limerick in the dark and then in Dublin, still in the dark. I'd be standing up looking out through the little window, the warm smell of the burning coal all around me. There'd be nothing to see but the track ahead and not another person in the whole world except the fireman with his coal shovel, glowing in the red of the fire. Anyone hearing the train would be thinking about me, keeping my lonely vigil better than the Apostles in Gethsemane, behind the big light to make sure there are no cattle or horses or asses on the line, making sure the gates at all the level crossings are open.

It's still coming, from the sound of it, but in a minute now, it'll reach that point where it begins to fade. The sound of it coming is better than the fading. Of course, if I were driving the train I wouldn't hear it coming or going; I'd be in the middle of the same noise the whole time. But I know I'd love that. I'd love it; all those moving pieces connected together, all the huffing and puffing and clacking.

It's terrible living in a place where there's no sound, where the silence plays tricks on you. There's times when I think, all of a sudden, that I've been hearing myself talking for a long time. And then I think I haven't been talking at all, that whatever I've been thinking in my head is what I've been hearing, but not with my ears.

Last night around twelve I discovered myself awake and I listening to myself in the dark. I couldn't figure out whether I'd been talking out loud or not. I held my breath and put a hand over my mouth. All I could hear was the blood drumming in my ears getting louder the longer I held my breath. I couldn't hear myself talking when I listened like that, and I began to think that when I don't have my mouth covered, I must be talking out loud. If anyone ever heard me, they'd think I was gone mad, or at least going.

I couldn't go back to sleep last night, so I lit the candle and tried a bit of *Paradise Lost* for a while. When that didn't work, I made myself think about the Hippwell One for half an hour. I did everything I could think of doing to her, but I couldn't even get a gasp out of the dragon. I only made myself more awake, and I heard myself saying out loud, "I'll get up and go to Derlamogue Bridge to see the train." I had two hours to get there and only four miles – that's after walking the bike across the two fields out to Derrycloney Lane.

It wasn't my first time on Derrycloney Lane in the middle of the night, but I've never heard it so silent. Even when I was passing Johnny's yard, there wasn't the sound of a beast rattling its chains nor the bark of a dog. All the houses were dark, except for Crissy the Widda's red Sacred Heart lamp through her kitchen window. Maybe she was reading the letter from Lieutenant Colonel Edwin Pickwoad. I never met or passed one person between here and Derlamogue Bridge, never saw light nor sight of fur or feather. Of course, I didn't turn on my bike light till I was at the top of Derrycloney and out on Wolfe Tone Street.

The minute I got to the railway bridge I hopped up on the parapet; that's the little wall that keeps people from falling off the bridge, but if you used that word around here they'd all look at you with their mouths open as if to say, "Who do ya think yaar, using a big word like that?"

Up on the parapet I hopped and dangled my legs over the tracks. Well, I heard the train when it was miles away, heard it coming a lot longer than I hear it in the bed. It was a rumble for a long time, like thunder miles away. The whole world slowly filled up with sound, and it kept filling until I could feel the air trembling, and the train not even in sight yet. I kept looking for the light, but I was looking too close altogether. It was off on the horizon that I saw a glow and thought to myself, that can't be it. But it was, and it seemed to take ages for the light to drive out of its own glow and become a clear speck. I'd swear the parapet started trembling in my arse when the train was still a mile away. I said to myself, if it's trembling with the train that far away, it will all fall down by the time it gets here. But I wasn't afraid. And then the whole world was full completely with the noise of the train, and the whole world was shaking and trembling. When the train went under me and smothered me inside a cloud of coal smoke, I was hard, and the Hippwell One wasn't even in my head. It was like the end of the world was happening and I was getting a bird's-eye view, the shaking and the noise and I not able to breathe for a minute. It was like what hell must be like when you walk in through the front door for the first time. Your man, Virgil, wouldn't have been out of place if he'd been standing beside me, showing me around. Oh, God! I could have died with the excitement. And the train was so long that after a while the sound of the engine was gone and it was only the sound of the wagons on the tracks that I could hear, a different kind of rattling altogether that I never heard in the bed. It must have been a mile long, and when the last wagon was gone from under me everything changed.

The level of the noise fell off all of a sudden. I hopped off the parapet, skipped across to the other one and hopped up on it. I listened till it was gone, and I wondered why the sound of the going-away train didn't last nearly as long as the coming train. It was all gone in a minute, the noise and the red light and the smoke.

On the way home I was feeling so good I had to think about it. It wasn't just the train that had done me a world of good. I was feeling terrible free, and it was because I had gone out of Derrycloney for maybe the first time in my life without anyone knowing about it. I had made an adventure for myself, and I hadn't to worry about what anyone would say. As I turned into the top of the lane between the maltings and Miss Moran's, I turned off the flash lamp, just in case someone would be up taking a piss and see the light.

I said to myself, I'll have to do this again; go for a spin in the middle of the night, go anywhere. No one will know where I was. For a few hours during the night the anhedonic uncle won't know where I am. It'll be like being out from under his thumb for a while.

It's not hard to find your way along the lane in the dark when there's no clouds, because all you have to do is follow the track of stars between the tops of the hedges on each side. When I came to Missus Brady's house, I thought for a minute I could hear another train in the distance, but before I got to Crissy's I knew it was an aeroplane. I love looking at aeroplanes, especially at night when I can see the green and white lights on the ends of the wings. When one goes over, I look at it till it disappears. But you have to be out in an open field to see it. The top of the lane is too narrow and, if you did see it at all, it would be only for a second. By the time I got down to Johnny's the aeroplane was nearly over my head, and you could tell from the sound it was off up high in the sky.

The Burnses' house was as dark as pitch and, after I passed it, I was listening to the aeroplane and at the same time thinking about Paddy Burns calling Missus Brady an oul cunt, and wondering what it was that made him do it – out of the middle of nowhere call her an old cunt. The next thing I knew I was on the flat of my back on the lane, and someone was letting fly with a whole string of words sounding like he was terrified, his voice getting higher and quicker the more he said, sort of whingeing. I definitely knew it wasn't me who was talking, nearly shouting, sort of praying and frightening the shite out of me. The minute I heard "frig" and "frigging" I knew it was Quigley, the mad fucker, mad enough to cut the beaks off his hens. I never heard the taciturn Crip being so verbose.

I was just going to shout at him, "What the shag are ya doing in the middle of the road in the middle of the shagging night, ya shagging eegit?" but something in the back of my mind stopped me.

"Who's there?" Crip says, and his voice as cracked as a hen's squawking for water after a feed of crushed oats.

"Who the shag do ya think it is?" I nearly said, and I on my hands and knees feeling around in the dark for the bike, hoping to God Quigley hadn't a flash lamp with him.

The second I felt the handlebars, a whole lot of things flashed through my head at the same time. The main one was that, if Quigley discovered it was me, then everyone would want to know where I was coming from at half-three in the morning; especially Duncle, and I forty-two. The first thing you'd know, everyone would be saying I was riding the Hippwell One for half a crown in the bushes at the lake. I didn't say another word, only threw my leg over the bike and pedalled off like a hure out of hell, one of the pedals all bent worse than an esshook and my foot slipping off, skinning my ankle off the bent-up end.

I wasn't up the lane today to hear anything, but I'm sure there's going to be a strange story coming out of Quigley to explain what happened to him last night. I wonder what was he doing out on the lane at that hour. He's as mad as a shagging hatter.

The sound of the train is gone for another night and the silence is pressing down again like a big flat stone. It must be three o'clock. Maybe if I think of riding the Hippwell One I'll be able to do it and fall asleep.

I've never seen what a woman looks like between the legs, so when I think of the Hippwell One I have to think she must be a bit like a sheep or a goat down there; hardly like a cow, at least not as big, or else it would be like doing it to a letterbox.

The first thing I do is grab her by the tits from behind and pull her in against me real tight, and she squeals like a sow bit by a boar, and she tries to kick me in the shins with her heels. But I know she loves it. She's only pretending so I won't think she gives in easy. Some night, some way, I'm going to get her to meet me at the lake, and the first thing I'm going to do is feel her between the legs to see what it's like. Oh, God. There must be a billion women in the world. Am I the only man in the world who has never seen a woman with nothing on? The closest I've got to a naked woman is a drawing of a Greek statue in a book, and you can't tell anything from that, besides the tits. Am I the only shagging man in the world who will die without looking between a woman's legs? But I suppose neither Crip

Quigley, nor Cha Finley, nor Duncle Murt for that matter, has ever seen one either. But that doesn't make me feel any shagging better.

While I was thinking about the billion women, the Hippwell One got away from me and I'm left holding nothing.

17. Paddy Burns

Jazus! I'm sweating.

I've been chopping the shite out of that elm without stopping once. And all the time it's been in my head that we'll have nowhere to live in November unless Lizzie's plan works, and I know damn well in my guts that it won't. The look in Parkingston-Shaw's eye when I gave him the will – you'd think I was handing him a day-old cat shite.

Leaving Derrycloney is all I can think of, and I feel as helpless as a blade of grass floating in a quick river. There's not a council house to be had in the whole fecking county, never mind in the town.

Lizzie's plan is too mad altogether. I just don't know what the feck we're going to do. I'm always good at finding a way to do things, of finding a way out, but with this I'm at a total loss for an answer.

If the fecking solicitor discovers what we're up to, we're going to be up to the neck in shite altogether. The first thing he'll do is call in Johnny, because Johnny's name is on the two wills. I hope to God Johnny says the second one is the real one. It all depends on Johnny, whether he'll tell a lie or not.

God, he'll hardly say it's not his signature, because it'll be the same as saying, "Throw Lizzie and Paddy and their children out on the road."

Please, God, let him say that the second will is the real one. Please, God. Please. I'll do the nine First Fridays for the rest of my life. If Johnny doesn't tell the lie, we'll be like Jesus on Christmas night with nowhere to go only a stable. Yourself knows what that's like, and it snowing and everything; the cow and the ass and the manger and the dung. Please, God. I'll give up the pipe for Lent. I'll give it up entirely. Please, God.

We're fourth on the list, but that means four council-house families have to die or go to England. We could never go to England. There'd be no hedge-cutting, no turf-cutting and no drills of spuds to weed, no houses to thatch, and I'd be lost altogether. Lizzie couldn't do it either. She's too bad on the feet to go anywhere, and anyhow, she just wouldn't go and that's the end of it. Women are in charge, no matter what men think. Men are just stronger in the muscles, and that's the only reason why the women pretend men are the bosses. But the women are always getting around men's muscles. Always.

Feck it! I was chopping so hard, and the grinding in my brain was so bad, that I wasn't listening for Kate's whistle. I hope she didn't blow it, but she must have; it's surely an hour since Teddy Short rang the Angelus. Even Teddy has a house with no one besides himself in it since the mother died; all by himself and the four of us with nowhere.

Kate'll blow the whistle again if she didn't hear me blowing mine back at hers. I'll sharpen the hatchet and billhook while I'm waiting, have them good and sharp for when I come back after dinner, listen for the whistle at the same time.

Even with my head full of the twelfth of November and the solicitor – such a fecking Protestant name he has, Parkingston-Shaw – I have to keep trying not to think about calling Missus Brady an oul cunt. I must've been mad entirely. An oul cunt! Jazus. I won't be able to look at her again, but that won't stop her, hasn't stopped her. She shouted at me last night from the kitchen door when I was going by on the bike. "Happy fecking oul twelfth of November, from the fecking oul cunt," she says. She must have been practising that one all day.

As sure as God, she told the Glanvils what I called her, but, thank God for small favours, Johnny hasn't said anything to me about it. I don't know what I'll say if he does. But, come to think of it, this morning, when we were eating the breakfast – Benny and myself – Kate said she had to go out to feed the calves, and she always stays in and talks. Jazus. She left me alone with nothing but the ticking clock and the silent Benny for company; asked me would I mind getting up and pouring the second cup of tea myself. Maybe this is their way of . . . The way they'll handle it is, they'll say nothing about it to me, but it'll be right there at the back of their eyes the whole time. I've never had to pour my own tea in Kate's kitchen before. Anyhow, I made Benny get up and get the teapot.

I was such a fecking eegit to call Missus Brady that. God, I'm more ashamed about it because of Johnny and Kate. Missus Brady surely told Kate about it before she even got as far as the little hob yesterday, couldn't limp fast enough down the lane to tell. And then Kate couldn't wait to tell Johnny.

Am I codding myself? Everyone on the lane knows about it, the same as they know everything about everyone else. What must they think of me at all? Shite. I'll have to get it out of my head some way.

The belly's falling out of me with the hunger. I hope Kate has a bit of rabbit today; rabbit and spuds and cabbage and butter and a mug of buttermilk. Johnny got two rabbits on Sunday with the ferret and the dogs out in Ockaboe. He never stops going, working all the time. He calls it hunting, but it's just a different kind of work; going off for miles across the fields carrying the spade and the ferreting bar and the ferret in a bag, the two chaps traipsing along behind. The stink of the ferret! It's so strong you'd think you had your nose buried up its hole. He asked me to go with him once, and we spent most of the time digging the fecking ferret out after it wrapped the line around a root in the burrow. Why Johnny ties a line around the ferret's neck at all is beyond me. Everyone else puts a bell on its neck and can tell from the ringing where the ferret is. "But they're always losing their ferrets," Johnny says. I'd rather lose the fecking ferret than spend all day Sunday digging up half the country looking for it. Still and all, he gave me half of what we caught that day, four, even though he owned all the tools and carried most of them there and back. All I had to carry was Mick Cosgrove's old double-barrelled shotgun, and I never even got one shot the whole day.

I'd never go hunting again with Johnny. It's too much like work for me, and anyhow, Lizzie burned the feck out of the rabbits. I had to bury them in the dunghape, and then Quigley's dog dug them up and et them. I should have given them to the fecking dog in the first place. There's nothing worse than looking forward to a good feed of rabbit and then not getting it. Lizzie can boil a spud, and that's the length and the breadth of it. I suppose she can fry black pudding too, only it's so fecking lumpy!

Johnny still gives me the skins. I never saw a quicker man at skinning a rabbit – you'd swear he was slipping them out of their fur coats.

"Y'oul cunt," I shouted at her, and I not even knowing it till I was halfway up the town. Jazus. I was up at Furlongs' before I heard what I'd shouted.

I'd better put on my coat. A fellow could catch his death of cold standing around in the cold air after sweating. Sharpening a billhook never kept anyone warm.

There might be a bit of currant cake with the mug of tea after the rabbit and spuds. Kate's a great woman; a currant cake every Saturday night she makes for Sunday, and it lasts half the week.

Johnny's a terrible lucky man, terrible lucky with Kate, and the wonder is that she amounted to anything at all, coming as she did from the likes of old Hoppy Hopkins's house. It was like Johnny saw from a distance how good she was in there in the middle of all that misery and hunger and drink and want. When he started courting her, everyone wondered why he was going after her at all, instead of a woman from a better family. But he was right, or he was lucky. I'd say he was right more than lucky, because he's been right too many times to be just lucky.

I wish I had half his luck. I wish I had his farm. I wish I had his house, seven rooms and one of them a parlour with good chairs and a fireplace and a wooden floor. And the gramophone! The music! There's a grand smell off the records.

And coal in the fireplace at Christmas for the children, instead of wet sods of turf.

A cunt is what I called her! I was so fecking blinded with crossness. On one side was Lizzie at me about doing something to keep us in Benny's, and Missus Brady at me on the other side about not staying one minute longer than the twelfth of November. That's why I was so stupid with crossness; I'm in the middle, and no matter what I do I'm going to be wrong. Any man that ever landed up between two women lost his balls, one way or the other.

And why am I even bothered by what Missus Brady has

to say, I ask myself. And the answer is – holy Jazus, I'm only thinking this now for the first time – it's because she's talking for everyone else, not only for Benny Cosgrove, but for the Glanvils, for Quigley and Finley and Dunkle McHugh and Bigword and even Crissy. They're all standing back and letting Missus Brady talk for them. She's the one who's as tough as barbed wire, who has harrow teeth in her mouth and a tongue like the blade of a scythe.

They mightn't put her up to it, but they're all behind her. She is every one of them. It's like they had a silent election; no one ever said a word, but they all voted for her. She was elected because the rest of them will still have to live together for years, and none of them wants it ever thrown in their face that they caused the Burnses to be evicted. Missus Brady and Jim are only renters and could be gone in the morning. Johnny owns that house, always has, because it's a part of his farm – cash rent every month for him. So, as far as the rest of them are concerned, Missus Brady is still an outsider and it's as an outsider that they're using her, and as an outsider she's glad to do it, because she's hoping like a dope that in the end it will make her one of them.

And me and Lizzie are outsiders too. They're all on Benny's side, no matter how nice they are to us. They knew Kitty before Mick Cosgrove ever came courting her, before he ever married into the place. They know Benny better than we ever will, because they knew him when he was a baby. Johnny and Bigword knew Mick Cosgrove since they were chaps.

And Jazus! I never thought of this before either: when I called Missus Brady a cunt, I was calling them all a cunt. Well, not cunts, but I was shouting at them all when I called her an oul cunt; telling them to feck off and leave me alone. That's how they heard it when I called her a cunt.

Even though Johnny and Kate haven't said anything to me about it, even though Johnny still hired me today to cut the hedges, and even though Kate will bring Lizzie to Mass next Sunday in the pony-and-trap, they are all on the lookout, all making sure that Benny gets the farm on the twelfth of November.

I'll have to stop thinking about it or it'll drive me mad. That fecker, Parkingston-Shaw, the way he looked at me.

Rabbit and currant cake. Jazus, how will I be able to go into the kitchen and eat and pretend that everything is the same as yesterday?

There's Kate's whistle.

I was the one who came up with the idea of the whistles. I even made the whistles and put rings of blue and red paint around them. I made one for all Kate's children, too.

Who would ever have thought that fifteen years would go by so quick, and that at the end of it we'd still have nothing? No matter how hard we worked, no matter how much we tried to save, we have nothing out of the whole thing. Not even a fecking ass-and-cart.

I'll take the shortcut up through the fields and I won't run into anyone. I suppose I shouldn't be worried about Johnny and Kate. They'd never even ask me how the looking for a council house is going, because they'd be afraid I'd think they were reminding me that I have to get out of Benny's. They'll never mention the twelfth of November to me. They're leaving all that to Missus Brady. She's going to be the one to suck up any shite that starts flying about the twelfth of November. She'll be like a sheet of blotting paper to a drop of ink.

I'll just have to keep thinking about the rabbit and the currant cake. But, I'll have to say this first. No matter how hard Missus Brady tries, she'll never be one of *them*, no more than Lizzie or myself, because if you don't own, you don't belong. Lizzie and myself know that only too well. They have all been here at least since the times of their grandfathers; they are Derrycloney, and Lizzie and me and Missus Brady are not. *We* can tear the guts out of each other and *they'll* go on as before. It's just like the song about the river, "Men may come and men may go, but I go on for ever." In a few years Missus Brady and Paddy Burns will only be people in a story that happened a long time ago.

Rabbit and currant cake. Rabbit and currant cake.

Like she's a soldier for all the old-timers, Missus Brady stands between me and the town. No matter when I go up the road she's there. I can't get away from her or them.

Currant cake and rabbit. Currant cake and rabbit. Buttermilk. Parkingston-Shaw.

If Johnny doesn't eat his dinner with us, I'll know for sure that I'm being pushed out for calling Missus Brady a cunt. God, I hope he's there. As well as everything else, if Johnny doesn't sit at the table with us, I'll be left with no one but Benny, have to watch him moving the food around inside his mouth trying not to eat with the teeth that pain him. He'd sicken a dog, the way he does it.

18. Kate Glanvil

Maybe it was because she was feeling so sorry for herself, right after Paddy Burns called her that name, that she told me more about herself in an hour than she'd let escape over all the years I've known her.

Such a long route she took to tell me! But then, I suppose when a woman, or a man for that matter, is telling things about herself, she takes her time approaching the pains, doesn't run up to them and blindly drag them out of hiding in case they would devour her all over again — like an eegit of a man sticking his hand into a burrow feeling for a badger. Such running up little side-roads with different stories she did, the nearer she got to the strands of her own story!

Sometimes a woman will tell another woman things she would never tell anyone else, and what Missus Brady told me I would never repeat, not even to Johnny. No matter how wretched someone's story is, there will always be someone else to pick it apart and laugh at it. I would never forgive myself if Missus Brady ever heard someone sniggering at what she told me about herself. Of course, you could have knocked me over with a feather when she told me, after she had collapsed on to the hob, that Jim wasn't her husband at all.

It was like she was wounded when she came into the kitchen. And it was because she always gives the impression that she's able to laugh pain away that I was so taken aback when I saw the tears on her face. It crossed my mind that Paddy's terrible word had run through her like a spear, and it was out of the wound it made that the old pains she had been covering up for so long were oozing out.

She sat on the hob with the snuff rag jammed against her mouth, trying to steady her body against the sobs shaking her, or else trying to stuff the words back in about herself and Jim not being married.

I didn't know what to say, or what to do, so I busied myself making her a mug of tea, and that was the first time she ever took tea from me outside of threshing day. Imagine that! And I've known her all these years.

After a few mouthfuls she was steady enough to talk again. Her father and mother, who weren't her father and mother at all, had adopted her out of the workhouse when she was five, two years after they had adopted Jim out of the same place.

"Oh, Kate," says she, "I think I've been hurt all my life, and it's only at a time like this that I feel it. When Paddy hit me with that name, it wasn't the word just there by itself. It had behind it all the hurt I do be keeping stored away in a deep hole."

To tell the truth, I was waiting breathless for her to go on, because I wanted to hear her explain how Jim and herself ending up living together, everyone thinking for ever that they're husband and wife. Of course, I couldn't ask her any questions, because that would have meant I was just being curious while she was crying.

"I've no notion who my real father and mother were. I've no notion when I was put into the workhouse. I can only remember being there all my life until I was five, as old as Benny was when the mother and father died."

Missus Brady took off into one of the side-roads of her

story about things that went on in the workhouse: there were fighting, biting, hair-pulling and screeching women; sodden mattresses; broken windows letting in the dampness and the cold; food that seemed to have been prepared to make it as tasteless as possible – swill, she called it.

"At the time, I didn't know how bad the place was, how cold. It was always a normal place for me. There were all these big people, any one of them as likely to scrape their nails across your face as they were to pat you on the head. They were all women wearing long black dresses and shawls around their shoulders and heads."

Then one day a man took her by the hand and walked her out to his ass-and-cart. Nobody said goodbye, nobody told her where she was going. She had never been in a cart, never been out of the workhouse before. The man didn't speak to her. She kept looking back at the workhouse getting smaller. When they stopped at a house, a woman came out and asked her name.

"I told her Marguerite, but the woman said, 'That's too posh a name altogether. Daisy will do.' It wasn't until I was fourteen that I knew Jim was adopted, too, even though Papa Brady, as we had to call him, had always been as harsh to Jim as he was to me. I'm reminded of Papa every time I see a bit of sandpaper. Everyone had to keep Mama Brady comfortable. She was the queen bee, and Jim and myself were her two drones. She was a delicate creature, and by the time I was six she was bedridden. I don't know what her ailment was, but whatever it was it didn't kill her till about ten years ago. I happened to see her death notice in Doctor Mansfield's paper one day; pure chance. The minute I saw her name, a big glob of spit landed on the paper and, I declare to God, I didn't know it had come out of me till I thought about it – there was no one else in the office."

When the older woman took to her bed, the child learned to carry a loaded chamber pot, never spilling anything over the sides. She emptied it, scrubbed it out with a rag. The child cleaned the woman's body all over, wiped her after she had used the chamber pot, washed her hair, cut her toenails.

"Papa Brady was a stonemason and he taught Jim the trade. Whenever the building work was slack, he sent me to work in de Lacy Hall to keep the money coming in. I was a scullery maid, with chapped hands. That's when I heard the lobsters crying when they were dropped into the scalding water."

Jim didn't come home from work one day, and Daisy couldn't sleep because, at seventeen, she had never been in a room all night by herself. Even though Jim was a mean and bitter person who used ugly language at her, he had never laid a hand on her. Even though they had never liked each other, their enslavement had knitted a bond between them – they had allowed each other to survive by not throwing obstacles in each other's way. It may not have been much of a bond, but it was something. Jim never came back.

"Of course, Papa Brady was in a rage for a long time about Jim. If he told me once, he told me a hundred times, that if I ever ran away he'd follow me till he found me and then he'd tie me across the kitchen table with nothing on me and he'd skin me alive. And to show he meant business, he swiped at my arm with the curled end of the leather-knife he was using to mend a pair of shoes on the kitchen table; not a big cut, only about an inch long, but it was deep enough to leave a scar." She pulled up her sleeve and twisted her arm to show me the ridge of white skin just below the elbow. "He never let me work at de Lacy Hall after Jim ran away, no matter how scarce the money was."

When Papa Brady couldn't work any more, the three of them eked out an existence on his Old-Age Pension. The woman in the bed got older and greyer and thinner, but wouldn't die. When Daisy was thirty-two she heard from a neighbour that Jim was married, had been married for twelve years, was living in the next county and had no children. One morning, when Daisy was forty-nine, the breadman told her that Jim's wife had died, that Jim was bringing her back to be buried from the local church.

"I went to the funeral and edged up beside Jim at the grave. During the Rosary, when the men were filling in the grave with their shovels, I begged him to take me with him, said I'd be his servant for the rest of his life if he would only feed me and let me live in his house; that no matter what happened I would never complain. And I never have, Kate, and I never will. I think it was only because he was wounded at that very minute that he agreed. When he's in one of his rages or drunk, he's locked me out of the house above more times than I can remember. But he's never laid a hand on me. I never went back to the Bradys' house again." She took a deep pull through the snuff rag. "I know I shouldn't wish anyone bad luck because I know what goes around comes around, but I've always hoped the Bradys died in the same kind of misery they made me live in."

Be the Lord Harry, says I to myself, this is as close to Charles Dickens as ever I'll get: the orphans, the workhouse, the adopting parents, the pretend husband. But I was desperate to say something, to tell her I wouldn't tell anyone, that I was sorry she'd had to suffer like this, that I was sorry Paddy Burns's word had hurt her so badly. Then she said something that made me more speechless entirely.

"Kate, on this hob in this kitchen with you is the only place I've ever felt safe and warm."

Suffering duck! I looked at the floor, at my feet, at the brown laces I'd put in my black shoes that morning because there were no black ones in the house. I had no notion at all what to say, but I cleared my throat to get ready to make some sort of sound because I had to say something, the same as I'd have to do something if I was standing at the lake and a child was drowning.

But it was Missus Brady who spoke again. "The only time I ever felt like a woman was the few months Benny Cosgrove lived with me when he was a child. It was the only time in my life when I knew I was loved."

Before I knew it, there were fat tears running into my mouth; the salt of them! This was the most intimate thing either a man or a woman had told me, and I felt very awkward. One second I was cross at Missus Brady because I was at a total loss for words; the next second I was embarrassed that an older woman would trust me like I was being trusted; the next second I was all shy about what I was being told, as embarrassed as if she had started showing me secret parts of her body.

Even though it was still fairly early, the kitchen was beginning to get dark – there's only one window and the chimney to give light – so we couldn't really see each other's faces. But, when I glanced at her, I could see she had the snuff rag against her mouth, that she was looking off into the darkness in the corner on the other side of the fireplace. I was still standing at the kitchen table, with my backside half on and half off.

"Missus Brady," says I and, I declare to God, she herself started talking at the same second, as if she had heard me taking in the breath to talk on and wasn't sure she wanted to hear what I was going to say.

"Kate, I had no one to stand up for me, and Benny is the

only one who ever loved me. I don't know how to go about protecting Benny. The only thing I can think of doing right now is to keep reminding Paddy and Lizzie Burns that the place will belong to Benny on the twelfth of November. It never crossed my mind that Paddy would fight so dirty, and when he came out with that word I wasn't ready for it."

"Missus Brady . . . I'm sorry . . . Johnny drops the buckets on the floor when you're here," I blurted out. "And Cinders lifts his leg to your white bucket when you put it out on the lane before you come in here."

Suddenly, in the silence, the ticking and tocking of the clock was ferocious loud. What had I said? There's times, when I don't know what to say, I should say nothing.

"Sure, what's a little drop of dog pee in a whole bucket of water, Kate? Cinders has been doing that for years, and Jim and myself are still alive. But, I may tell you, Kate, that sometimes I think the pee takes away some of Jim's contrariness, like it was a magic mixture."

I couldn't help myself. If someone told me I'd go to hell for all eternity for laughing at that moment, I still wouldn't have been able to stop myself. At first it was a titter. Then I was shaking all over. And somewhere in the middle of the storm of laughter that swept over Missus Brady and myself, I realised it was funny little things like a dog's pee curing contrariness that had helped Missus Brady keep her head above the threatening waters all her life.

The next chance I get, I'm going to talk to Johnny about throwing the buckets on the floor. Missus Brady doesn't need such a rude and loud hint that it's time to go. And whenever she comes and Johnny is across the fields, I'm going to give her tea, sit down myself and have one with her.

19. Missus Brady

God be good to her – Lill-the-aunt, as we called her – the woman next door to Papa Brady's. She showed me how to string onions. I can't help but think of her whenever I sit down to string, and every time I sit down to do it I say to myself, the next time I string onions I'll think of Lill-the-aunt again. That means I'll think of her the last time I ever string onions before I die.

I'd better sit by the door and keep a sharp eye out for Becky on her way for the messages. That one goes by like a hare.

Lill-the-aunt had nothing when she was born, and when she died she owned nothing. She earned her living working like a labouring man. Her hands were livid frying pans. She died in the poorhouse, roaring, as they say. Cancer, but you can't say that word. People think if they hear the word spoken their chances of getting cancer are worse, as if the evil spirit of the thing is wakened up when it's named.

"Becky! Becky!"

Bloody into it, I nearly missed her.

Thank God she heard me! She goes so quick, sawing from side to side, that it takes her ages to stop. She's ashamed to be seen on a bike that's too big for her to reach the saddle, thinks the girls in the town laugh at her for being a farmer's daughter, for riding a farmer's wife's big bike. "They're jealous, child," is what I told her that day she came in, afraid to go home with the dead hen in the basket, and Billy Bates – Earthquake Face – after frightening the life out of her up the lane. If she wasn't so upset I would have died in knots with the laughing.

Kate had sent her for a clocking hen to Sarah Nannery off out at Traigue – the one they call the Infant of Traigue because she's forever eating the altar rails. The Glanvils are anything but unprepared – a thing they all get from Johnny. He'd have made a great general, up there with Napoleon himself. So when Becky went for the clocking hen, she had an old barley sack and a piece of twine to tie the neck. Off she tore like a hare, with her stuff in the wicker handlebar basket. She got the hen from the Infant all right, but the sack was caked with dust from the ground-up barley. The air couldn't get in and the bird started to smother. When the child was coming down the town, didn't the hen start to squawk. "It wasn't cackling, Missus Brady, it was squawking," Becky told me, and her face wet with crying. A squawking hen can be every bit as loud as a squealing pig with its snout caught under a gate.

The poor child was so embarrassed to be in the company of a squawking hen that she put one of her hands into the basket and pressed the sack till the hen stopped. When she got to the top of the lane above at Miss Moran's, she took her hand off. But by the time she got near our house, there wasn't a stir out of the bird. Down off the bike she got and opened the sack. When the hen didn't move, the child thought it was after fainting. Of course, she was terrified of going home with the Infant's injured hen; afraid Johnny would kill her. And I don't blame her for thinking that. He can be a terrible impatient man with them, with everyone.

I hate it when he comes into the kitchen below with his two metal buckets and drops them on the floor to get rid of me. If I see him coming through the window, I get off the hob before he gets to the door. I hate them buckets and what he does with them. Kate knows it's rude, too. But talk about rude! Paddy Burns calling me an oul cunt! I try not to think about it, but it's hard not to.

At least I felt better after talking to Kate below.

The Infant's hen. Becky dragged the sack over to a lough of water. She pulled out the hen's head and tried to revive it in the water. She was so taken up with bringing the hen back to life, she didn't hear Bigword Earthquake Face arriving on his bike, and when he spoke the child thought the sound was coming out of the hen. She jumped up in the air with the fright and, when she recovered herself, she threw the bag into the basket and took off. Then she came in here to me to find out what to do, still shaking from the fright the big eegit had given her.

Sure, the hen was as dead as a maggot, died for want of air, its red feathers white with barley dust. But it all worked out all right. I went down below with the child and the hen and, before I finished telling them what happened, they were all in stitches on the floor. Kate got another clocker to hatch her clutch of turkey eggs.

A few months later, Kate gave the Infant back a different hen, but that one spends so much of her time with her head above the clouds talking to the saints she never noticed the difference.

At last Becky comes back, wheeling the bike.

"Good girl," I tell her, as I hand her the seven pennies wrapped up tight in the piece of paper. "Don't look at that now, and give it to no one but Ivor Thompson. The next time I'll have a penny for yerself. Go on now, like a good girl, and don't run into a bush on that bike. There'll be a ha'penny change."

Ivor Thompson, the shopman, kept his promise about not telling anyone, and he's the only one in the town who knows I take a pinch. You can always trust a Protestant better than a Catholic. A Protestant would never call a woman what Paddy Burns called me. A Protestant wouldn't call an animal a cunt, and I'll bet anything a Protestant wouldn't even know what a cunt is. The balls of Paddy Burns to call me that. That fellow has no more class in him than I have in my arse. But, in the long run, it'll hurt him more than it'll hurt me. They all know why he called me an oul cunt, and now they'll all be keeping a sharp eye out to make sure Paddy and Lizzie move out on the twelfth of November. The fecking oul bastard. I try not to think of it too much or I'd go down there and claw the appendix out of him. Like Kate Glanvil said, I have to be patient, and in the end Paddy Burns and Lizzie will be gone and Benny will have the place back, and that's all that counts.

Lill-the-aunt, God be good to her. The day she showed me how to string the onions was the day she got her first turn, fell down on the kitchen floor like she was nothing but a skinful of water. At least it wasn't out on a dunghape she fell, like Cha Finley below. Sweet Jesus tonight! When Murt McHugh told me about Finley, I thought I'd burst a gizzard trying to keep a straight face, and Murt droning on like he was a war hero who'd rescued Cha from death's door, dragged him across no man's land under fire. McHugh going on about Cha as if the midget deserved to be saved after what he did to his own sister so the threshing plans wouldn't be upset. Doctor Crippen is what I'd call him, not Little Cha Horner, as Bigword calls him. If it was me who had found Cha unconscious up on his dunghape, that's where the bugger would have died.

"Cha," says Murt, "is always bound up in the gut because he ates nothing but bought bread and rashers. He gets so bound up he doesn't shite from one end of the week to t'other.

"I was going down," says Murt, "to see about buying the new calf offa him, and when I got to the other side of the field I could see this yoke up on the dunghape. In the name of the good Christ, says I to meself, but what the hell could that be at all up on the dunghape. I was thinking after, that it was only because I wasn't expecting to see what I was seeing that it took me so long to figure out what it was.

"Never in me life before," says Murt, "did I ever see a man lying on top of a dunghape with his hat on, and his trousers down at his ankles, his shirt-tail and short coat up at his chest and not a stir out of him. 'Cha,' says I, 'Cha, are yawlright?' says I. I said it a couple of times. Then, be God, says I to meself, shure I'll have to climb up there and see what's wrong with the poor hure; shure he could be dead. I nearly never got up the dunghape, he has such slithery shite down there, and I was covered with shite meself be the time I got up to him. The first thing I noticed, he was wearing a tie, and, says I to meself, it's bad enough to be prostrated – aye prostrated – on top of a dunghape with yer things hanging out all over yer belly, but to be wearing yer tie! That, says I, takes the biscuit entirely.

"There wasn't a budge out of him," says Murt, "when I poked him with the toe of me wellington. But his hairy belly was going up and down so I knew he was alive. His mickey on his belly was going blue with the cold. And what, says I to meself, in the name of the sweet Jesus, am I going to do now? It would be terrible to leave him there, and

maybe dogs would come and start aten him, says I. Be the
time I'd get back to Derrycloney Lane, and then up the
town for Mansfield the doctor, shure the bugger could be
half et. Then it struck me straight between d'eyes, as shure
as I'm standing here. I'd cut across Cha's two far fields and
wait on the tarred road till someone came along, and I'd get
him to go for the doctor. So down off the dunghape I went,
like them lads you'd see in the paper coming down the
mountain in the snow, and off as fast as I could across the
fields and out through the thorniest hedges I ever
encountered in me life."

"Did ya cover up Cha, Murt?" I asked him.

"Cover, me arse!" says Murt. "Shure, I had nothing to
cover him with, and who do ya think comes along on his
bike but Pad Lehan, the tram conductor, Crip's brother-in-
law. You'd think I was one of them lepers out of the bible
with no ears or nose or fingers, the way he looked at me, and
he in his blue serge suit in the middle of the week. When I
was telling him about Cha up on the dunghape, the
conductor kept moving away like he'd get a disease offa me.
When I toult him he had to get the doctor, he says, 'Shure,
I'm going home from the town, not to it. Wait till someone
else comes along that's going to the town.'

"'Well, ya fucking thoughtless Protestant hure,' says I to
Lehan, and he not a Protestant at all. 'Go on home with ya,
ya scallywag, ya scut, and ya with a neighbour after having
a turn up on his dunghape and his trousers down and his
shirt up. Go on home, Pad Lehan, and when Cha Finley's
mickey is et be the dogs or he dies of the coult, what will
people think of ya then when ya went on home and could
have got the doctor and saved him?' I gave the old bollicks
such an aten that I shamed him into it, and off he went with
his tail between the legs of his blue serge suit for Mansfield.

"To tell the truth for Mansfield," says Murt, "he was down to Cha's nearly as soon as I was, after tearing through the hedges and trotting across the fields. Between the two of us, we slid Cha down off the dunghape and got him in on the settle bed in the kitchen. Cha came to himself after Mansfield covered him with a blanket he got out of the room.

"It turned out that Cha was up on the dunghape trying to make a shite, but he was all bound up. The doctor said, 'Ya were trying so hard, Cha, that ya gave yerself a black hout. That's what happened ya.'

"Mansfield got an empty porter bottle off the dresser and put three or four powders in it. Then he shook the hell out of it with his thumb holding in the dose, after sinking it in the water bucket and nearly filling it. He made Cha drink it there and then, and he says to Cha, 'Yed better be ready in about half an hour to run.'

"Then the doctor," says Murt, "said there was nothing wrong with Cha at all except constipation. 'That's the same as hardbound,' says Mansfield, and he out the door with his bag. But no sooner was he out than he was back in. 'Cha,' says he, 'did ya ever think of making a lavatory where ya could take a shite in cumfort?' 'Ah no, doctor,' says Cha. 'Shure, I've backed up on a dunghape all me life, and I'll back up on a dunghape for the rest of me life too, like me fadder and mudder before me.' 'Right yaar, Cha,' says Mansfield, and out the door he went, not to come back again. And no sooner was he gone than Cha says, 'Lavatree me arse. He must think I'm as big an eegit as Johnny Glanvil with his lavatree in the garden; spend munny on a place to take a shite in! Did ya ever hear such a horseload of shite in yer life?'"

Thank God for favours big and small, but there's Becky back already and the longing just coming on me for a pinch.

"Thank ya, me girl," says I, and I always imagine the Glanvil children stand well away from me when I'm working with onions.

"We have a new lamp," Becky says.

"I know," says I. "Yer mother told me about it when she was going home with it in the pony-and-trap this morning."

"It's an Aladdin lamp, and it's going to be real bright, like an electric one," she says.

"Better than an electric one," says I, "and yeel all be able to read yer own books at the same time now, instead of queuing up for yer turn near the old double-wicker." Off she goes on the bike, sawing, and she doesn't even know how lucky she is with that mother of hers. Kate's a great planner, and she has great ways of making a few extra bob. With the Aladdin she has the latest in paraffin oil lamps, and she has the Brownie box camera too, and a Singer sewing machine that must have cost fifteen pounds. And the gramophone. It's from the duck eggs and the butter and the Children's Allowance that she saves the money, and when she has enough for what she's saving for she's not afraid to spend it. It wouldn't surprise me at all if the next thing she got was a wireless. Sweet Jesus tonight! but wouldn't that be great. They say you can hear the pantomime in Dublin at Christmas on the wireless.

I'll finish up this string before I take a pinch. But I'll have to wash the hands first. There's nothing worse than a nice pinch of fresh snuff with the whiff of an onion off it.

Fecking oul cunt, I ask you!

20. Johnny Glanvil

I love coming here with the barley to be ground and the oats to be crushed.

I love the smell of the place, and the dryness, and the way everything is planned out; the whitewashed walls and the wooden floors always swept clean; the rows of flooring nails shining from the soles of leather boots; sacks of ground barley all in neat rows, lying against each other like fat pigs asleep.

My twenty-stone sack of oats, at the end of a chain, is whisked up through the trapdoors in the second floor as if it weighed nothing. The trapdoors close under the sack, and Watty Wrenn's waiting there with the rubber-wheeled hand-truck, not a bockety iron-wheeled yoke like we have. The sack has barely landed back on the closed doors before Watty has it gliding on its way over the smooth floor to the grinder, balanced on the hand-truck, making it as light as a sack of straw. Then there's the hum of the machinery, and the whirr of the wide belts going from one floor to the other through holes in the floor. The machinery groans like a satisfied pig flopping down in the straw after a big feed of mash.

Watty Wrenn trots down the clean, dry and worn wooden steps to kick the sack attached to the chute to make sure the corners get filled, and the white dust makes him sneeze.

It's terrible hard for me to keep Paddy Burns out of my mind – what he called Missus Brady. Jakers.

There's times I say to myself that I'd love to work here; nine hours a day, off on Sundays and a half-day on Wednesdays; aye and completely off the minute you step out through the door, too, not having to worry about rain or wind or anything; always dry and with a weekly wage that you know is yours even before the week begins – instead of the muck and rain and hard labour of farming, and the whole thing depending on the weather and praying.

It's only on wet days that I come up here to get the oats and the barley done. This is one of those jobs you can't afford to spend fine weather on and, as well as that, there's hardly anyone out on the roads in the wet, except Bigword Billy. Maybe that's why this place always feels so warm and dry, because it's always wet outside and maybe windy, too, when I come here.

Watty Wrenn may be dry and have a weekly wage but, for all I know, he probably has his own version of a coalminer's black lung from the corn dust; for all I know, he might be living hand to mouth and never has a chance to save up to buy something extra like a gramophone, or an Aladdin lamp.

That was a great idea of Kate's – the Aladdin lamp. The kitchen was never so bright. It's as good as an electric light, only it has to stand on the table instead of hanging out of the ceiling. "Will ya get out of me light," someone is always saying. But it's still a hundred times better than the double-wicked lamp; you had to be sitting on top of the double-wicker if you wanted to read, especially if the book had small print. Even Bigword had something good to say about the new Aladdin lamp the other night when he was in with

Bleak House – at least it was good till I met him this morning. It's the first time he said something good about anything we own. He's one of the quarest men I ever met in my life. It's no wonder they threw him out of the seminary.

On the way up here this morning! Here was Bigword, coming home from the town with his messages in a cardboard box without a lid, tied to the carrier on the back of the bike with a bit of binder twine, and nothing would do but that he stop me in the pouring rain to talk. For an educated man, he's a terrible eegit. It's a good job I had the cape on, and the extra sacks spread over the bags of corn. But Bigword wasn't even noticing the rain, and it soaking into the loaf of bread in the box and into whatever else he had in it, too. I could see a small jar of Bovril. I'd never let on to my neighbours what I bought in the grocery shop; I'd always make sure it's covered up. But Bigword doesn't mind displaying his ball bag and connecting rod to the tinkers down at the lake, so why should he mind displaying his groceries to the world.

I hate the way he says my name; I feel like he has me by the throat, is pushing me up against a tree to get my attention. And once he gets started it's like he throws up block walls around me with his words, and escaping would cause more hardship than staying. "Let me tell ya something, Johnny," he says, and his big lips and cheeks flapping all over the place full of noise and spit. What could I do but stop? He grabbed the wingboard with one hand and sat there on his bike like it wasn't raining at all, hat all drooped down around the rim making him look like he had a bucket upside down on his head.

Once he starts talking there's no knowing when he's going to stop. "D'other night when I came out of yer kitchen, I

couldn't see a thing after such a bright light in me eyes."
Then he told me how he had to stand on the lane outside
the wicket door for ages, holding on to the handlebars of his
bike, waiting for his eyes to get used to the dark, "and me
bearings gone altogether," as if it was my fault he couldn't
see.

When Bigword tells you something, he doesn't know what
to leave out. He tells you so many details that, after a while,
you begin to wonder does he think you're a complete eegit,
or if he's a worse eegit than you thought he was in the first
place. And his face! The way it changes all the time – it's like
looking at a pot of oatmeal boiling, always moving, always
changing and bubbling, always shooting hot air out of little
volcanoes. No wonder Missus Brady calls him Earthquake
Face.

Then he tells me he was talking to Benny Cosgrove
yesterday, but I knew right away this was his way of getting
around to talking about Paddy Burns and what he called
Missus Brady. "Benny's so thin, I always say he must have
been reared on a consumptive cow," he says, and the eyes
going from side to side, like they were disconnected from
the machinery behind them; and the head nodding all over
the place as if the strings attached to his backbone had been
suddenly cut; the wrinkles coming and going on his forehead
like they were waves on a lough of water in a storm; and even
a big wrinkle between his eyes – one that starts halfway up
his nose and ends above the eyebrows – moving like a worm
twisting on the end of a fishhook. And then, the worst of all,
when he says something that he thinks is very, very
important, he grabs you by the arm to make sure you're
listening, as if daring you not to hear what he's saying.

But, this morning when I met him, he couldn't grab me
by the arm because I was up in the pony's cart. Instead, he

grabbed me by the leg above the knee when he told me Paddy Burns had called Missus Brady a dripping cunt.

I had to stop myself from whacking the back of his hand with my knuckles. It's a real bugger when someone grabs you above the knee; it's so tickly, but, besides that, I don't like it when someone grabs at me like that – it makes my skin crawl and I want to say, "Get yer bloody hand offa me, ya thick eegit!" Of course, if I said that, Bigword would be so insulted he'd never talk to me again; he'd go around telling everyone I shouted at him, called him an eegit, and for ever after when I'd meet him I'd have to not talk to him. That would be worse than talking to him.

Bigword Billy seldom says good things about anyone. The first thing he does is clobber them by saying something like what he said about Benny: reared on a consumptive cow! That's his roundabout way of saying Benny can be laughed at. I know damn well if he says not-nice things about everyone else to me, then I'm no exception to his blackthorn wit.

On purpose, I didn't even give a hint of a smile at what he said about Benny. Then I said, "No, Billy. Paddy didn't call Missus Brady that," and I edged across the seat of the cart until his hand fell off my knee.

"Let me tell ya something, Johnny," Billy said, like he was the pope going to tell me what I have to believe, like it or not. "Missus Brady told Dunkle that Paddy called her a drippen cunt."

"No, Billy," I said. "He only called her an oul cunt."

"That's what I'm saying, Johnny, an oul cunt. It's a terrible thing to call anyone a cunt, drippen or oul, wouldn't ya say? Now, let me ask ya something, Johnny. What has Missus Brady ever done to Paddy Burns that he would call her a drippen cunt?"

"Ah, Jakers, Billy," I said. "Shure, you'd have t'ask Paddy that." Bigword knows as well as anyone else in Derrycloney that Missus Brady has been bothering the hell out of Paddy about the twelfth of November. But Billy likes to talk about it, sort of roll around in it in a gossipy kind of way, like a dog rolling around in another dog's dung; it must make him feel good to wallow in the miserable goings-on of other people, puts him above the ones he's talking about. Billy knows how Paddy and Lizzie ended up living in the Cosgrove house. He knew Mick Cosgrove and Kitty, too, before they were even married, knew them when Benny was born, and knew them when they died.

"Let me tell ya something, Johnny. If Paddy is cross enough to call Missus Brady a drippen cunt, then I'm not going t'ask him anything meself. He might ate the face offa me entirely."

Then he started telling me how Paddy and Lizzie were "dog-arsed poor" before they moved to Derrycloney to take care of Benny, sixteen years ago; that Mick Cosgrove's dying was "a gift from God" for them. And I knew damn well that Bigword knew that I knew everything he was talking about. But he loved rolling around in it, kept inviting me to say things, expected me to agree with him too, roll around with him in the dung, but I said nothing at all. I just sat in the bloody rain trapped in the words charging off his tongue like fresh cement blocks spitting out of one of those new block-makers at the Spring Show in Dublin. As he went on and on, my mind wandered, his words after a while slithering off his tongue like scoury dung shooting out of a force-fed bullock's arse. I had to listen to him for a certain length of time to make sure I showed the proper neighbourliness, even though on the inside I was fit to be tied, and I thinking, "Bad cess to ya,

Bigword Billy Bates," as his words shot out faster and more watery.

He talked about how the Burnses never had a cow in their lives until they came to Derrycloney; they never even knew what a churn was until they saw the little one Kitty Cosgrove had, the one she'd set on the kitchen table every Saturday morning to churn the cream; Paddy and Lizzie never had hens or eggs, never had growing potatoes, nor rhubarb, nor apples; they never had an ass-and-cart.

"And do ya know what makes me laugh, Johnny? Even the dunghape was something they never had, and it was the dunghape that gave them great notions altogether. Shure, the dunghape is the one thing that all the people in the town are jealous of; it's what they can see and, like a scientist deducing because he can't see what he knows is there, they deduce there's great wealth behind the dunghape, even if they can't see the wealth. A dunghape is a great sign of prosperity. A dunghape is pure prestidigitation that separates the labouring man from the farmer, divides the man with nothing from the man with something. There's nothing like a good dunghape, and the bigger it is the better, and all it is, when ya think of it, is a pile of shite. But there's no beating it to bespeak wealth."

Inside my brain I rolled my eyes as Bigword took off after his favourite subject – that great symbol of class distinction. What depth of loneliness was he in, when he stumbled across the symbolism of the dunghape?

Maybe an educated man would call Bigword a philosopher; maybe a visitor from another country would call him a poet; maybe in a thousand years he will be canonised because some pope will think he was a mystic; maybe a doctor from Saint Dympna's Asylum would say he's a lunatic.

No matter what all those people might think of Bigword, I can't help but feel he's in terrible want of living with other people. But that doesn't mean I felt bad for Bigword. I didn't feel bad for him at all. I just wished to hell he would shut up and let me get out of the bloody rain. Like Father O'Shea said to Kate about Crissy, "There's people who get paid good money for looking after lunatics."

It was a strong gust of driving rain staggering Bigword's flow of words that gave me an opening without it seeming I was brushing him off. In a sort of dramatic voice I said, as the tail of the gust whipped around us, "Billy, yer going to ketch yer death of cold if ya don't get out of this rain. Hurry up and get home and dry yerself." I didn't give him a chance to answer, and the pony trotted off when I dropped the reins on her rump.

Dunghapes! Dunghapes! And the notion Bigword might be canonised some day isn't so outlandish at all. Look at Saint Francis; there was a man half-naked, going around talking to birds, and look where it got him. Hundreds of years after he died, people made him into a saint.

Saint Bigword Billy of Derrycloney. It doesn't sound nearly as smooth as Saint Francis of Assisi, not enough esses in it. Saint Billy Bigword of the Dunghape.

Jakers! Watty Wrenn has the sacks all tied up and ready to go in the pony's cart. I like to slip Watty a shilling for himself. I hope it makes him feel as good to get it as it makes me to give it. He seems glad to get it, anyhow.

Watty always grabs the end of the sack where it's hard to get a grip. I grab it by the neck. We swing the four sacks up into the cart, and the sleepy pony lays her ears back crossly on her head when the bellyband snaps into her without warning.

Out into the bloody rain again I go and, like I always do

when I'm leaving the Crusher Yard, I think to myself, "I came up with two sacks of corn, but I'm going home with four sacks of meal. It's like the miracle of the loaves and fishes."

I pull the rainhat down tightly, make sure the cape is spread out taut so the water won't run on to me. The pony bends her head against the rain and trots off down the empty street, the sound of the tacklings and chains dulled in the damp.

21. Crip Quigley

There's sometimes I'm a ferocious eegit, and even while I'm doing the eegity thing I know it's eegity, but I still go ahead and do it anyway. Now, why is that, I ask you?

Why do I tell things to Murt McHugh when I know that any time I've ever told him things about myself he made a laugh of me; went then and talked to everyone on the lane about me and had another laugh. Once bitten and I'm not twice shy, as oul Mangan would have said, because I didn't learn my lesson.

I've often wondered about it, and the only thing I can think of is this: when I start telling him whatever it is I'm telling him, I can't see how it could be laughed at at all, and it's only when he starts grinning that I feel very eegity for even thinking for one minute that what I'm talking about is serious. But how is it that I don't see it is not serious till Murt starts grinning? Then again, maybe I'm not making an eegit of myself at all. Maybe Murt makes an eegit out of me. He's quicker with the words than I am, and a noisy man is always in the right, as oul Mangan would have said.

Like when I told Murt about the night of the terrible loud noise, about going out to see what it was all about with nothing only my shirt on, and somebody started beating the jow out of me in the middle of the lane in the dark.

And then about walking into the ditch and into the stable door and the pump before I could find my way back to bed. And my toes. And the more I told him the more he grinned, and that made me keep talking all the more, trying to make him serious again. By the time I was finished, he was hissing like a train letting off steam, and I felt like a terrible eegit altogether – stupid. I couldn't see at all how it was funny, what I was telling him.

"The noise, Crip!" says he, and he grinning like a stuck pig. "The noise," says he, "was a naeroplane."

"A naeroplane?" says I, because he took me by surprise.

"Aye," says Murt, "a naeroplane; one of them yokes that flies from Gander ta Rienanna down at the Shannon river, and then flies on to the big cities in London and Paris and Germany. Shure as God, that's what ya heard, Crip – a fucking naeroplane and ya didn't know what it was. Shure, they've been going over for ages."

But then I tell Murt, says I, that it wouldn't be a naeroplane in the middle of the night because a naeroplane couldn't see where it was going in the dark.

"Dark me arse, Crip," says Murt. "Shure, they have yokes that tell them where they are and where they're going and even where they're coming from."

"Well," says I, "it couldn't have seen me, because it was so dark I couldn't see my own hand."

"What do ya mean?" says Murt, and I knew by the sound of him that he thought I was the biggest fool that ever lived in Ireland. "What do ya mean? Shure, the naeroplane wasn't looking for ya, Crip. Why would the naeroplane be looking for ya?"

"Sure, Murt," says I to him, "whatever was making the noise is the yoke that hit me."

"Ah, Jazus, Crip," says Murt, and he threw back his head

and laughed, and I could see halfway down his throat, all that wet red stuff and the black teeth. "Shure, it wasn't the naeroplane that hit ya, Crip. How in the name of the good Christ could a naeroplane hit ya?"

"Well, I don't care what you say, Murt," says I, "but whatever it was that was making the noise, that's the yoke that hit me." And then like an eegit I says, "Do you take me for an eegit or what?"

"How could the naeroplane hit ya, Crip?" Murt sort of shouted, and the way he shouted was like the way you'd shout at a terrible thick ass that won't do what you want it to do.

"Maybe the driver stuck out his fist and hit me in the head and then another fellow beside him hit me in the chest," I says.

"And how could he do that?" shouted Murt, as if he knew everything about naeroplanes. "Do ya think he opened the door when he was going over ya, and stuck out his foot to hit ya? Jazus, Crip, don't ya know anything about naeroplanes at all?"

"I know they make terrible noise, Murt," says I, "and I know when they go by in the night they are terrible loud, and you can get hit in the head and the chest. And I know that, Murt," says I, "because look," says I, and I showed him the lump on my head and then I opened the buttons of my shirt and showed him my chest.

"Well, God between us and all harm," says Murt, and he blessed himself real quick, and his voice was all changed. "That thing on yer chest is like the footstep of a goat."

"The footstep of a goat, Murt?" says I. "Shure, the nearest goat is off out on the bog at Shem Scanlon's, six miles away. His goats don't ramble this far at all."

"The devil has the same footstep as a goat," says Murt.

"Maybe it wasn't a naeroplane ya heard at all, Crip. Maybe it was the roaring of the devil just before he jumped on yer chest, and maybe it was his tail that hit ya on the head. Oh, Jazus, Crip, yer finished, true as God." But I could see Murt was trying hard not to grin, and I was so cross at him for treating me like that that I had to get away from him.

"I have to go down the fields, Murt," says I, and I turned around and left him, and I was kicking the shite out of myself for telling him anything at all about the noise in the night. I kept saying to myself, "Yer a ferocious eegit, a ferocious eegit," and I was so cross I could have ran back after Murt McHugh and kicked him up in his arse. And I was so cross I heard myself saying out loud, "And do ya think yer a genius yerself, Murt, ya big gobshite?"

Well, the minute I heard myself saying that, I began to remember the times when Murt made a ferocious eegit out of himself. There was that time he got some of the lads up in Beglin's workshop to make a kitchen table for him, ten years after a calf broke the old one in two when Murt had it tied up, the calf on its back on the table, trying to cut a piece of barbed wire out of the skin of its belly. The calf gave Murt a poke in the balls with its nose and, when he fell on the calf roaring and holding on to himself, the two of them went down through the table.

Murt told Beglin's men that the new table had to be made out of larch and that he wasn't going to pay for it unless it was.

"And don't be trying to cod me," says Murt. "Don't be trying to palm off a piece of cheap, knotty-pine shite on me. And I'll know if ya try, because I can tell ya the name of any bit of wood from the taste of it."

One of the young lads serving his time with Beglin was a terrible chancer, Jamie Harrigan, the fellow that put the new slate roof on the Methodist church up the town. Harrigan says to Murt, "I bet ya a half a crown I can give ya a piece of wood and ya won't be able to tell me the name of it."

"If it's a bit of Irish wood," says Murt, "I bet ya five shillings that I'll tell ya the name by tasting it. Do ya have five shillings, sonny boy?" says Murt, sounding like he knew everything in the world.

When Harrigan said he had the money, Murt says, "Well, where's the bit of wood?"

"It's hard to get," says your man, "but I'll have it for ya when ya come for the table."

"Right yaar," says Murt, "and it'll be a gentleman's bet."

"What do ya mean?" says Harrigan. "There's no gentleman around here that I can see."

"Whoever loses pays d'other, ya thick fucker of a carpenter," says Murt, sort of getting carried away with himself.

"Ah Jazus no," says your man. "Mister Beglin, there, will hold the money and, when ya do the tasting of the wood, Mister Beglin will give the money to the winner."

They say Murt took a long time to count out the five shillings, that it was full of shiny pennies and ha'pennies that had been in the corner of his pocket for years with bent nails and the chaff of last year's threshing. The Harrigan lad went over and stood in front of Murt, watching him counting out five shillings exactly. Then he had to get the loan of a few shillings from Mister Beglin to have enough himself.

When Murt came back at the end of the week for his larch table, the first thing he asked for was the bit of wood he was going to win five shillings with.

But Mister Beglin said, "Business first, Mister McHugh," and Murt forked out four pounds for the table, after making sure it was made of larch by running his tongue along the edge of one of the legs. All Beglin's men were standing around sniggering at Murt with his big tongue like a cow licking her itchy elder, one leg held up to let her at it. Then they all loaded the table into Murt's horse-and-cart.

"Now," says Murt, and he sounding like a big cattle jobber in a new suit talking to a crowd of farmers covered in cow shite. "Where's the bit of wood, young fellow, till I win my five shillings?"

Hadn't Harrigan varnished a bit of flattened-out dog shite that he'd mixed with glue, and all the men knew it. "Mister Harrigan's me name, Mister McHugh," says he, and he handed over the dog shite.

Murt bit into it and started smacking his lips together like he was the king's cook tasting the soup for salt, and he put a look on his face like he was thinking very hard. Then he spoke in the real important voice he uses when he's showing off. "Are ya sure this is Irish and not Norwegian?" he asked your man.

"Oh, it's Irish all right," says Harrigan.

Murt smacked his lips again. "Of course," says he. "It's pedunculate oak, not a doubt in the world about it."

The minute he said that, didn't Mister Beglin say, "Yer wrong, Mister McHugh," and he gave the ten shillings to your man Harrigan.

Well, Murt flew into a rage and got all red in the face. "Hold on a minute there, Mister Beglin," he says. "If it's not pedunculate oak, then what is it?" he roared.

And your man Harrigan says, "It's a bit of pedunculate dog shite, Mister McHugh, with a bit of pedunculate varnish on it, ya thick fucker of a farmer."

All the men started to shout and clap. One of them belonged to the pipe band and he had the big drum ready, hidden all the time where Murt couldn't see it. They lifted Harrigan up on their shoulders, and carried him out on to the street like he was after winning the Sweepstakes and his hands up in the air. They made a great commotion altogether, your man beating the shite out of the drum on his chest till half the town came running to see what was going on.

Murt sort of sloped away and never said a word about the whole thing to anyone, but of course everyone in the town knew about it in five minutes. "Big Chief Dog-Shite-Eater" is what the young lads in the town started to call him, the ones who go to the pictures.

When Murt laughs at me, I wish I had the balls to say that to him: "Big Chief Dog-Shite-Eater", or say to him, "What will ya be having, Sarge?" I wish I could say them things to him, but I'd be afraid. Of course, if wishes were horses, beggars might ride, as oul Mangan would say.

Even though I would never remind Murt of the times when everyone else thought he was an eegit himself, it makes me feel a bit better to think of them things when Murt laughs at me. But, good Christ, just once before I die, I would like to say to him, "Pedunculate dog shite". I may be able to answer back to the nephew, but I can't to Duncle.

The old bollicks. I'll never tell him anything again as long as I live. And it wasn't the devil that hit me. It was someone in the naeroplane. I hope it wasn't the devil.

I nearly forgot about the slithering sounds I heard.

22. Liam Glanvil

Dear Sister de Monfort,

The record came last Tuesday, and there wasn't a mark on it. We all love the music and we make each other laugh when we imitate the animals. I like *The Swan* the best. It is as sad as a swan looks. I asked Father O'Shea who Saint-Saëns is, but he never heard of him. You'll have to tell me. The name of the composition is "Speaking from Experience – What It Means".

I remain, Your nephew, Liam

SPEAKING FROM EXPERIENCE – WHAT IT MEANS

Every Sunday morning, I go to Cha Finley's house with Benny Cosgrove. Cha pays Benny one shilling for cleaning out the pighouse and the asshouse and for getting two buckets of water from the well in the well field.

Cha Finley's kitchen door is at the end of a narrow lane that splits off from Derrycloney Lane at the far side of Crip Quigley's haggard. The first half is so narrow that the tops of the hedges meet each other over your head and make the lane as dark as a church when the lights are not on. No one is allowed to go to Cha Finley's house by themselves, and the children always run past his lane because he might be in there in the dark waiting for them.

Every Sunday morning at half-past ten, Cha Finley drives up Derrycloney Lane in his ass-and-cart to the last Mass. Cha never stops to talk to anyone, just waves, and his head bobs up and down to the trot of the ass as if he has no springs in his body. He doesn't know how to balance a cart. He keeps all the weight pressed down on the ass's back by sitting too close to the front. Instead of loose chains rattling and making music as the ass trots along, the tight chains make quick noisy jerks, and you want to shout at Cha to move his weight off the ass's back, to place the seat over the axle. Cha is deaf and he can't hear the chains not making music. When his cart goes by on Sunday mornings, I run out to Benny Cosgrove's house.

But before I go, my mother tells me the same thing every time. "Keep out of Benny's way and let him get the work done before Mass is over. Be home before Cha Finley comes down the road in his ass-and-cart, even if it means you have to run up the dark lane by yourself."

Cha Finley doesn't know I go down to his house with Benny. Even though Benny is nearly twice as old as I am, he's afraid to go to Cha's house by himself. Benny says it's too lonely down there. But I think it's because Cha's sister died in a room in the house.

At the end of the dark lane there is a wooden, tarred gate with barbed wire stapled to its boards to keep the cow from scratching against it. When we see the gate in the distance, Benny and I start to run, because on the other side there is light; the rest of the lane goes across an open field from one corner to the other. From the gate, it looks like it runs right through the middle of Cha's house.

The dungheap in his yard is as high as the top of the kitchen door. Whenever the kitchen door is open, the hens fly up and roost on the half-door. Sometimes there's three or four hens asleep on it, their heads under their wings. Cha has one ass and a cart, eleven acres and he always has two pigs fattening.

Benny makes me stay near him while he is doing the jobs. But one day in the winter, when there was snow on the ground and the birds had no food to eat, I asked him to make a bird trap for me. But Benny was afraid Cha might come home early and catch us. I kept begging him till he got fed up listening to me. He made me promise never to tell anyone.

Benny took off the top half of the pighouse door while I looked in the hedge for a short stick. We couldn't find Cha's leftover roll of binder twine anywhere, and the only place we hadn't looked was in the spare room. Benny wouldn't go into the spare room, because that was Nan's room before she died. But I opened the door a little bit, and there was the roll of twine on a chair with a wicker bottom at the far wall. There was a narrow bed against the wall, too, and Benny said that's the bed Nan died in. We stood looking at the twine for a long time.

I stepped into the room the same way I'd step on to the ice on the lake to see if it was strong enough to hold me up. A big picture of the Sacred Heart, all faded yellow, was hanging over the bed, a long string of dusty cobweb hanging from the bottom of the frame. In the windowsill there was a candlestick just like the ones we have: white, enamel saucer with a ring at the edge for your finger to carry it, and the holder in the middle for the candle. Nan's candlestick still had the stub in it, and the saucer part was full of melted wax and a lot of mouse droppings.

I found the cut end of the twine and pulled it over to the doorway. After Benny had wrapped enough into a ball around his good hand, I said I'd get a knife off the kitchen table. But Benny wouldn't let me move. He pulled the ball off his hand and gave it to me to hold while he got the knife.

When he was sawing the twine with the blunt knife, Benny said, "Did you ever hear of Little Cha Horner?"

"Little Jack Horner is a lad in a rhyme," I said.

"Why does Bigword Billy call Cha Finley Little Cha Horner?" he asked.

"I don't know," I said, "but my father said he would skin us if we ever mention Little Cha Horner."

When the twine was cut, I went back into Nan's room and pushed the cut end of the twine back into the roll. We ran back out to the pighouse door and the stick.

Benny cleared the snow off a piece of ground beside the dungheap with the side of his boot. I dragged the door over to the bare spot while he tied the end of the twine to the middle of the stick. Benny ran into the kitchen and came back with a handful of crushed oats. He put it in a little pile in the middle of the bare spot. Then he held the stick while I walked backwards to the asshouse letting the twine roll off the ball. When I got to the asshouse door, Benny put the pighouse door down on the bare spot, lifted one side and propped it up with the stick.

Benny went back to cleaning out the pigs while I hid in the dark in the asshouse, peeping out. Every few seconds, a forkful of dung came flying out through the pighouse door and landed up on the dungheap. Two willie wags, hopping around with their annoying tails going up and down, jumped up in the air every time the dung came flying.

I didn't want to catch a wagtail, but I knew a blackbird or a thrush wouldn't land while Benny was cleaning out the pighouse. At last, Benny finished and, after he had carried in a forkful of fresh straw and bedded the pigs, he said he was going down to the well field for the water. He went into the kitchen for the two buckets and, when he came out again, he shouted to me, and I was afraid he would frighten away every bird in the country.

"If you get one, the door will kill it. Don't jump on the door or you'll squash the guts out of it."

I kept wishing real hard Benny would stop shouting, that he'd go away and get the water. And the minute he stepped out of the yard, a fat blackbird swooped down and landed on the edge of the door, right above the spot where it was propped up with the stick. I got so excited I was afraid I would shake the twine by accident and frighten off the bird.

The blackbird was a cock, because it had a yellow beak. I was already imagining it plucked and baking on the red coals on the hearth; the tiny drumsticks; my brother begging me for a piece; my mother warning me about the bones; me pretending the meat tasted nice because it was my blackbird and I had caught it; the search for the tiny wishbone.

The blackbird hopped down off the door and jerked its head around looking for food first out of one eye, then out of the other – turning the looking eye towards the ground. I asked God to let him see the oats, and at that second the blackbird hopped in under the door and pecked once.

I gave the twine such a pull the stick from under the door came flying toward the asshouse door. But when I'd pulled the twine, I'd twisted my head away from the trap and I didn't know if the bird had got away. I ran over to the trap and looked around. There were no little feathers that you'd see when a bird has been whacked. I looked down towards the well field, but there was no sign of Benny. I couldn't wait to lift the door, but I was afraid if the bird was still alive it would fly out and frighten the life out of me.

I jumped up in the air and came down, two feet together, on the door. Then I lifted it up.

The blackbird was there. It was as flat as a pancake, and its guts was lying there near its tail. I gently lowered the pighouse door, and stood there thinking. I had done what Benny told me not to do, but I didn't want him to know. I would pretend that I had caught a bird, but that I was afraid to look under the door. When Benny would lift up the door he'd find the bird with its guts out and think the door had been too heavy.

When I saw him puffing his way up from the well field with a big bucket in each hand, I ran towards him pretending to be all excited. "Benny," I shouted, "I got one, I got one."

Benny put down the buckets and blew on his hands. "I told you not to jump on the door," he said.

"I didn't," I said.

"I heard the door falling first and then I heard you jumping on it. When the weather is frosty the sound travels."

I felt very ashamed for having tried to trick Benny. Everyone says he's stupid, but I know he's not. Everyone says he never talks, but when only the two of us are together he talks like anyone else.

"Is the guts squashed out through its tail?" he asked.

"How do you know, Benny?"

"Because I did the same thing one time," he said, "and the bird was flattened and its guts was out."

"Were you able to pluck it and eat it?" I asked him.

"No. The bird was so flat and broken that everything was mixed up with everything else."

Benny picked up the buckets, and I caught the handle of the one in his bad hand.

"I should have listened to you, Benny," I said.

"Yes," he said, but he wasn't cross at me the way a grown-up gets cross at you when you do something you were told not to do.

When Benny told me not to jump on the door, he had been speaking from experience. From now on, if I see someone going to jump on a trap with a bird underneath, I will be speaking from experience when I say, "If you do that, you'll break up the bird."

On our way home, Benny asked me to teach him the rhyme about Little Jack Horner.

23. Billy Bates

Sometimes my brain isn't working when a thing first shines on my eye. When that happens, I feel I'm not rightly connected to the rest of the world.

One Sunday, one summer, down at the lake, all the swimmers from the town had gone home, and I was looking around in the bushes to see if anything fell out of pockets while the people were changing into their togs. One time I found a blue comb shaped like a cowboy's gun; it even had a trigger. But what I was really doing in the bushes was sort of hanging around to see if the Hippwell One would show up. They're always saying in the town that she's often down at the lake before dark.

The midges were ateing me alive and I had no money, but I thought that maybe if the Hippwell One did come, and that if I did work up the courage to talk to her, that maybe she'd let me at her with the promise of a couple of chickens. I could always throw in a bag of spuds if the chickens wouldn't do. In the meantime, my mickey was straining at the reins at the thoughts of doing it to her. There I was, looking out through a hazel bush with more young nuts on it like little eggs in little eggcups than I've ever seen on a hazel bush, and I slapping at the midges on my face and on the back of my neck and on my arms, when suddenly there were twelve men jumping out of the bushes on the far side of the lake, every one of them with one arm up in the air and their mickeys and balls caught up in the other hand. Not one of them had a stitch on, and all were cheering and running, and bucking up in the air like horses running and bucking and farting after rolling on the ground at the end of a long day in harness.

Some of the men had long hair and beards, and some were bald with no beards. All of them had hairy chests and bellies, with thighs as thick as stumps of beech trees. They were like a pack of savages, and for one tiny part of one second I thought they had spears in the hands above their heads.

The first thing that went through my head when I saw they were bare was that, with a bunch of fuckers like this around the place, I wouldn't stand a chance with the Hippwell One. These fellows looked like they'd all mount her and be off her again before I'd even get the safety pin in my trousers opened.

When they got to the edge of the lake, the savages didn't hesitate. Down came the hands out of the sky, and up went the hands that were covering their parts. Such an array of swinging blue mickeys and balls I never saw, and it not even cold. If they were any bluer, the mickeys and the balls would have been like the string of lights you'd see in the window of Eamon's Emporium at Christmas. Into the water they went, head first, the whole lot of them, the cracks of twelve white arses the last thing I saw.

It was like I fell asleep for a minute, because, the next thing, they were all standing in the water scrubbing each other's backs with the mucky duck and swan shite they kept scooping out of the lake. The ones getting their backs scrubbed were washing their own fronts with muck too, holding their mickeys and balls out of the way to get between their legs. Such a sight, and they all chattering like monkeys in the cage in the zoo in Dublin the year of the Eucharistic Congress, shouting at each other to scrub this side or that side or down along the middle, and they squirming and shaking like a dog when you scratch it behind the ear and it can't stop the spasms of pleasure, beating the floor with a back paw.

"They're all tinkers," is what I heard myself saying out loud, and hearing myself talking is what made me see there was nothing quare going on at all. A crowd of tinker lads, who'd no swimming togs, had waited for the townies to go home, and here they were having a good wash, cleaning themselves like sows in muck. The next thing I know, I'm taking off my own clothes and running bare out of the bushes towards the water, and all the mucky tinkers looking at me with big eyes and open mouths like I was a savage or something, their mickeys and balls hanging there on the surface of the lake at the bottom of their bellies like things sewn on as an afterthought.

I sort of like it when that kind of thing happens to me, as long as it doesn't last too long, seeing something and not being able to see right away what I'm supposed to be looking at, like one of those trick pictures that one minute is clouds in the sky and the next is Jesus rising from the dead, or ascending into heaven, or blessing the loaves and fishes. Jesus is always in there doing something. No one ever sees Rasputin or Jack the Ripper. Missus Brady told me one time she saw Jesus in the clouds relieving himself behind a bush. Missus Brady said she looked away real quick herself, but not before she saw the holy water splashing off a flat rock. I'm never too sure when that one is codding me.

The best one was yesterday when I went into Johnny's to ask about getting the loan of his big mare to draw the sugarbeet up to the train. When I went in through the wicket door, there was nobody and nothing in the farmyard except a landrace sow, a long, thin, hairy, big-eared animal, the bits of its backbone sticking up out of the skin like the teeth in a cross-cut saw. I don't like pigs. The sow had her scabby and hairy back to me, with her two crubeens up on top of the half-door of the pighouse at the far end of the yard. She was screeching like a hure.

Be gob, I held my ground, knowing that a sow with young ones can be a dangerous animal, and I knew there was a litter of pigs on the far side of that half-door. There's stories, says I to myself, of sows ateing children. So I wasn't going to do anything that would give the sow the impression I was coming between her and her young ones.

Then, all of a sudden, the sow dropped down on to all fours and spun around. I couldn't get my feet to move off the ground with the fright, and I stood there as stiff as an icicle. The sow charged up the yard and, I declare to God, I very nearly made a shite in my trousers. Then she stopped so quick that she sent pebbles and sand flying from the tips of her trotters. It was the squeal of one of her litter that spun her around and sent her roaring back to the pighouse, her big ears flapping like rhubarb leaves in a storm. Up she went again on the half-door, like a dog with his paws on your leg.

Be the holy fucking Christ, says I to myself, I better get the shag out of here, because the next time maybe one of her young ones won't squeal in time to save me. I was so knocked about with the fright, it never crossed my mind I could be making an eegit of myself. Up on the edge of the pump trough I leapt, and then up on to the wall of the water tank, and from there I put my arse up on top of the farmyard wall that the wicket door's in, my legs dangling.

I had a different view altogether from up on the wall. I

could see into the pighouse, see Johnny and the oldest girl, Becky or Ruthie. Johnny was sitting on a chair with a young pig on its back between his knees, the back legs towards him and they splayed apart. I didn't have to wait to see the light glinting off the cut-throat razor in his hand to know what he was doing. It was the same as down at the lake with the tinkers: everything suddenly fell into place. Johnny was castrating the young pigs and annoying the shite out of the sow at the same time. When he'd cut the balls out of the pigeens, he'd throw them over the sow's head out into the yard; the sow'd drop down off the door, run up the yard after the little balls, slobber them up, and then go galloping back when she'd remember she was supposed to be going mad about her young ones screaming.

The thing about it was this: when I'd seen the sow first, I hadn't seen the pig balls flying out over her head just before she dropped off the door. And there, for one terrible minute, I had thought the sow was running up the yard to attack me with that snout of hers. And here I was, perched like an eegit on top of Johnny's wall. So, I sort of sloped down as quick as I could, trying to act like I was a snake, hoping no one had seen me.

Just as I stepped off the edge of the pump trough, Kate stuck her head out through the kitchen door. To distract her from what I was doing, I said, "Be gob, Kate, it's a salubrious day that's in it."

"It is, Billy," says she, but I knew damn well she didn't know "salubrious" from "salutiferous", even if she does read Charles Dickens to the children. She may be a great reader, but she doesn't have the education, and everyone knows you can't beat the education.

"Yer man's doing the pigs, I see," I said. I would never say "castrating" to Kate.

"Aye," says she, "but I think he did the last one. The sow just ran up the yard for the seventh time, and of the twelve seven are hogs."

When I'm talking to someone and looking at their eyes, I don't know where to look after a while. Kate has grand eyes, ones you could fall into, and I had to pull away or I'd get red in the face, embarrassed-like. Dragging them off her was like pulling on a strip of rubber that's snagged on something and, when my eyes snapped off Kate, they got entangled in a wire going from the corner of the loft, across the yard to the kitchen chimney, a wire I had never seen before in my life, and I've been in Johnny's yard more times than a cow farts in a lifetime.

Kate must have been looking at me looking at the wire, because, just as I was going to burst out and say something about a new clothesline, didn't she say, "That's the aerial for the new wireless, Billy."

Oh, thanks be to God and his most blessed mother, says I to myself, for not letting me put my two feet in it. If I'd let Kate know that I was thinking the wireless aerial was a clothesline, and it twenty feet up in the air, I'd have been the eegit of the year in Derrycloney.

"Ya have a wireless, Kate? One of them newfangled yokes," says I, and I knew I was talking like a dose of scoury shite coming out of a bullock after having its first feed of fresh spring grass after a winter of bad hay, on account of my near escape about the clothesline and being up on the wall, and because I know nothing about a wireless, but I wanted to pretend that I did. I was dying for Kate to ask me to go into the house to see it, so I could tell her, "Ah, once yev seen one of them yokes, Kate, yev seen them all." I'd never let the Glanvils even think they had one up on me. "I wouldn't spend me money on a wireless meself, Kate," says I. "A lot of these newfangled yokes die out very quick. In a few years' time, the shopkeepers won't be able to give a wireless away; they'll be paying people to take them off their hands." I didn't know what to say next to let Kate think I wasn't in the slightest bit impressed with her wireless or her aerial, but at that very minute the sow let a squeal out of her that made me think she'd caught every one of her twelve mammaries in a slamming door.

But it was only Johnny after giving the sow a puck in the snout with his fist. The sow sort of fell back off the pighouse door, and Johnny and the child came out, he holding the chair in front of him like the lion tamer in Duffys' Circus, and the girl trying to keep him between the sow and herself, holding on to the tail of his short coat with one hand, the other hand in her mouth trying to keep herself from screaming with the fright, the hairy snout of the sow with its two big snuffling holes and wicked-looking pig-rings only a few feet away. No sooner had Johnny stepped out of the doorway than the sow went charging in to count her young ones, to see they were all right, and she snuffling loud enough to make you think there was a whole herd of her.

Johnny's a terrible man to have a child in the pighouse with him when he's cutting the balls out of the young ones. The sow could've gone in over that half-door in a flash, and done a job on Johnny and the child. A couple of good chops from a sow that size could do a lot of damage. But who was I to say anything of a reprimanding or advisory nature to Johnny? I'd come to borrow the horse.

"Yer a tough man, Johnny Glanvil," says I, because I knew that was the right thing to say, the thing I knew Johnny would like to hear.

"Hello, Billy," he says, as if he hadn't heard the compliment. But I'm a bit of a student of human nature, even if I say so myself, and I know damn well that Johnny likes the bit of flattery the same as the next man.

The little girl, whichever one it was, ran past me into the kitchen without saying a word – the same one I saw that time up the road the far side of Bradys' with the hen's head in the lough of water. Kate followed the daughter into the house.

"Cutting the pigs, you were?" says I.

"Aye," says Johnny, and he rubbing the pig-ball blood off his hands in d'arse of his trousers, but moving all the time up the yard to the boiler house. Never let it be said that Johnny Glanvil wasted one minute of God's daylight in his entire life. And knowing the nature of the man, I went with him, followed him into the boiler house, with its two pulpers for turnips, one coarse, one fine; and bins of crushed oats and ground barley; the bin for bran and the one for pollard; the barrel of bonemeal and barrel of beet-pulp; and the boiler for boiling a quarter of a ton of spuds at a time for the pigs; and even the rafters in the roof being used to hold neat lines of folded tow sacks, so high up that a pitchfork's needed to put them there and get them down again. "Highly organised", is what I'd say about Johnny Glanvil, if anyone asked me.

"Getting the pigs ready for the fair next month in the town?" says I.

"Aye," says Johnny.

He went over to the bit of a workbench between the two pulpers and cleaned the cut-throat razor in a rag.

"How's the price of bonhams these days?" says I, as much as a way of doing something about the silence as looking for information. But Johnny has never given a straight answer yet to a straight question about money.

"I'd say no more than three pounds, give or take a few

bob," says he, and I knew enough to add on two pounds to what Johnny had said. Johnny's always making poor-mouths. But every farmer I know is the same. It must come from the time of the English, from the time of the assessment man, who'd even put a tax on the panes of glass in your windows. And even though those days are long past, the farmers still do it, poor-mouth everything in case anyone might think they had something. They even curse their neighbours by wishing them a bad assessment. Johnny "bad cesses" everything that doesn't go the way he wants it to; better than saying "fuck it", I suppose, with young children all around the place.

So, I knew damn well that Johnny was going to get at least five pounds a skull for his twelve little piggies. That's sixty pounds. No wonder he can afford to have a pulper that pulps the turnips fine, so the pieces won't stick in the throats of his calves and choke them; no wonder the Glanvils can have an aerial going from the corner of the loft to the chimney; no wonder they have a new Aladdin lamp and a gramophone and a Singer sewing machine and a separator for taking the cream out of the milk. The maddening thing about it is this: if Duncle Murt wasn't so bloody tight with his money, I could have the same and more. I'd love to be the first to have a tractor on Derrycloney Lane, and, by Christ, the first thing I'll buy when I get my hands on Murt's money is a great bloody tractor and every bit of equipment that was ever invented to be pulled after a tractor too.

"I was wondering, Johnny," says I, and I hating having to ask him for the loan of anything, "if I could get the loan of the big mare next Tuesday to draw the beet up to the train. Duncle got the notice from the factory that we have a twelve-ton wagon on Tuesday."

Johnny was putting the folded razor into a hole high up

in the wall so the children wouldn't get to it and, without stopping, he says, as I knew he would, "'Course, Billy."

I know he gets a perverse delight out of being in the position of having to be asked for the loan of something, and I know too that, when I come up to get the mare-and-cart on Tuesday morning, the mare will have the tacklings on her, the cart will be ready with the creels on it, and it'll have fresh grease on the axles. The runners on the shafts, where the backband is attached, will even have grease on them, too. You're sure to get goosegrease all over yourself when you're using something that belongs to Johnny.

I'd feel better about it if I had to tackle the mare myself, and drag the cart out of the shed, and put the creels on. But when you get the loan of something from Johnny, he lays on the butter real thick, makes you feel that he'd love to come and do the work for you. He has a way of crushing you altogether.

Johnny cleaned the oil off the bit of broken roof-slate where he'd sharpened the razor for the pigs' balls, and he put it in the hole along with the razor. I'd bet he has that bit of slate for a hundred years, he's so careful with the money. I'd say he'd be as tight as Murt, only he's married to Kate. A good woman would get the money out of Murt too, spend it on things she'd want, instead of putting every bloody shilling in the bank to rot. Money's no better than a heap of steaming dog dung in a clump of grass on the morning of a white frost, unless it's being used for something.

"I suppose you'll be starting early," says Johnny, knowing damn well that, with a twelve-ton wagon to be filled, I'd have to be going up with the first two loads by eight o'clock, Dunkle Murt's horse-and-cart behind Johnny's. Everyone knows that a twelve-tonner means two more horseloads than a ten-tonner, and that each journey to and from the station takes an hour and a half. "Elementary mathematics, my dear Watson," I wanted to say to Johnny, but of course I wouldn't and I didn't.

"Around seven, I suppose I'll be up for her," I said.

Johnny rubbed the oil off his hands on the back of his trousers. "She'll be in the shafts, Billy," he says, and I knew it would be useless to ask him to let me put the shagging tacklings on the mare myself and yoke her to the cart.

To get away from the treacly situation Johnny creates when he's loaning you something, I said, "And did you think any more, Johnny, about Paddy Burns calling Missus Brady a stagnated cunt?"

"He didn't call her stagnated, Billy."

"It's all the same thing," I said. "A cunt is a cunt, whether it's stagnated or not. Well, did you think any more about it?"

Johnny headed out through the boiler house door and I followed him. "I did, Billy," says he, "and, shure, I think he didn't mean to call her that at all; it just slipped out when he thought he was going to hit her with the wheel of the cart. I don't think Paddy would ever call anyone a name like that on purpose."

"Ah, Johnny," says I, seeing that "cunt" made Johnny wince, "he would have called her an old bitch or something if he was only all excited. But he called her something far worse – a stagnated cunt – and for good reason, too. Missus Brady is driving Paddy mad, telling him about Benny's birthday and about having to leave the house on the twelfth of November, and him with nowhere to go, himself and the Missus and the two daughters."

"Even so," says Johnny, "I don't think Paddy meant to call her a name like that."

"Then why didn't he call her something softer like a bitch. It's a quare thing what a man will do if he's driven to it," says I, and I getting all pissed off at Johnny for defending Paddy, and he knowing damn well that Paddy meant every word he said. And then, without thinking about it, maybe just because I was pissed off at Johnny for pretending, for being so superior about loaning me his shagging horse-and-cart, for having a new wireless, I said, "Shure, it wouldn't surprise me at all if it was Paddy who attacked Crip Quigley the other night at three o'clock in the morning, and all because Missus Brady had driven him to it."

This stopped Johnny in his tracks. "Jakers, Billy! Shure, Crip has nothing to do with it at all, with whatever went on between Missus Brady and Paddy."

"Ah, be gob," says I, "I don't know about that, now, Johnny. It wouldn't surprise me at all if Paddy Burns is as cross at everyone who lives on Derrycloney Lane as he is at Missus Brady for tormenting the shite out of him."

"But why would he be cross at the rest of us, Billy?" Johnny asked the question in such a way that I was meant to know he thought I was the biggest eegit in the world for even thinking such a thing. Johnny was beginning to get my dander up.

"Well," says I, "if Missus Brady keeps telling him about the twelfth of November, then Paddy is bound to think that we all feel the same as she does, only we're afraid to say it."

Johnny suddenly remembered he was wasting daylight by standing there in the yard talking to me, so he started to walk out to the haggard.

"But that doesn't mean he attacked Crip," says Johnny.

"Be gob, Johnny," says I, "when a man thinks he's under attack by all his neighbours, he's going to do the quarest things, things that neither you nor I would think of doing."

By this time Johnny had reached the ladder lying against the hay rick. He started up and, when he stepped on to the bench of hay, he turned around and looked down at me from twelve feet up. "Shure, Jakers, Billy," says he, "how would Paddy Burns even know that Crip Quigley was out standing in front of his house at three o'clock in the morning? And how would he have seen Crip, it was so dark?"

I started up the ladder myself and, when I stepped on to the bench, Johnny was down on one knee with the hay knife and the stump of a sharpening stone. Never let it be said that Johnny Glanvil threw away anything just because it got worn away in the middle and broke in two.

"Well, Johnny," says I, "how can you explain what happened to Crip, if it wasn't Paddy who clobbered him?"

Johnny kept sharpening the knife. "It was an ass or a bullock," says he, "running down the road, and Crip happened to walk out in front of it." Before he got halfway through his explanation I knew Johnny wasn't believing what he was saying himself.

"Well, then, Johnny," says I, and I making it up as I went along, and I more pissed off at him the more I talked, "here's what I think happened and what's going to happen. Missus Brady kept nagging Paddy until Paddy got tired of it and called her a cunt. But he knows everyone is watching him and Lizzie to make sure they move out when Benny turns twenty-one, so he knows everyone is thinking the same way Missus Brady is thinking, only they're not saying it. He called Missus Brady a stagnated cunt because he can't clobber her. He clobbered Crip in the dark because Crip's a bit of an eegit, and Paddy was sort of practising on him, and between now and the twelfth of November, Paddy's going to do something to everyone else, get even with us all."

By the time I'd finished talking, Johnny had stuck the sharpening stone back into the face of the hay rick and was down on his knees driving the hay knife to the hilt along the edge of the bench. He stopped cutting and looked up at me. "Be Jakers, Billy, I don't think you're right about that. If Paddy shouted at Missus Brady, it was because he was afraid he was going to run over her with the ass-and-cart, and he got all excited. Shure, Paddy would never hurt any one of us. We've been his neighbours for the last fifteen years."

"Well, Johnny," says I, "if that's what you want to believe, shure there's nothing anyone can do about it. But you just wait and see; when a man's in a spot like Paddy's in, he'll do quare things. First it was Missus Brady, then it was Crip, and God knows who's next. Remember, Paddy has a wife and the two girls to think of as well as himself."

Johnny had cut his way across the width of the bench by this time. He stood up and plunged the hay knife into the face of the hay rick like he was plunging it into the belly of someone who was annoying the shite out of him. I took the hint to get off the hay rick so he could throw down the hay that he'd cut. When I got to the bottom of the ladder, I shouted back up to him. "Do you want to put a bet on it, Johnny?"

He stopped rolling the hay to the edge of the bench. "On what, Billy?" he asked, red in the face and puffing from the work, as if he didn't know what I was talking about. I hate it when someone does that.

"That Paddy will get his own back on someone else very soon," I said.

"Ah, shure, you know yourself that I'm not a betting man, Billy," says Johnny-the-careful.

Aye, says I to myself, you're too tight-arsed to bet, Johnny; as tight as a bull's hole in August, and that's tight. "Well, I'll be seeing you early on Tuesday, Johnny," says I. "And, Johnny!" I called up to him.

"What, Billy?"

"Keep an eye out for Paddy."

"Ah, Paddy's all right, Billy," he called down to me, and I couldn't even see his face.

When I was walking out of the yard with one eye on the aerial, I thought to myself that someday soon I'll have the biggest shagging tractor in the county and everyone'll listen to what I have to say then. And I'll have a wireless, too.

24. *Kate Glanvil*

Suffering duck! There's going to be ructions, wigs on the green.

When Johnny came into the kitchen with the bike clips still on the cuffs of his trousers, I knew there was something wrong. Then, before he even spoke, I saw the furiousness in him. He was mad, as far gone from himself with crossness as I've ever seen him; nearly frothing at the mouth. I declare to God, I thought he was going to have a heart attack.

The two of us had been anxious since yesterday's letter asking him to go up town to the solicitor's office at his earliest convenience. That meant right now, and Johnny would have gone the minute he read the letter, only it was too late. Mister Parkingston-Shaw would already be in the snug in Nelligan's Pub, fondling his double brandy. It's peculiar how things happen: Owen McIntyre, the postman, got a puncture in the front wheel of his bike out at the lime tree. If he hadn't been late getting here with our stuff, Johnny and myself wouldn't have lain awake half the night worrying about what Mister Parkingston-Shaw, Esquire, wanted.

We hardly slept a wink, each of us trying to come up with a reason for the solicitor's letter. Of course, we never thought it was anything but trouble; there's no one in America to die and leave us money. In the end, we thought it was about a right-of-way or the flow of water or fences or something that farmers are always too cross to talk about to each other and make matters worse by getting solicitors to talk for them.

I don't think Johnny was even up at Mister Parkingston-Shaw's office before I started looking out to see if he was on his way home. And then around twelve, before I pulled back the curtain on the hall window, I knew it was him in the distance – the hat and the high bike. And I didn't even have to move the curtain to know he was boiling worse than Dunphy's steam engine on a hill, knew it from the way he was riding the bike; heaving down on the pedals like he was trying to push the whole machine and himself down to Australia through the earth. It took all I could do not to run out into the yard to ask him what was going on. "No," I said to myself, "I'll wait here in the kitchen so he won't know how worried I am."

Well, when he didn't put the bike in the shed, just sort of let it fall against the side of the house, I knew there was trouble. And then the bike clips; he doesn't like them and always takes them off the minute he gets down off the bike, says anyone who walks around with bike clips on looks like one of those ballet dancers you'd see in photographs in the paper with thin legs.

He came in through the door like a wild horse, puffing and frothing and so red in the face I wouldn't have been surprised at all if sharp spurts of blood had come shooting across the kitchen at me. He threw his hat across to the window and it whacked the glass. Then he used the word I had never heard him saying before.

"That fucking Paddy and Lizzie," he said, and he ripping off his tie as if it was a hangman's rope with a hangman swinging out of it. He even pulled the thin end out of the knot that's been on the tie for at least four years – five years, the day Mick Dempsey married the Lynch one from Ballynahinch. Then he started pulling at his collar, trying to get it off the stud. It was like his Sunday clothes were killing him in the middle of the week, like Sunday clothes worn on a weekday were a magnet for trouble and had to be got out of in a hurry. When the two ends sprang off the stud, the stiff collar flapped out like the wings of a seagull. I became afraid of Johnny's crossness.

"Paddy couldn't be that stupid. He couldn't be. Do you know what he did?" Johnny asked, and I bursting at the seams with the wanting to know. But Johnny wasn't asking a question. "He went up to Mister Parkingston-Shaw last week, the day he called Missus Brady that name, with a will that says Mick Cosgrove left the farm to Lizzie." Johnny tore the collar off the stud at the back of the shirt. He scrunched it up in his fist, and it crossed my mind that's what he was doing to Lizzie Burns in his head.

I had heard what Johnny had said, but I wasn't able to see yet what it all meant for ourselves and the Burnses. And when I didn't get swept up into his crossness, Johnny quickly made it clear why I should be as raging as he was.

At seven o'clock one morning fifteen years ago, when Benny Cosgrove was six, he appeared at Johnny's cowhouse door – Johnny under a cow milking her – with his fingers in his mouth, and he looking at the ground. After a lot of coaxing, Benny said his father was sick in his bed.

It only took one look to see that Mick Cosgrove was after having a stroke, and a bad one at that. Johnny took Benny up to Missus Brady on the bar of the bike, and then he went on up the town in his old workclothes for Doctor Mansfield. The doctor came on in his car and, by the time

Johnny got back to Cosgroves', Mansfield had told Mick he was dying, gave it to him straight, as Mansfield always does; straight between the eyes no matter what it is he has to tell you. He must think it's a waste of time trying to soften the approaching footsteps of death. "There's not a thing in the world I can do for ya," is what he said. Then he took Mick's good hand and shook it. "It won't be long till I'm after ya meself, Mick," he said, and that was it. He made Mick as comfortable as he could, and then went off leaving Johnny standing there beside the bed.

Between hopping and trotting, Mick got it across to Johnny that he wanted to make his will, the spit drooling out of his twisted mouth while he rounded up his face muscles and forced them to shape a word. Johnny said it was like looking at the man in Duffys' Circus trying to get ten dogs to do ten different things at the same time.

The only paper in the house that could be written on was a brown envelope that the rates had come in. And the only thing to write with was the stub of a pencil that Johnny always carried with him, still carries, in the same pocket as his penknife.

Johnny couldn't figure out what Mick was telling him, so he said out loud what he thought Mick should be saying. And when Mick nodded or blinked or moved his hand or whatever it was he did, Johnny wrote down the words, and then helped Mick to write his name at the bottom. I leave everything I own to my son Benjamin who is Benny. Then Johnny wrote the date and his own name. When he started to put the envelope under the pillow, Mick gave Johnny to believe that he was to take care of the will. Johnny put it in his pocket and the next day Mick Cosgrove died. The day after that, Johnny went up to Mister Parkingston-Shaw and gave him the will. The day after the funeral, Lizzie Burns went to Mister Parkingston-Shaw to find out what her brother had done with his farm. Mister Parkingston-Shaw showed her the brown envelope.

"Paddy told Mister Parkingston-Shaw they found the new will in one of the little jugs hanging on a hook on the front of the kitchen dresser. I leave my farm and house to my sister Lizzie who is Elisabeth. My name is at the bottom beside the date that Mick died."

"But . . ." says I.

"It's all too stupid for there to be a but," says Johnny, and he threw his suit coat so hard against one of the chairs that it nearly fell over backwards. "It's such a brazen lie, and Paddy knows it, and he knew Mister Parkingston-Shaw would know it was a lie, and he knew that Mister Parkingston-Shaw would ask me about the new will, and Paddy thought he would have me in such a spot, with being his neighbour and knowing him so well and all, that I wouldn't say he was telling a lie, that I wouldn't do anything to make him lose the house and farm. That's what Paddy did – he made me pick between the four Burnses and Benny, between what the Burnses want for themselves and what Mick Cosgrove wanted for his son. That's what the bastard did. He thought I wouldn't have the nerve to tell the truth, that I wouldn't be able to face him and Lizzie if I was the reason why they'd be put out on the road. The bastard. How did he think we would ever be able to face each other again if, between the two of us, we stole the farm out from under Benny?"

Johnny flopped down on to a chair and belted the table with the side of his fist. "The bloody bitch!" he shouted and, to tell the truth, I was afraid he'd be heard on the road through the chimney.

I didn't know what to do, so I just stood there in the

corner of the kitchen with my hands in my apron pockets. I was so expecting Johnny to let go with another explosion, I was surprised when he said real quiet, "That Lizzie! She must be terrible clever. She nearly got it word for word. I leave everything I own to my son Benjamin who is Benny, and I leave my house and farm to my sister Lizzie who is Elisabeth. After one look at the brown envelope fifteen years ago, she very nearly got it word for word."

Whenever there's a long silence in our kitchen, you can almost see the ticks and the tocks of the clock hopping off the hard walls and the concrete floor like cold hailstones. The edginess of the ticking changes, too, depending on what has been said last and with what harshness. After everything that Johnny had said, I was at a total loss about what would happen next between ourselves and the Burnses, and the ticking of the clock had become as loud as the clacking and hissing and groaning and moaning of the train engine just as it's setting out from the station for the beet factory with forty full wagons behind it.

When I couldn't stand it any longer, when I had to stop the loudness of the clock, I said, "What are we going to do?"

Johnny answered in such a contrasting tone to the one he'd burst into the kitchen with that it struck me he might as well have taken a couple of Doctor Mansfield's powders. He sounded like he'd been pitching hay for fourteen hours on a hot day. Like he always does when he's dead tired, he rubbed his open hand up over his forehead and left it resting on the top of his skull, his elbow on the table.

"I don't know," he said. "I just don't know." He rubbed his forehead against the palm of his hand, and it was so rough it sounded like the noise of the grease paper when I'm getting butter ready for the town. "I don't suppose Mister Parkingston-Shaw will be talking to Paddy for a few days. He'll have to write a letter, and then the letter has to get to Paddy through the post. Say he posts the letter tomorrow, Paddy could get it the day after, if Owen McIntyre doesn't get a puncture or fall off his bike or something. The minute Paddy gets it, they'll know Mister Parkingston-Shaw talked to me. So, for at least two days we'll have to pretend to Paddy and Lizzie that we know nothing."

The clock took over again, filled every space in the kitchen, filled the cups and mugs and pots and jugs and jars, the enamel basin, the half-empty galvanised water bucket, the red globe of the Sacred Heart lamp. But, in the middle of all the sound, I got a brain wave. "How many times a year do you put on your suit and tie and go up the town in the middle of the week, Johnny?" I asked. "No one makes a move on the lane without everyone else knowing about it. It wouldn't surprise me at all if Paddy and Lizzie know already where you were; that since Paddy brought the will up to Mister Parkingston-Shaw they've been watching to see you going up town all dressed up."

"You're right," Johnny said to the table-top. "What are we going to do at all?"

I stood there wishing the clock would stop. I kept thinking Johnny would jump up and pull it off the wall, throw it on the floor and stomp it to death. It was like the clock was just sitting there with its loud mechanical ticking and tocking jeering at us for being in such a stew. Then I began to wonder about Paddy Burns, about how I always thought I knew him to be a nice man, pleasant. But he'd fooled me completely. I began to wonder did I even know what he looked like; when was the last time I had really looked at his face. As I tried to picture him in my head, the first thing I saw was the long moustache, the colour of turf ashes, covering his mouth entirely. Even though I had seen him many times at our table with his cap off, I couldn't get the cap off him in my head. I've often seen a man laid out at a wake without his cap on, and stood there trying to persuade myself that the fellow in the bed is the one I'd known all my life. A man's cap can be a part of him as much as the shape of his nose or the colour of his eyes or the hump on his back. As I put Paddy's face together, his pleasant smile turned into a sneer, his eyebrows were pointed arches, and his eyes were little pools of sly planning. When I imagined him walking, I saw him sloping along, leaving an unpleasant trail behind him like a slug's.

It's strange how a person changes very quickly when we find out something about them that's not nice. The picture of Paddy in my head began to run, as if his picture was made of ink and splatters of water had started falling on it.

With his full weight still on the chair, Johnny suddenly pushed himself back from the table. The bottoms of the wooden legs ground along the concrete floor and it seemed Johnny was inflicting his crossness on Paddy and Lizzie Burns. If it had been one of the children who moved the chair like that, Johnny would have growled at them, told them to take their weight off the chair before pushing it along the floor; that they were breaking the chair apart at the joints; they were setting everyone's teeth on edge with the noise; they were distracting everyone in the kitchen. When Johnny gets something between his teeth he shakes the living life out of it, like a terrier shaking a squealing rat to death, still shaking it long after it's dead.

As he used the table-top to push himself up straight with the motions of an old man, I knew everything would be different from now on between ourselves and the Burnses. We were all in for a time of terrible awkwardness, because everyone would be pretending that no one knew anything, pretending that things were the same as they normally were. The great pretending game; it takes so much energy to play it. Sometimes, I think it would be easier on everyone if an all-out war was fought in the open, instead of having to watch every word you say for the rest of your life on Derrycloney Lane.

"The lousy bastard," Johnny said, and he began to gather up the clothes he had thrown from himself in anger when he'd come home. He went to the door to the side of the fireplace. When he looked down and saw the bike clips still at his ankles he snatched them off.

"Mister Parkingston-Shaw asked me how many cattle are on Benny's farm," he said. "I wonder why he wanted to know that." Johnny went up to the bedroom to change his clothes. Even though I didn't know what was going to happen, I knew it was going to be awful.

25. Missus Brady

I never saw such white sheets in my life; I can even hear them crinkling, feel them as smooth as the collar of a shirt just after ironing. I can even smell the cleanness of them, feel it when I move – not that I can move that much.

This is what a holiday must be like for rich people, only they don't have to break a leg to get it. I can't believe how nice the nurses are. Nothing is too much for them. It's "Are you comfortable, Missus Brady?" and "Would you like me to do your hair, Missus Brady?" "Is your foot warm enough, Missus Brady?" and, I declare to God, "Would you like me to rub your back, Missus Brady?" Rub my back! They are all so nice to me there's times I nearly cry.

I don't remember everyone being so nice when I was in here, years ago, after breaking the hip. But, then again, maybe they were and I was in too much pain to see it.

And the food! There's a boiled hen egg for breakfast with toast; toast, mind you, and a spot of marmalade to go on it. After eating nothing but Kate's duck eggs for so many years, I had forgotten how mild a hen egg can be. Meat of some kind and potatoes and a vegetable for dinner; and then a dessert – every day a dessert after dinner – and a cup of tea with a biscuit. You never know what you could get for supper. Sometimes it's a bit of a fish, or sausages or bread and jam. And all the time there's lashings of sweet tea, only I found out the first day the more tea I drink the oftener I have to call for the pan. That's the only thing that's bad about the place, and it's only bad for people like me who can't get out of the bed. I hate having to do my business in the bed. First of all, there's the other three people in the ward hearing every sound I make; then there's the smell slowly rising and spreading all over the place and everyone knows it's me. And then there's the worst – calling the nurse to take this terrible thing away, and she seeing what I did. The last thing in the world I want anyone to see is the stuff that comes out of me; it's so personal!

But, even though I broke the leg at the wrong time – when I wanted to be in Derrycloney to make sure Benny gets what's his – and even though there was the terrible pain and the muck and such a fuss when I did break it – I'm having a great time here. I've never in my life had such a comfortable time. I was just thinking last night that this is the second time ever in my life, since I was a child, that I haven't had to do anything. Anything! Not even fill the kettle; keep the fire going; not take care of someone else. Sweet Jesus tonight! It's the best thing ever happened to me. I just wish there wasn't the Benny thing. That's the only thing that worries me, especially since Kate told me last night about the new will Paddy brought up to Parkingston-Shaw; she rode over here on the bike, eight miles, to see me after she fed everyone at home. With the help of God, I'll be home at least a week before Benny's birthday and I'll be able to take command of my post at the door to keep Paddy and Lizzie on their toes. They're two bigger melts than I ever suspected.

Only for the Aladdin lamp I wouldn't be in here at all, my leg up in the air in a cast with weights hanging out of it. The weights keep pulling me down in the bed. When people ask me how did I break the leg, and I say, "It all began with a new Aladdin lamp," they look at me like I'm quare or something. Then I tell them about Kate and how she rears turkeys and saves her money and how she bought a Singer and a gramophone and a wireless with its wet and dry batteries, the stereoscopic photographs showing people in India cutting the head off a young goat, and a separator and the Aladdin lamp. Of course, most of the people in here are real bog-trotters and have never heard of an Aladdin lamp. When I'm done explaining it to them, most of them say, "Sure, ya mean a paraffi noil lamp." "Yearra, it might be a lamp that uses paraffin oil," I tell them, "but it's the way the flame is made that's different." I might as well be trying to explain the Trinity to some of them, they're so thick; boggers. They just look at me with their mouths open.

Kate asked me to go down last Friday night to see the new lamp. "Come down around half seven and we'll have a cup of tea, " says she, and before I could say anything, she said, "Johnny has to go to Rathmount with a set of tacklings he got mended for them." Johnny's sister is married to a fellow in Rathmount, a real good-for-nothing who imagines he's a gentleman farmer; he goes shooting rabbits and pheasants in the middle of the week wearing a special hat. Johnny's always pulling him out of the hole he's managed to slip into. Of course, Kate told me about Johnny and Rathmount because she knows well that I'm not comfortable in her kitchen when Johnny's around.

Well, I couldn't believe my eyes when I went in through the wicket door and saw how bright the light was in the kitchen window. It was a white light. When I knocked and went into the kitchen, I had to put my hand over my eyes the same as you do when the sun's shining in them. I oohed and aahed for the girls' sake, and they showed me how easy it was to read, even over at the fireplace. "You can be warm and read at the same time," says Becky. No matter how much the Glanvils have, their house is the same as everyone else's when it comes to dampness and breezes under doors. In the winter, they're like the rest of the country sitting on top of the kitchen fire – too hot in the front and too cold in the back.

The two chaps, Liam and Jayjay, had gone to Rathmount with Johnny, because they wouldn't have to get up for school the next day, being as it was Saturday. So the four of us women, the two girls and Kate and myself, had the place all to ourselves, and, I declare to God, if she didn't have high tea for us all, the four of us giggling away.

I wish I'd known, and I would have made scones and put my raspberry jam on them. Kate had sliced up cuts of shop bread and put a sardine on each piece; she had a Gateaux Swiss roll with cream, a dainty, thin apple tart with Bird's custard, and Jacob's Goldgrain biscuits with chocolate on one side. It was more a feed than it was a high tea. I wondered if Kate was trying to make me feel better after what Paddy Burns called me the week before, and that thought alone made me feel good; someone was on my side.

We dug into the grub, and on account of the new lamp and the brightness of it I told them about the time the electric came to de Lacy Hall, and about how all the people went up Begses' Hill in droves to look down at the big house floating like a big ship on the sea; people even coming on their bikes and asses' carts from miles around to look in the dark.

Then I told them about the lobsters again, about how they cried in the boiling water. It's funny how children want to

hear the same story all over. They know there will be no
surprises, and they don't have to be on edge in case
something terrible is going to happen, and they can look
forward to the funny parts.

When the girls asked me to tell them about riding the bike
over the Protestant's dog, I threw my eyes at the clock to
make sure I'd be out of there before Johnny arrived home.
Kate must have seen me. "We'll hear the pony-and-cart in
the chimney," says she, and she gave me the nod to go ahead
with the story.

So I told them again about Shep, made them laugh about
what the Protestant said to me and what I said to the
Protestant; about that eegit, Jimmy Griffin at the garage,
with his car for hire, pulling me into the back seat and me
screeching like a banshee with the pain in my hip. Every
time I think of Griffin, the pain comes back. I'll tell you
one thing, and I don't say this to the children when I'm
telling them this story, when God was making eegits, he
spent a lot of time on Jimmy Griffin. And when I think of
that fool of a Protestant and his dog! I wasn't just riding
along a smooth road one day and made a sudden swerve to
miss the dog and fell off the bike. The Protestant's fecking
dog, or the fecking Protestant's dog, ran out into the street
and under my front wheel. No matter how you look at it,
one was thicker than the other, the dog licking my face with
his sloppy tongue while the Protestant kept asking, "Did ya
hurt yerself, Missus?" And me with such a pain in my hip
that I couldn't talk. The Protestant kept at it until I was
able to shut him up by asking him to get his bloody dog out
of my face, only I said "fecking". "Will ya get yer fecking
dog out of me face, ya heretic, or I'll give him such a kick
in d'arse he'll get piles on his front teeth." And I was in no
condition to kick anything. All the pain and the rage are

gone out of it now; the dog is dead and the Protestant is gone to limbo. But when the children get me to tell the story about Shep they do be laughing out loud; and in the corner of my eye I can see Kate in stitches.

When I was finished with Shep, I looked at the clock again and Kate made no effort to delay me any longer; she could tell I wanted to be gone before the lads came back. She wouldn't hear about it when I offered to dry the cups and saucers. But I did stay another few minutes and listened to the girls' latest compositions for school. Becky used a few words I never heard of. It's all from the reading they do, I said to myself. Soon she'll put Bigword Billy to shame.

I was feeling nice and warm about Kate when I started for the kitchen door. And, of course, when the three of them came with me to show me out, I felt very nice altogether. It was different from being there with men around the place. When I stepped out into the yard, I was as blind as a bat after being in the bright light for so long. Even though the moon was flashing through thick clouds now and then, if it hadn't been for the light in the kitchen window giving me my bearings I wouldn't have known which way was which.

They walked me out to the wicket door, the girls holding my hands, and we stood there in the breeze stretching out the goodbye, the way we do, so the goodbye is not sudden, so there's really no goodbye at all, just an easy stretching of the apartness, making us like two things at the end of a piece of elastic that will pull us back together again. For a while, we looked at the wind in the sky ripping the clouds apart, the full moon flickering from very bright to solid dark in the same second, making you blind like someone shining a flash lamp in your eyes. Then one of the girls said, "There's the pony-and-cart," and we all listened.

Sure enough, I heard the sound of the cart off the far side of the town. Even though the lads were still nearly two miles away, the rattling of the pony's chains brought our nice evening to an end. Without anyone saying anything, Kate and I knew that I would just about get home and off the lane before Johnny and the boys came trotting by. Kate closed the wicket door and I started off.

How many times have I left Kate's, even in the early dark of winter days? I know it's in the thousands. Wouldn't you think I'd know every step of the way, every pothole, every briar sticking out of the hedge waiting to grab me by the stockings! And I do. But last Friday night, after the terrible brightness of the Aladdin lamp and from looking at the moon, my eyes hadn't got used to the dark, even after talking to Kate at the wicket door for a few minutes, and I didn't know it.

I thought I was facing up the road towards my own house, but all the time I was facing straight across the lane. I was lying down before I knew I'd even fallen. It took a few seconds for me to feel the cold muck under the side of my face, on the hand that was under me, along the leg twisted up under me that I didn't yet know was broken. Then I got the smell. Sweet Jesus tonight! The smell was so bad I could hardly breathe.

When Johnny unplugs the big stone pump trough in the farmyard after he washes the pig-spuds, the mucky water flows across under the lane and into the ditch I was lying in. He cleans out the ditch once a year, and when he disturbs the muck, everyone on Derrycloney Lane knows what Johnny is doing. It's a smell that's worse than anything that comes out of an animal, and when it travels it takes it a long time to scatter about in the air.

For the first few seconds, I just thought, "Oh, God, I'm

going to stink for a year." Then I was trying to figure out how I would get into the house when I got home without bringing the clothes in with me; I'd get Jim to throw me out something and I'd take the clothes off in the turf shed. Then I started to move, to make an effort to get myself out of the ditch, but I might as well have been stuck like a fly in a bit of honey. And not only could I not move, but I could feel myself easing down into the muck. That was the first time I got a bit panicky. I thought I might drown, choke on the muck; can you imagine choking on that stuff! But I turned my head so I was looking straight up; and the arm that was under me, I pushed it down until I felt the solid bottom of the ditch. It was very strange feeling stuck like that, but I still thought I'd be able to climb out by myself.

I made another plunge, but I only made matters worse. When I caught my breath I called, "Kate!"

If I was a man, and a coarse one at that, I would say I might as well have been pissing against the wind. Here I was at the bottom of a three-foot ditch, with the farmyard wall and the kitchen wall between myself and Kate. She might as well have been in Siberia. Then I felt the pain in my leg, then I heard Johnny's pony-and-cart, and then I said, "Thank God, I'm saved."

Kate must have heard the pony-and-cart getting near in the chimney, too, because I heard the bar that locks the galvanised gates being drawn back.

"Kate!" I called again. "Kate!" and, I declare to God, she didn't hear me. Maybe it was the noise of the gate or the noise of the cart and the pony and the chains and the wheels. Suddenly it sounded like the pony's cart was going to come in on top of me, it was so close. I could see shadows moving on the hedge above me, so Kate must have had the yard lamp with her.

The cart wheeled off the lane into the yard and, the minute it was gone in, Kate started closing the gates again.

"Kate! Kate!"

Then I could hear the children's voices disappearing into the kitchen. There was nothing left but the sounds of Johnny untackling the pony. I heard the stable door, heard him telling the pony to "gup". He pushed the cart into the car shed, the hanging draughts jingling along the stones in the yard. I knew I had only one chance, and when I heard his footsteps coming up the yard to the kitchen door I shouted as loud as I could, "Johnny! Johnny!"

I couldn't even tell if his footsteps hesitated, because the ditch was full of the sound of my own shouting. But then I heard the kitchen door closing, and I said, "Sweet Jesus tonight." What could I do but cry, and that's what I did; I felt so sorry for myself that I started to cry like a little girl.

I don't suppose it was long, but it seemed like a year to me, before I heard the wicket door opening and saw the light on the hedge.

"Hello?" Kate's voice said softly, as if she was afraid someone would hear her talking in the dark and think she was an eegit.

"Kate," I called, and, I'll tell you, I started crying like I've never before in my life cried.

"Is that you, Missus Brady?" she asked.

"It is, Kate."

Then she sort of whispered again to make sure no one would hear her. "Where are you?"

"In the ditch."

Then Kate and Johnny were standing up there on the edge of the ditch, the yard lamp between them giving all kinds of strange shapes to everything I was seeing from that angle.

Without even thinking about it, Kate handed the lamp to

Johnny and she slithered down the side of the ditch, stepped over me, turned around, bent down, stuck her arms into the muck under me, lifted me up on the bank like I was a sack of straw and put me down at Johnny's feet. I didn't know she was so strong or that I was so light. I still didn't know the leg was broken. Isn't that a good one, and it paining the life out of me.

That's as much as I tell anyone here in the hospital. I just say the ambulance came and got me. I wouldn't tell them the goings-on that got me from the side of the ditch into this bed.

I hate remembering how smelly I must have been when I came in here, even though Kate did her best to clean me up before Doctor Mansfield came to tell me I had a broken leg. He went away and telephoned for the ambulance.

I have to call for the pan again. Suffering duck! I hate even thinking about the thing, much less having to get the nurse to come and push it under me. No matter how slow I try to go, some of the wee-wee always manages to get on the sheets.

26. Paddy Burns

The fecking solicitor. The minute he called me "Mister Burns", I knew the game was up, and I thinking up to that very minute he was going to tell me the farm was Lizzie's. Talk about being a fecking eegit!

Mister.

It was like he put five miles between himself and myself with the one word. I wanted the floor to open up and swallow me. And it was because I was drowning in embarrassment and shame that I didn't hear what he was saying for a while. The fecker. The fecking Protestant. His voice was going on for a long time before I heard "fifty-one pounds", and right away my ears pricked up.

I asked him, "What fifty-one pounds, Mister Parkingston-Shaw?" Of course, his answer went all over the place, and me shaking with the waiting. But before he got within a mile of the point, I knew the fifty-one pounds were not coming to me.

"It's my duty as a solicitor and a citizen to inform the authorities you have attempted to defraud Benjamin Cosgrove, known as Benny, of his rightful inheritance," is what he started with. "That means, Mister Burns, I have to tell the guards you tried to steal Benjamin Cosgrove's farm from him, like Esau. You'll certainly get the jail."

The shame and the embarrassment ran out of me like a loose shite after me eating a feed of Lizzie's turnips that she didn't know were got at by the frost.

"Mister Burns, I have no interest in you going to jail. So, if you pay my fee for the time you have taken from me with this scheme of yours, I'll not trouble the guards and a judge with your sordid little story."

Parkingston-Shaw, the fecking Protestant solicitor, had me by the balls and he knew it. He twisted.

"Mister Burns, before half-past five tomorrow, you will have my fee of fifty-one pounds on this desk in ten English five-pound notes and one English one-pound note." Parkingston-Shaw, the hure, stood up. The fecker smiled. "Tomorrow, Mister Burns."

I couldn't move. Fifty-one pounds. Fifty-one fecking pounds. I couldn't stand up out of the chair. My mouth was dry down past my navel, and I think I was even a bit dizzy. "Mister Parkingston-Shaw," I said, croaked like a goose with barley dust in its windpipe.

Parkingston-Shaw was moving bits of paper around on the top of the desk. He hadn't heard me. "Mister Parkingston-Shaw," I said again and, when he glanced at me, I went on real quick while I had his eye. "I could no more get fifty-one pounds for you than . . ." but he didn't let me finish.

"The fifty-one pounds is not for me, Mister Burns," says he, the little squinty Protestant eyes of him. "It's for you, to keep you out of jail. At half-past five tomorrow I'm walking out of here and straight over to the guards' barracks. If you don't want me to do that, then pay my fee. And now I will ask you to leave, sir, unless you want another ten pounds added on to my fee; I have another client waiting to see me."

You fecking Protestant cunt of an English hure, I nearly said to him. You black bloody Protestant of an English fecker, that your balls may rot and slide down the leg of your trousers.

I staggered up out of the chair, and I missed the doorknob the first time, I was that shook. When I did get the door open, your man starts talking again, and I didn't have the nerve to look around at him. Maybe I hadn't moved fast enough.

"Mister Burns," he says, and I looking at what looked like a spider shite on the wall in front of me outside his office door, waiting for that extra ten quid to hit me between the shoulders. "Benjamin Cosgrove will be twenty-one on the twelfth of November. If you or any members of your family sleep in Mister Cosgrove's house on the night of the twelfth of November, I will bring you to court, if I have to, to make you pay rent at the rate of a half a crown a night, per person."

I felt like I'd been hit across the knees with a double swingletree. I swear to Jazus, I had to hold on to the wall while I made my way to the front door. By the time I got out on the footpath, I thought there was a flock of ducks gone mad in my head.

It took every bit of strength I had to walk over to the electric pole where I'd tied up d'ass-and-cart. And again, by Jazus I'd swear, when I put my foot on the axle to get up in the cart, I couldn't pull myself up the first time. Only for my fingertips getting caught on the edge of the wingboard at the last minute, I'd have fallen on the road on the flat of my back. And all I could think of was, "I hope to God no one's looking at me," even though I knew that was the same as hoping d'ass would turn into a bird and fly away with me on its back; fly away for ever over the mountain and never come to Derrycloney again; fly away over the sea to a new country where no one would know me, or know that I was thick enough to do what Parkingston-Shaw had caught me at, what Lizzie had put me up to.

Now that I was seeing how the plan had so easily crumbled, I couldn't believe that I'd gone ahead with Lizzie's mad idea. I should have done what my guts told me to do the morning after she first told me the plan that sounded so great in the dark. I should have figured out . . . I did figure out – a man with a brain the size of a babby rabbit shite would have been able to figure out – what would come of her plan. Fecking Jazus. Never throw another man's snowballs, is what my mother always said. I had thrown Lizzie's snowballs after my mother saying it so many times to me; never throw another man's snowballs, and I never knew till that minute outside Parkingston-Shaw's what she meant.

I put my foot back on the axle and climbed into the cart like it was the last act of a desperate man. I suppose I was desperate; desperate to get out of the town; desperate to turn the clock back five days. Parkingston-Shaw was surely at his window looking down at me, laughing like a fecking English fecker, thinking about the fifty-one quid that had fallen out of heaven at his feet. The minute he saw me stepping through his door with the made-up will in my hand, he must have said to himself, "Here's an easy fifty-one quid stepping through me door." Thick, thick, thick.

Sitting there in the ass-and-cart, all I wanted to do was beat my head against a tree, to beat it until it broke apart like a rotting turnip that you'd throw against a wall. Thick thick. How in the name of the sweet Christ could I be so thick, so fecking thick?

With a fierce jerk on the reins, I twisted d'ass's head and drove the heel of my boot into her arse. Off she went, across the market, bucking like a hure and, just as I was pulling out on to the street, who should be coming straight ferninst me with his two horseloads of sugar beet than Bigword Billy fecking Bates, his own horse-and-cart tied by the reins to the back of Johnny's horse-and-cart. He brought everything to a halt and, of course, I had to stop d'ass.

"Be gob," says Bigword, loud enough for the whole town to hear, "I've been looking all over the country for ya, Paddy Burns, and here yar negotiating yer way out of Parkingston-Shaw's; of all the places I'd a thought of looking for ya, Parkingston-Shaw's is the last. Dunkle wants to know if ya'll be able to load the beet into the wagon for us. It took till now for me to persuade him that I'd never be able to draw up the twelve tons and load them into the wagon be meself before the train leaves." Bigword always takes very long to say nothing, and I didn't give a shite what he was saying with all of Parkingston-Shaw's ducks still quacking in my brain. I couldn't wait for him to finish, and before he even got near to finishing I knew what answer I was going to give him.

"Dunkle said he'd pay you seven-and-six for the rest of the day that's in it, feed yerself."

I couldn't wait for the bollicks to finish his speech. "Yarra, feck Dunkle," I said, either to Bigword or to myself, and I cut d'arse off d'ass with the end of the reins. My brain was taken up with fifty-one quid, and here was this mean bollicks of a farmer talking to me about earning seven-and-sixpence for throwing twelve tons of sugar beet up over the side of a train wagon with a beet fork from ground level. "Feck Dunkle, the stingy hure," I muttered to myself, as d'ass trotted off down the street. "And feck you too, Bigword. And feck you, Lizzie," I heard myself saying out loud. I looked around to see if someone had heard me.

That's what the whole thing was: Lizzie's mad plan. She kept at me every minute of every day and night until I wasn't able to bear it any more; her non-stop nagging for letting an eegit like Benny drive us out of the house; what kind of a man was I that my family wouldn't have a place to live, no place to rear a few animals for money to save for a wet day, no place to grow spuds and no place to work? I shouldn't have listened to her. I should've listened to my guts that morning. And Missus Brady was in there in my guts, too. It was that skinny, gimpy bitch, with her constant yakking like a crow about leaving Derrycloney, that stupefied me into bringing the made-up will up to Parkingston-Shaw. I wanted to get back at her; to be able to go up and down Derrycloney Lane for ever in d'ass-and-cart thumbing my nose at her.

Just outside Jack Connor's house, the ass stumbled over a lying down dog dying of the mange in the middle of the road. For a minute I thought d'ass was going to go down and, with the screaming of the dog and because I'd been off in my own head cursing Lizzie and Missus Brady, I got a terrible fright. I was sure I was going to go flying out of d'ass-and-cart head first. At the last minute d'ass caught up with her feet and I got my balance back, and I knew the whole town was looking at me slinking out into the country like a cur with its tail between its legs.

I could picture myself sitting in the cart with the gabardine pulled around me as tight as a suit of armour, the cap pulled down over my eyes like a helmet. I didn't want to see anyone and I didn't want anyone to see me.

Good Jazus! The fifty-one quid was belting me non-stop across the back of the head. Not only had the solicitor found out I was as thick as a double ditch but, into the bargain, he had twisted fifty-one quid out of me. In the name of Christ, where was I going to get fifty-one quid?

I have to admit there was a feeling of satisfaction in the crevices of my belly about having to tell Lizzie we had to cough up all that money. "Look where yer mad bloody plan got us," I'd say to her, and I'd beat her with the words, punish her. "I'm going to be pointed at for the rest of me life for the one who tried to steal a farm from me own wife's nephew. And tell me," I'd say to her, "where are we going to get fifty-one quid before tomorrow night for Parkingston-Shaw? Not only don't we have Derrycloney any more, but we now have to find fifty-one quid because of you." That last part, I knew, would put her back in her place, send her with her head down to the dark corner of the fireplace. A man shouldn't be bossed around by his wife.

The ass trotted past the fancy iron fence outside Miss Moran's house and headed on to Derrycloney Lane without me even giving a nudge to the reins. But, no matter how hard I tried, I couldn't get the will and Lizzie and Parkingston-Shaw and the fifty-one quid out of my head. It kept going around like the rim of an old bike wheel being run after by a boy with a flogging stick in his hand, no shoes on his feet and the arse out of his trousers: Lizzie at the kitchen table with a page out of one of the girls' composition books; the oil lamp six inches away on the table giving strange shapes to her face with short shadows; her tongue caught between her teeth at the side of her mouth, the red tip sticking out between her red lips; the wooden handle of the pen gripped between her thick fingers; the flame of the lamp making bright blue the ink in the inkwell; Lizzie's eyes squinting to the smallness of a pig's eyes with the effort to see; the poisoned wisdom squeezing out of the tip of the tongue and dripping on to the paper through the nib of the pen; me sitting over at the fireplace, sitting where she had told me to sit out of the way. "And shut up for God's sake and let me remember."

Then I remembered Johnny Glanvil. Johnny. Fecking Johnny. Lizzie had been counting on Johnny to tell Parkingston-Shaw whatever it would take to leave Lizzie and me and the girls in the house. And now he knew . . . he had known for a few days what I'd tried to do, get the farm from Benny, and that I'd tried to get Johnny himself to tell a lie for me. I felt myself sinking deeper into the gabardine, and I pushed my head deeper into the cap. I knew now everything had changed. I wouldn't be able to face Johnny, ever face him again, and all the times I worked in his fields and all the times I et in his house and all the times his children came into our house to see the toys I made, the rabbit skins he'd given me to line the girls' boots in the winter.

But it wasn't just Johnny. I hated facing them all – the Bradys, Cha Finley, Quigley, Bigword, Dunkle and Kate, too. Feck Crissy. I knew what they'd be thinking. They'd have me worse than King Herod and the Slaughter of the Innocents. Those pictures in the holy books used to frighten the hell out of me; the Roman soldiers holding the babies upside down by the feet and running their swords through them or cutting their throats, the mothers tearing at the soldiers' clothes like mad animals. That's what they'd make me worse than. King Herod. I should never have done it, never, never, never. Oh, Jazus. I was so thick to even let Lizzie talk about it the first time she mentioned it. Jazus, Jazus. Feck! They'll make the whole thing sound worse than it is. You'd think forty-one acres was half the country the way they'll tell it.

I wish I was dead. I wish I'd never heard of Derrycloney. If they'd treat me like I was King Herod, then feck them all. Feck them. Feck. Feck. Feck me for being so thick. Oh God.

And who the hell is Esau?

27. Crip Quigley

The short red flames in the turf fire throw jumpy shadows around the kitchen, and they remind me of Mud; about how different it was then, when she was alive; she'd sit there and I'd sit here and maybe say nothing all night, but she was there.

In the dark, when it's only the turf flames lighting up the kitchen, everything looks as clean and neat as she used to keep it. The place isn't the same without her; Mud. When I was small, she'd go to town on a Saturday for the messages, and I'd feel the house was terrible empty without her. I'd stand on the lane waiting for her, looking up the lane till I'd see her at the Furry Hill. It was always great when she came home.

I never got over her dying. It's like she went for the messages on a Saturday and never came back and I'm still waiting for her. Poor Mud.

There's something about the dark; sounds are different. The fire is hotter when it's dark, hot on my face and hands and shins. I still have to wear the cap and throw the topcoat over my shoulders, because, no matter how hot it is, the fire only warms me in the front.

When my shins get too hot inside the wellingtons, I turn sideways to let the boots cool off. That's when I watch the jumpy shadows that the short flames make. After a while, when the shadows have taken ahold of my eyes, the table and chairs and the dresser go away; the kitchen is a cave with black things jumping against the walls, like frogs jumping against something that's too high for them to get over, jumping and jumping and falling back down all the time, never learning to hop a few feet to the left or the right, until a duck comes along and ates them. You can't teach an old dog new tricks, as oul Mangan would say, nor old frogs either. There's been times when I saw a frog jumping against a wall for so long that it got on my nerves, and I gave it a good kick and sent it flying, guts and frog all over the place. You can't teach your granny to suck eggs. Thick yokes, they are. I don't like frogs. Mud said frogs could curse you.

Besides being in the bed, the next thing I like best is looking into the fire when it's dark, staring into the hot redness.

Last night I burned five more sods of turf because I stayed up till ten to have a gander inside the lavatory in Johnny's garden. I wanted to snake up there for a look myself, not ask Johnny or Kate for a look. I was afraid they'd think I was an eegit for not knowing, and I wouldn't please anyone to let them think I'm a thick.

At first I wondered about going out in the dark after what happened to me on the night of the big noise. But then I said to myself, "In the name of God, Crip, yev lived on Derrycloney Lane since the time ya were born, and ya were never afraid before. What kind of an eegit are ya becoming at all?" As well as that, Johnny told me what he thought happened that night, and I believe him; it was an ass or a bullock running down the lane that hit me – McHugh and his naeroplane, d'eegit.

I got a lot more than I bargained for when I went to look at the lavatory. First there was the whispering I heard, and then there was the roars of the Glanvil young lads. By the time I got home again, the wind was puffing out of me. I jumped into the bed with everything on me, and lay there, afraid of my life for an hour that Johnny would come and bang on the door looking for me, ready to straighten me out with a swingletree. But, thank God, the young lads must have been so frightened they didn't know it was me.

Anyhow, I'm ahead of myself. Last night I made myself sit on the chair in front of the fire till the minute of ten, and then I took the flash lamp off the mantelpiece. There was only a dim yellow light in it, but it was better than good enough because no one would notice it from a distance. I put the lamp in the topcoat pocket and went and stood in the door for a minute listening. There wasn't a sound in the whole world, not even a breeze or a bird squawk in the bare ash trees across the lane. I stood and listened again when I stepped on to the lane.

Just to be on the safe side, I walked along the grass verge beside the hedge, and that's what saved me. I was so taken up with snaking past the Burnses' house that I'd swear the whispering was in my ears all the time, and it wasn't till I was past their house and standing across the lane from Paddy's henhouse that I heard it.

"Whisper, whisper, whisper."

Maybe I thought it was the swishing of my rubber boots in the grass at first. Well, a fright came on me that put all the hairs standing up like needles on me. I couldn't move backward or forward, I was so stuck to the ground by the feet, and I'd swear I started sweating like a pig – and it the end of October and I doing nothing to make me sweat, not forking dung or anything. Good Christ! All I could think of was the night of the loud noise, and for a minute I stood there in the pitch black waiting to be hit in the chest again.

I waited, and while I was waiting with my arms out in front to protect myself, didn't my heart slow down and the blood in my ears stopped making noise like the noise you hear when you put a cockle shell to your ear.

"Whisper, whisper, whisper." I thought of ghosts, and little bumps came up on my skin.

The whispering was coming from the far end of the yard where the barn is, where the Burnses keep d'ass's cart and the turf and the few yokes they own they want to keep dry.

"Whisper, whisper, whisper."

And then, from the sounds I started hearing, I knew their tackled ass was in the yard. I could hear the jangling of the short chains of the breeching.

"I'll hold the shafts, and ya back in d'ass," Paddy said real low.

"Will ya not be talking so loud," Lizzie hissed like a goose hissing, its head nearly touching the ground and it looking up at you like it was a snake. I hate when a goose does that to me.

"Get d'ass."

"I'll get d'ass, and will ya keep yer voice down." Lizzie's a hard woman at times.

"Just get the fecking ass before somebody comes."

I thought of slipping away up the lane on the grass verge. The fright had gone off me, even though I still wouldn't want Paddy or Lizzie to know I was standing there listening to them.

But I was too full of curiosity. Curiosity killed the cat, but information made him fat, as oul Mangan would say. So I held my ground.

I heard the noises of an ass being yoked to a cart; the backband falling into the wooden bridge on the straddle; the draughts being pulled along the ground and hooked on to the hame at the collar; the short chains of the breeching getting hooked on to the shafts.

"Here's the bellyband," Lizzie whispered and, even though I couldn't see my hand in front of my face, I knew she was bending down at the far side of the shafts and handing the chain across under d'ass to Paddy for him to take and hook on to the shaft at his side. "Is it going to take ya all night or what? Will ya take the bloody yoke?" Lizzie's worse than my own sister, Bride.

"Did ya hook the britchens?" Paddy whispered.

"'Course I did." You could hear the blunt edge of her teeth. "Will ya get going, and be sure to hold on to the top of the creel to keep the cart from swaying and knocking sods off."

They had the creel on the cart and it was full to the top with sods of turf. Where was he going at all at this hour of the night? And then I turned into a dead stick with the fright, because, wherever Paddy was going with the load of turf, he'd have to pass me and I'd only be inches away.

"Don't go into the pump trough."

"I'm not an eegit."

"I'll open the gate," Lizzie whispered.

What gate? says I to myself. There's no gate to open for Paddy to come out on the lane. But he didn't come out on the lane at all. He went out through the gate that hangs on the corner of the henhouse, that goes out into the fields. He went down the cart track at the side of the field, because I could hear the axle of the cart rocking in the wheels from all the deep ruts. Then I heard the kitchen door opening and closing, and I said to myself, "Thank God, thank God."

But where the hell was Paddy going with the turf? There was no place down the fields to take it to.

Then I started to think. First of all, there was me getting

hit in the middle of the night. Then Missus Brady fell into the ditch and broke her leg. Then there's Paddy Burns's cow and calves all getting sold all of a sudden. Now there's this. If you ask me, I said to myself, there's something quare going on in Derrycloney.

You know, I should have come home and gone straight to bed, after nearly getting caught by Paddy and Lizzie. But at the time I never thought of that. So I snaked on up the road, wondering to myself what the hell Paddy and the Missus were doing drawing a load of turf down the fields at this hour of the night. That track down the field beside the hedge goes nowhere in the end, stops at the thick hedge that separates Paddy's big field from the tarred road. Maybe I wouldn't have thought it was so strange if Paddy hadn't drove his cow and two calves up to Coleman-the-cattle-jobber a few days ago, drove them up and sold them and left himself without even a cow. What was the man thinking about at all? And the next day he had to go up to Cavanagh's shop for a bottle of milk in d'ass-and-cart; didn't go into Kate above for a drop in the bottom of a jug. A terrible quare carrying-on altogether, I was thinking to myself. He's hardly taking the turf off to sell it, says I to myself, and anyhow he can go nowhere with it down the fields.

I couldn't stop thinking of Paddy and Lizzie and their goings-on, and before I knew it I was standing outside Johnny's garden gate. Just to make sure of everything, I stood there for at least five minutes listening. Then I drew back the latch and let myself into the garden. Across the gravel I walked as careful as a turkey stepping in stubbles, out through the little gap in the box-hedge; on to the clay where he sows the early potatoes in the spring. When I got to the third apple tree, I stopped and listened for a long time again. The lavatory was only about ten yards away in the corner of the garden. I turned on my flash lamp and walked over to the green door.

I could get the smell of the new paint. There was a latch that you put your thumb on, and when the door swung in there was this terrible screeching, so bad that I nearly did everything in my trousers. There was a yard lamp on the floor, there was a chap sitting down with his trousers at his ankles, and there was another chap standing beside him. The two of them had their mouths open, and their eyes were as big as buckets.

You know, I took off like a kicked dog. I don't even remember if I went out through the garden gate or whether I just went straight through the hedge. I know I was in bed with the sheet over my head and my boots still on before I stopped to think. Two narrow escapes in the one night. I'll never go out in the dark again.

28. Billy Bates

I'm still boiling, seething. I'm as alive in my belly as the raindrops get when they fall down the chimney and land in the fire, hissing and steaming.

The old bollicks. It's the first time I've ever talked back to Duncle, the first time I've ever been so cross that I didn't care if he took his farm and left it to the ISPCA as a home for stray cats. I told him to go fuck himself, that if he wanted to be so stingy with his payback days to Johnny that he could go up there himself and say to Johnny in the spills of rain, "I'm here for the day, Johnny, to work for all the times yev helped us and for all the times we've borrowed the horse and the machinery from ya."

I was calm at first but, the more words were said between us, the crosser I got. "All he'll be doing is sharpening tools, or mending sacks or tacklings," I said.

"Do what I bid ya!" Dunkle said, and he turning purple in the nose.

"I'm no good to him on a wet day," says I.

"Yer not much good to him or me on a dry day either," the old shagger said. "Now, do what I bid ya!" and he turned around to walk into the cowhouse, a stream of rain running off the back of his hat as strong as a yellow flow out of a mare.

"I'd be too embarrassed to walk into his yard to work on a day like today," says I. "He'll know yer sending me because it's a wet day and we have nothing to do ourselves. He'll have nothing for me to do either."

Dunkle stopped walking away, but he didn't even turn around. "I'll have nothing for ya to do for the rest of yer life if ya don't get out of me sight this minute. Maybe this will teach ya not to be running for Johnny Glanvil every time a cow farts sideways."

That's when I told him to go up to Johnny's himself.

"I can change me will anytime," says he. "I'll leave the farm to the Church just to spite ya," he says.

"You can stick it up yer arse for all I care," I said. "I'm fed up of ya sending me up to Johnny's on wet days for payback."

Then he thought he would get a move under me by shouting. "*Do what I bid ya, ya little scut!*"

"Go fuck yerself," I said.

While I was walking out of his farmyard, he was still shouting after me, calling me names. "Ya lazy cunt. Ya spoiled priest. Half the country knows yer a fucking lunatic. They all call ya Bigword Billy. Yer nothing but a bloody bastard. Ya bastard."

Autocephalous I am not.

I put my head down against the rain and came on home to my own place. My own place! Dunkle owns this place. He owns everything. I own nothing. Out of crossness at him, I put more turf on the fire than I've ever done in my life and, shag him, I'll keep it blazing all day, as long as it rains.

I'll sit here all day and listen to the raindrops hissing at me in the red turf. It's the only noise around here. The rain on the roof doesn't even make noise with the thatch.

It makes me blush to think about that wet day a year ago when Dunkle made me go up to work for Johnny. At that time I wasn't brave enough, or thick enough, to stand up to him.

When I stood there inside the wicket door in the spills of rain and told Johnny I was there to help him for the day, to pay him back for the loan of his horse and the drill harrow and the turnip barrow, and the spring grub, and for the times he'd taken care of Dunkle's sick animals, he looked at me with his mouth open, as if I'd made him speechless, or else as if he was letting his raging thoughts about Dunkle splash over his bottom teeth in silence.

"Is it not raining down at yeer house, Billy?" is all he said, and I could hear the rage in his voice. But Johnny knew what the situation was, knew Dunkle had sent me and there was nothing I could do about it. But he'd never say anything to me about Dunkle. Like everyone else, Johnny knows blood is thicker than water.

In my wet cap and topcoat, I sat on an upside-down bucket in his boiler house for two hours, trying to get a bit of warmth out of the fire under the boiler. Johnny had left me to look after the fire, while he went up to the crusher yard with barley and oats. I was feeling like my balls were in a vice, caught between Dunkle's stinginess and Johnny's crossness. I kept wishing I was in bed asleep.

Every now and then, I'd get down on my hands and knees and push another piece of tyre into the fire under the belly of the boiler. Johnny wouldn't waste good turf or sticks to boil spuds for the pigs. He gets old tyres from Jimmy Brady's garage and cuts them up with a beet knife. Nothing goes to waste on Johnny; he even saves the wire from the rims of the tires, uses it with weights to tie down the hay rick against the winter winds, and even the weights are bits of old ploughs and broken machinery that he finds and saves from one year to the other.

Above and beyond the feeling of being caught between the two of them, the rim of the bucket was cutting d'arse off me; the fire was too far under the boiler to give me any heat; the dampness had soaked down to my skin from the wet topcoat; I was perishing with the cold; I was five days away from my forty-first birthday; I wasn't wanted where I was, and I wasn't wanted down below at Dunkle's – the place I could come nearest to calling home.

If Johnny was raging because Dunkle had sent a payback man to him on a wet day, he was nowhere near as raging as I was. I was so raging I could have torn the guts out of Dunkle with my bare hands, tied them into Gordian knots with my teeth, and thrown them up into the bare ash trees to rot, for the crows to eat. The shagging old uncle; such a miserable old shite, and I was sorry, like I've been sorry many times before, for ever agreeing to work the farm with him, for not going out to Anthony in Pottstown when I left Maynooth twenty years ago. What a shagging eegit I was to pick Dunkle and his promise of the farm when he died, instead of Anthony in America. No farm was worth the work and humiliation doled out by Dunkle.

Forty I was, and I hadn't a penny in my pocket, and too old for Pennsylvania. I had to ask Dunkle for money every time I wanted to buy a loaf of bread. Once, when I asked him on a Sunday for money to go to a football match, he gave me sixpence. Six shagging pennies! Nobody knows it, but I hid behind a hedge and cried with crossness. It costs a shilling for a ticket to go into the football pitch, to say nothing about having a pint with the lads after the game. But I wouldn't please the old shagger to go back begging from him again, so I got up on my bike and went for a ride up the mountain. I spent the sixpence on ice cream in a little shop off behind the back of beyond where no one knew me. Ice cream!

There I was in front of the boiler, driving myself into a gale-force rage. I stood up all of a sudden and rubbed the bucket's rim out of my arse. I looked around Johnny's orderly boiler house, saw everything in its place, everything easy to get at, every bin with its own homemade scoop; the big wooden container for the boiled potatoes with its own black-handled chopper; the two pulpers at each end of the pile of turnips; the pieces of saved binder twine hanging from a hook in the wall; all the mash buckets lined up in their places like soldiers in a row.

I walked over to the arched double doors and gazed out through the spaces in the hen-proof lattice-work at the rain falling into Johnny's tidy, rectangular farmyard; the long family house making up one side; fifteen yards across from it, a line of animal houses; the feed and cart houses at each end of the rectangle; everything built with stone and slate; all the grey, stone walls pointed with lines of black cement; all the doors coated with tar. There's no rusting sheets of galvanised iron in the Glanvil place, nothing patched with the bottom of a metal barrel, no broken bedspring filling up a doorway in place of a door.

And there is no dunghape in Johnny's farmyard.

Each animal house has a window at the back – a hole in the wall with a wooden cover to keep out the wind in winter – and the dung is forked out through it every day whenever there's animals in the houses. Then the pile outside every window is spread around, levelled off. The dunghape is out of sight.

Even though I hate having to ask him for things, I love coming into Johnny's place. I love the neatness and the order. It must make it easier to start work every day when there's order, when everything's in its place. I'd never let on to Johnny how well he keeps the place. Never tell a man how good he is – only tell him how he could be better. That's the way it is around here.

Such a man Johnny is! Such an amount of work he does to get a simple job done. It has to be done right, down to the last detail. He's at it from morning to night six days a week, himself and a hired man most of the year. But besides all this neatness, what has he to show for it all? He still ploughs with horses, one sod at a time; up and down the field all day, moving across the field at the rate of nine inches a pass, crows and seagulls flying all over the place and the horses shiting in his face like they did in his father's face. When one time I said to him, just for the sake of keeping him in his place, that the day of the horse is gone, he looked at me like I was gone soft in the skull. But I let him have it. "It's all machinery now, Johnny," says I. "A tractor can pull a three-winged plough and go three times as fast as a pair of the best horses. That's ploughing nine times as quick as the old way. Nine days of ploughing down to one. Eight days saved." But all he did was shake his head and talk about the cost of everything. "Where would we get the money for a tractor and for everything that goes with it?" For all his hard work and for all his cleverness, that's as far as his thinking lets him go.

I often think of what I'll do to Dunkle's place when I get my hands on it – if I ever get my hands on it. Sometimes, when I can't sleep because of the terrible silence and the thickness of the dark, and when the Hippwell One won't do what I want her to do, I think of what I'll do to Dunkle's place to make it like Johnny's. But in the end I know it would take years; in the end I know I'll have no reason to tidy the place up. By the time I get the farm, I'll be so fed up I won't even notice the rusting, broken machinery in the hedges, where it was thrown when it broke; I won't see the holes in the roofs, patched with pieces of flattened-out barrels; the dunghape will still grow big every winter outside the kitchen door, the liquid animal shite running out of it in brown rivers every time it rains.

If I'd thought about those things any longer, I'd have depressed myself down through the floor entirely. It was the rattle of Johnny's pony-and-cart in the boiler house chimney that saved me. He was on his way home from the crusher yard, but I knew from the sound he was still up at Bradys'. I knew, too, that I should shake myself out of the black mood I'd sunk into, try to be full of good humour and helpfulness when he got home.

I had the painted, galvanised gates open by the time he arrived. The sogging pony trotted into the yard, her head bent and her nose so close to the ground that she, too, must have been feeling sorry for herself. Maybe it was the rain.

After I helped the sullen and dripping Johnny to empty the sacks of meal into their bins, he stood in his own puddle, the front of his topcoat white from the dust of the meal, the water dropping off every edge of his clothes and hat.

"How's the boiler fire?" he asked.

"Blazing away," I said.

He looked over at the boiler. "I'm going to untackle the pony, and then we're going to put a ring in the bull's nose, the two of us." He took a shining brass nose-ring out of his pocket and put it on his workbench.

How the hell are we going to ring a bull? I thought to myself, but I didn't say anything in case Johnny would think I wasn't willing to help. Putting a ring in a bull's nose might be a wet-day job, but it's more than a two-man job. How could one of us hold a two-year-old bull still enough, while the other burned a hole with a red-hot iron in the cartilage between the two nostrils? Had he just thought up something real hard to do, just because he was cross at Dunkle? Johnny went out into the rain.

When he came back after taking care of the pony, he told me the plan; Johnny always has a plan.

We'd put the bull in the middlehouse, tie a rope halter on him, throw the end of the rope out through the window, go around the back on to the dunghape and pull the animal's head out through the window. I'd keep the head pulled against the thick wall of the window and Johnny would do the burning.

So, Johnny got down on his belly and pushed the one prong of a broken pitchfork into the boiler's fire. Then we went to the middlehouse to wrestle the bull. After putting the rope on him, Johnny slipped the window cover off its hooks. I ran around to the back of the animal houses, stepped up on the dunghape, took the end of the rope from Johnny and pulled. I might as well have been pulling out an elephant's tooth with my thumb and finger, until Johnny gave the bull a few slaps on d'arse with the flat of his hand.

Suddenly, the bull's head was there in the opening, and I had the rope pulled tight against the stones in the wall. The bull's nostrils were flared, his breathing was very threatening, and the one eye that I could see was bulging. The way it was looking at me! That eye was telling me that, if the bull could get his head and hooves at me, he'd split me in two. Then Johnny came running along the top of the dunghape, his cap wrapped around the end of the broken fork, and the drops of rain hissing off the hot prong that had already lost its redness.

"Hold him tight," he shouted. "Hold him tight."

The rope was cutting into my hands, but I was willing to do anything to show I could be counted on, that I wasn't my uncle.

With his left hand, Johnny raised the bull's nose-flesh out of the way, and the instant he touched the hot iron to the cartilage there was hissing, smoke, and stink. The bull let out a roar and started to pull away. But I was performing for Johnny, against Dunkle, and no shagging animal was going to best me. The bull shook his nose away from the hot iron, and let out another roar that rattled the slates on the roof, Johnny shouting, "Hold him, hold him."

Then a whole lot of things happened at the same time and, maybe because I thought I was going to die, I saw everything happening real slow before my eyes.

The rope in my hands went as slack as if it had been cut with a knife and I plonked down on my arse on the dunghape.

Johnny backed away from the window, moving like an old man who's taking a long time to fall after stumbling, his hands flailing the air trying to keep himself up.

The bull's front feet appeared on the wide windowsill, scrambling to get a grip. Then his head was in the window and the front feet were free of the wall, pawing the air as they tried to get a grip in the surface of the dunghape. For an instant, it seemed the bull was balanced on the wide windowsill, his head out, his arse still in the middlehouse. Then, with a monstrous effort, he shifted all his weight, and the front feet sank into the dung. All the bull's movements were accompanied by the most fearful puffing and snorting; snorting that said, some fucker's going to die for this.

I was paralysed with the fright. The bull's livid nose was within a foot of my face, puffs of hot steam shunting out like curse words, every one of them starting with eff.

Only Johnny caught me by the scruff of the neck, I was finished. And it was only when he grabbed me that the words I'd been hearing, flying around in the air like excited bats, made sense.

"'Will ya get up and run. Get up. Get up, y'eegit."

Then I was on my feet, and Johnny was dragging me backwards. With its arse still high up in the window, the bull's own weight forced it down on its front knees. Then, as if the whole world had slowed down, the bull somersaulted – the back legs and tail beating the air, the bag with the big balls slapping over to one side, the head twisting desperately to keep the neck from snapping, and then the big *whoomp* when it finally landed on its side, the air smacking out of its body.

Johnny had pulled me to my feet, was still shouting at me. "Will ya run, for God's sake. Run!"' He pushed me in front of him, and the two of us high-stepped it along the dunghape, our feet sinking into the soft shite with every step taken. We didn't stop till we were on the other side of the haggard gate, the fear of God making our arseholes so tight that not even a man with a ferreting bar could get in.

When we looked back, the bull was on its feet, standing on its tippy toes. The chest was heaving as quick as the shunting of a train on a hill. The eyes bulged above the white-hot breath at the nostrils. The tail was curled over the back, exposing muscled thighs, puckered hole, and mighty balls. It's roars were the bellows of a wounded bull when it had fled the altar, shaking off an unsure axe, as yer man Virgil would have said. Everything about the animal was saying, "Try that again and I'll fuck your arse in two while I paw you to shreds with my knifey hooves."

Johnny and myself huffed ourselves back to normal, the teeming rain unnoticed by either of us, the dung on our clothes and hands unnoticed. Eventually, the bull lowered his tail, and all the tension ran out of his body. He sauntered across the dunghape, stepped off and walked over to the hay rick. As he pulled out mouthfuls of hay, he paid no attention to his nose where the hot iron had stabbed him. His lower jaw sawed from side to side, the way an old, contented cow will chew sweet hay.

Johnny said, and I knew damn well that he was seething to say something else, "Why don't ya go on home to yer own house, Billy, and if Dunkle says anything I'll pretend ya were here all day."

That's what I did. I hadn't the balls to go to Dunkle's house, curse at him and tell him I'd never be sent as a payback man on a wet day again. And I've never forgotten that Johnny called me an eegit, even if he did it when he was all excited.

But I had the balls at last this morning to stand up to Dunkle. He would never change the will, because he'd have to leave the farm to someone outside the family and he's too proud to do that. I wonder is anything going to happen to Paddy Burns for bringing the forged will up to Parkingston-Shaw. Wasn't he a terrible chancer to try that, to cheat Benny out of the bit of land? He'll be lucky if he doesn't get the jail. One thing's for certain; I'll never get the jail on account of Dunkle. If he gives the farm away, I'll pack up and go to Pennsylvania to Anthony, even if I am over forty. I'll get a job in one of those caves where they grow mushrooms. I could work for a farmer. I could be a labourer on the buildings. There are a thousand things I could do, if I only put my mind to it. And there would be sunshine.

Fuck Dunkle! Now that I've done it once, it won't be as hard to stand up to him again. I'll demand a wage, a weekly wage. To hell with this shite of begging every time I need to buy a loaf or a jar of Bovril. I'll tell him right out to his face, if he doesn't start treating me better that I'll pack up and take off. And, by God, I will too. I'll go to Pottstown. What's stopping me? Anthony told me a hundred times he would send me the fare.

Be gob! I feel better all of a sudden. I'll write to Anthony this minute and tell him to get ready, that I might be on my way at last. Where did I put his last letter? He had a great one in it about a cow shite. Pennsylvania. God, it sounds so good. Anthony sounds great every time he writes, like he's happy all the time.

> *Last Sunday I was walking along a footpath here in Pottstown where the Molly Maguires were hung, and I had my head down looking at the ground, just sauntering along thinking of everyone in Derrycloney. Then I heard someone calling and when they called a second time I looked up. A black woman was standing on the footpath on the other side of the road. She shouted over to me and asked if I was all right. I said I was. Then she told me to lift up my head and smile, that I shouldn't be going around looking at the ground as if the world was coming to an end. I told her I only walk that way out of habit, because I was born on a farm and you always had to watch your step because of the cow dung all over the place. Then she shouted back, 'Well, there ain't no cow dung in Pottstown, honey. You can walk with your head up.' I gave her a big smile and she gave me a bigger smile.*

There ain't no cow dung in Pottstown! Isn't that a good one.

I have a shagging choice. God!

29. *Johnny Glanvil*

It was in an August, I forget the year, but I'll never forget the date: the fifteenth, the Feast of the Assumption. Five yearling calves died over there in the haggard in twenty minutes, over there outside the middlehouse window, when the ground was clean and dry because all the dung was gone to the fields since the spring.

In the crevices of my stomach, I can still feel the remainder of the loss, the remainder of the crossness at myself for being so stupid. Five bloody calves: more than the profit for one whole year of farming. Can you imagine five – five – calves stretched out nearly on top of each other, their necks as long as a camel's and they coughing the life out of themselves in a few minutes.

I went into the boiler house where no one could see me, put my head in my hands and sank down so far inside myself it took me two years to come out again. It wasn't the loss by itself that buried me; it was because it should never have happened.

This whole business with Paddy Burns has given new life to the old pain of the loss of the calves, like a dry stalk coming to life after a shower and making a flower all of a sudden.

Tom Kirkwood, the vet, told me one time there was no

need to buy a special dose for the calves when they got the hoose. "A half a cup of paraffin oil kills nematode worms quicker than any dose you'll get from Matty-Moran-the-chemist," is what he said.

And it always worked. For years I'd dosed the calves with paraffin oil when they started coughing, their eyeballs bulging. But the year the five of them died! I felt very stupid when I found out what happened, when Tom Kirkwood told me I'd dosed the calves while they were still panting after all the running it took to get them into the haggard. "They inhaled the paraffin into their lungs, and that," the vet said, "was the same as throwing scalding water on a dandelion; the lungs melted."

No matter how hard I tried, those five calves sat in the pit of my stomach for two years – the regret of it all. Regret is a terrible thing once it gets into your system, worse than the worst nematode worms ever could be. How long will the regret over Paddy Burns be in my guts? Longer than the calves; till the day I die, blooming to life every time I hear his name or see him or think of him. Already, the whole thing feels like a splatter of acid burning a hole on the inside of my belly. I'll have to devise a way to distract myself away from it, train my brain to switch the instant it knows Paddy is in there, before he even gets within an ass's roar of my head; something that's nice to think about, or funny, or frightening; falling off the straw rick that time and missing the coulter of the plough by a hair; scoring the winning point when I was on the under-fourteen hurling team – how many years ago? – that day hunting with Jimmy Reilly when his shotgun went off by itself and I felt the wind of the passing pellets on the side of my head; Missus Brady falling into the drain; anything to get my brain away from what Paddy has created.

Of course, there was nothing funny about it for Missus Brady, but, knowing her, sometime in the future she'll sit on the little hob and everything about the fall into the ditch will be funny enough to make Kate and the children laugh.

It's a terrible state of affairs, the way the whole thing has turned out. I can't believe Paddy could have been so thick. I still think it was the Missus who put him up to it. But Kate doesn't like to hear me saying that. She thinks Paddy did it all by himself.

It was the night we'd been to Rathmount with the set of tacklings. The night started out terrible dark, but by the time we were coming home across the mountain road the wind had started tearing the clouds apart. Then it turned into one of those nights I love being out in, as long as there's someone with me; a night of high broken clouds and a full moon and a strong wind blowing off up in the sky, while there's only a bit of a breeze on the ground. When you look at the raggy clouds running over the face of the moon, it's the moon itself that begins to move in the sky after a while, going real fast till you think you'll fall over, everything gone backways on you. The chaps love it, too. The clouds become huge ships racing across the sea, plunging on and changing shape all the time.

When I was walking up to the kitchen door, after pushing the pony's cart into the shed, I heard her calling, but, of course, I didn't know what I was hearing; this whispery voice floating around the yard saying my name. At first, I thought it was a gust of wind whistling in the slates of the cowhouse roof. But, when I heard it again, the yard lamp nearly fell out of my hand with the fright I got. I took long steps into the kitchen, barging in through the door when I'd only half-lifted the latch. Kate took one look at me and left the children huddled with their books around the fire.

A terrible crossness at Paddy sprung up in me when it all sank in – what the solicitor was saying. I wasn't cross at the sneaky and mean thing Paddy had tried to do, but that he'd destroyed our friendship, betrayed it by trying to use it against me and for himself. From now on it we wouldn't be able to look at each other, and we next-door neighbours always bumping into each other. He had shoehorned me into a box where I'd have to tell a lie for him, where I'd have to swear for his lie in front of a judge. Perjury – calling God to witness a lie – one of the worst sins, and one you could go to jail for, as well as to hell. Bad cess to the two of them – Paddy and Lizzie. Bad scuttering cess to them.

I still feel ashamed that I let Kate go in front with the yard lamp. Outside the wicket door, we stood and listened again. Kate whispered in my ear, "I'm going to say hello." A shaft of moonlight tore down the lane, went on towards Crip Quigley's and got lost in the clump of elm trees at the far side of his dunghape.

Then, in a voice that sounded as if she was afraid someone would hear her talking in the dark and think she was a lunatic, Kate said, "Hello," like a little bird calling out in the dark, but afraid at the same time of giving away its position.

When she was answered, I felt myself turning white. "Kate!" the voice said.

"Is that yerself, Missus Brady?" Kate asked, only a little bit above a whisper.

"'Tis, Kate." I couldn't figure out where the voice was coming from.

"Where are ya, Daisy?"

Daisy! I never heard anyone calling her Daisy before.

"In the ditch."

I never gave it a second thought when Paddy asked me a few months ago about me being a witness to Mick

Cosgrove's will, the two of us sweating from cleaning out the crossdrain in the pasture, cutting our way with blunt shovels through sheets of thick watercress. I just thought Paddy was striking up a conversation when he asked me if Mick made the will on the day he died. I told him, "No. 'Twas the day before he died, right after Mansfield the doctor came to see him."

It was only when the solicitor showed me the new will, and I saw the date on it, that I remembered the leaves of the watercress stuck to my wellingtons and Paddy asking me about the day Mick signed his will. The new will, with my signature forged, had the same date as the day Mick died, which would mean it was his last will and testament, that the one I had witnessed . . . Jakers! Jakers!

In the light of the yard lamp, Missus Brady was lying on her side like a fish swept up on the muddy bank of the river, an ugly fish with its sickish white face turned up towards the sky, the black muck of the drain holding her in place as tightly as if she was set in concrete. There was something terrible about it; frightening, like looking down into hell and seeing a soul trapped for all eternity.

The stink! Pieces of potato are always getting swept across in the pipe under the lane when I let the washing water out of the pump trough. And there's nothing as bad as the smell of potatoes rotting in water; it's almost as bad as the smell of a dead animal; like that ass rotting in Paddy's drain in the tober field for months before he and Benny buried it, a whole jar of Vicks on the rags on their faces.

It was bad enough that Paddy and Lizzie tried to take Benny's farm from him, but the way they tried to do it! Their plan swivelled on whether or not I would tell a lie. Bad fecking cess to the two of them. We're all in a terrible situation; no one talking – they cross at me for letting them down, me cross at them for trying to steal the farm from Benny and for putting me in . . . Bugger, bugger, feck and bugger. They did it, and there's no way of changing that now.

For a minute I was real cross at Missus Brady for being such an eegit for falling into the bloody drain, and she after being up and down the lane twenty million times. But, in a second or two, I said to myself, "This is how things are. This is what has to be dealt with right now."

When we decided to carry her into the kitchen, she said, "Aw Kate, don't let the children see me like this, smelling like the back-end of a goat. I couldn't bear it."

I went into the kitchen and told the chaps about Missus Brady. Then, with a few tough words, I cleared the four of them into the parlour with the old two-wicker lamp and their books. They put on their topcoats and caps. Becky put on her gloves.

If Paddy had thought about it at all, he'd have known he'd never get away with it. How, in the name of God, did he think he was going to fool anyone with a new will? Didn't he know Parkingston-Shaw would have to ask me about my signature? Did he think I was going to stick a knife in a dead man's back and take away from his child the little he had, have Benny thrown out on the road with nothing? What the hell was Paddy thinking about? Bloody into it! I'd love to give him a good swipe with a swingletree.

The smell of her filled the kitchen the minute we plonked her down in the wooden armchair, the one Kate bought at the dead priest's auction. In the bright light of the Aladdin lamp she was a terrible sight altogether and, for the first time in my life, I felt sorry for her. I could feel her embarrassment so much I decided she would be better off without having me around; one of her stockings drooping away from her leg with the weight of the muck; one side of her head and face was caked with the stuff. So, we made plans to get her home, but first I was to go up the lane to prepare Jim for the arrival of his wife, and to ask him to go for Doctor Mansfield. By this time we all knew she had broken something.

I don't think Paddy came up with the idea himself, of a new will – he doesn't have that kind of badness in him. It was Lizzie who bullied him into it. Even the solicitor thought it was Lizzie who wrote the new will and wrote my name under Mick Cosgrove's. She might have been clever to think of stealing Benny's farm, but she was stupid to think the rest of us would believe she had accidentally found Mick Cosgrove's will stuck in a cracked mug hanging on a hook on the kitchen dresser, that she hadn't taken down the mug or washed it once in the last fifteen years.

Jim Brady was standing at the corner of the table when I knocked and walked into the kitchen. It took me a second to find him in the single-wicked flame of the paraffin lamp.

You'd think I went to visit him every night at the same time for all the surprise he showed. "'Lo, Johnny," he said, and he glassy-eyed drunk. "Do ya wan a bih av a nunyun?"

It was only then I saw the peeled onion, as big as a small turnip, on the table. He cut out a chunk with the blade of his penknife, held the piece of onion out to me, it caught between the blade of the knife and his thumb, enough dirt under the nail to plant five potatoes in.

"Ah, no, Jim," I said. I can't stand the smell of onions.

I thought he was going to stab himself in the eye when he chucked the onion into his own mouth. While he chewed as loud as a horse scooping a mangold, he cut out another chunk and held it ready.

When his mouth was almost empty, he said, "There's notten like a good unyun ta clear yout. If Cha Finley et a nunyun every day, he wouldn't be nokken himself ouh every time he took a shite."

I decided there was no delicate way to break the news about Missus Brady to Jim, so I told him straight out.

"Deh stewpid bitch," he said, as if I'd told him his wife had been caught out in a shower without her coat. "How many times has she gone hup and down dah lane, and she still doesn't know deh way?" He threw the second piece of onion at his mouth and impersonated the chawing horse again. He kept staring at a spot on the wall near the lamp as if he was anchored to it, that if he took his eye off it he would fall over. Without saying anything else, without looking at what he was doing, he cut into the onion again.

"Ya'll have to get the doctor for her leg, Jim," I said. "It might be broke."

The next piece of onion soared across the space between his hand and his face. He pushed it into the side of his mouth behind his teeth with his tongue. He looked like a child with an abscessed tooth. He said, "Johnny, I'm so drunk, I couldn't find me own mickey if I wanted ta make a piss as big as deh Shannon River."

I didn't even say goodbye to him. Maybe he thought I was just one of the visions he has when he's drunk.

It never even entered my mind that Paddy and the Missus would try to steal the farm. And then, all of a sudden, there I was in my best suit and boots sitting in the good chair in Parkingston-Shaw's office, my hat in my hands. I couldn't believe it when he told me; that Paddy would do such a thing. But how could I have suspected? What did he ever do or say that would lead me to think anything bad about him? I hate what he has done, what he has created in Derrycloney. I hate how he used me after all the things we did together. Ah, Jakers, Jakers, Jakers.

There's the sound of Tom Kirkwood's motor car pulling into the yard with the injection for the sow. Milk fever; it'll kill a sow in a day if you don't catch it. Tom's a terrible decent lad. He never charges if the sick animal dies that he came to cure, and he has a son a priest who is the secretary to the Archbishop of Dublin. I always wear my good hat when Tom comes around the place.

That fecking Lizzie.

30. Kate Glanvil

The new spokes flickering in the light of the flash lamp would nearly make you dizzy if you looked at them long enough. It's hard to drag my eyes away from them, especially when there's no other light in the whole world. Only I'd be afraid of running off the road, I'd switch off the light altogether so I'd be completely lost in the dark.

Suffering duck! but it's great to be by myself for a few hours, even if I'm out on the long and lonely mountain road, all dressed up against the rawness of the night in my Sunday hat and my gloves and scarf, and a bag of sweets in the pocket of the heavy topcoat. There's not a soul on the road. It's a great comfort to be out here in the dark, feeling like I'm gone from the world, especially when the world is full of crossness. It's like slipping into a secret room.

Even though I'm glad to escape from Derrycloney for a few hours, I can't wait to tell Missus Brady about all what's going on.

I hate it when there's such crossness in the air that you could cut it with a stick, that no matter where you turn it's staring you in the face. After Johnny getting called in by the solicitor and finding out about the new will, no matter what we did, we did it with the Burnses in mind; we couldn't go out on the lane without peeping first to see if the coast was clear; we couldn't go down past their house for the cows without stirring up a hive of bees in the belly, knowing right well that Paddy or Lizzie was behind the curtains staring out in anger; I couldn't go out on Sunday morning with the pony-and-trap to bring Lizzie to Mass, like I've done since I married into Derrycloney.

But on Tuesday, when Paddy walked into the kitchen at dinner-time, the crossness got so thick it was hard to breathe. Without saying hello or anything, he said, like he'd said it a hundred times when times were good, "I want to get the loan of the billhook, Johnny."

I never heard such a silence before a storm; I never heard Johnny shout so loud before; never heard him mix up his words and sentences so much as he tried to get out his crossness at Paddy, blaming Paddy for things he never did, the children around the table forgotten in the middle of the war with their mouths open, their eyes swimming in glistening lakes as big as frying pans.

The first thing that went through my head when I saw Paddy was, "How could you be so stupid? You're more stupid than Daniel to think you can get out of this lion's den alive." Of course, it wasn't till long afterwards that I realised Paddy was using the billhook as an excuse to see how things stood between himself and Johnny; testing the waters, he was, as only an eegit would think it was needful to do, and it as clear as the nose on your face that the waters were boiling mad.

Poor Paddy! Despite everything, I nearly felt sorry for him when I saw Johnny rising up out of his chair like a giant with his hair on fire, his eyes sightless with rage. Before Paddy had even finished saying the word, Johnny snapped it from him and slapped it across his face.

"Billhook!" he roared. "Billhook! You come in here looking for a billhook!" Johnny kept saying "billhook" as if the word meant more than a tool for cutting bushes, as if billhook meant mercy or pity or forgiveness. But then the meaning of the word changed quickly.

"Billhook! I'll give ya a billhook all right across the back of yer neck. I'll give ya a billhook up and down yer belly like a hung pig after getting stuck to let its guts out."

The air was so thick I couldn't move, couldn't make my way over to Johnny to put my hand on his arm, remind him about the children. But even if I had been able to reach him, I think he was too caught up in the swirl inside his own head to be able to notice anything else. The fury spewed out of him like blue smoke shooting out of damp turf on a wet day on the bog, and there was no stopping it.

"You have the nerve to come in here looking for a billhook! You have the nerve to even come in here! You have the nerve to even talk to me! All yev been doing since ya came to Derrycloney is using me and using me and using me until ya thought ya had me in the spot where ya could make a liar out of me."

The more Johnny said, the worse I felt. After all these years of being friends, of telling each other things about ourselves, of giving Paddy and Lizzie a pair of plucked chickens every Christmas, here was the whole thing going up in flames as quick as a sheet of newspaper in a drafty chimney. Johnny was red in the face, his arms swinging all over the place like he was fighting off anything that Paddy might even try to say. Bits of food and spit were falling off his words as he flung them across the kitchen at Paddy with as much force as a terrified mother throwing shrieks to protect her child against a wild animal.

"That's why ya were friendly to me since ya came to Derrycloney, you and that wife of yers with her thick bread and lumpy butter. It wasn't enough that I gave you work when there was no work to be had anywhere else. No! You nuzzled yer way into our lives so that I'd take yer side when it came to the will that that wife of yers concocted. I'll give ya a billhook all right. I'll give ya a billhook where ya deserve to get it. Ya were never a neighbour, ya were never a friend. All ya were was a user, you and that wife of yers with her gristly black pudding, with her bad legs that are good enough to get her into our trap every Sunday morning. Go on with ya. Go on! Get out of here and don't come back, and if ya try to frighten my lads again when they're out in the lavatory ya'll be getting the billhook all right. All ya can do is jump on top of Crip Quigley in the middle of the night and beat him because ya can't beat any of the rest of us. Well, come up here in the middle of the night and ya'll get a billhook where ya deserve it. Go on with ya. Go on! Go on up to Missus Brady and drive yer cow into her garden to eat her flowers. Go on, ya lazy bugger, and leave a dead ass to rot in yer drain for months before yeh bury it, the rest of us breathing the stink every time we passed. Go on and push Missus Brady into the ditch in the dark of the night so she breaks her leg and has to go to hospital, and then ya won't have her around when ya try to steal Benny's farm. It wouldn't surprise me if ya galloped the calves on purpose that time so they'd die from the paraffin oil. It wouldn't surprise me at all. Go on and laugh at Crissy when she gets stung with her bees after ya turn her beehives over in the middle of the night, and she never did anything against anyone in her life. Go and laugh at Billy Bates when he puts his foot in his mouth. Go and tell everyone in the town about Cha Finley and his sister. Yev been laughing at everyone since ya came to Derrycloney, laughing at me and Kate, too, but the shoe's on d'other foot now. Get out of my house and never darken my door again, you . . . you . . . you blackguard."

This new bike is a delight to ride, especially after putting up with the wobbly front wheel for so long on the old one. I can feel a bit of a slope on the road, and in a minute I'll see the shape of Meaney's big tree. This is the spot where Murt McHugh says one night he caught up with a woman walking her bike because her carbide lamp had run out of water, and she asked Murt to do his wee-wee into her lamp. He says he went into a pub in Rathmount a month later and the woman behind the counter winked and told him she owed him some liquid infusion, and then gave him a pint of Guinness for nothing. That Murt's an ass, if you ask me. Now, he says Paddy Burns was right to have a grab at Benny's farm, that Paddy and Lizzie have squatters' rights. Johnny said that would mean Billy Bates would have squatters' rights to half of Murt's farm.

In our kitchen that day, if I'd been Paddy I'd have been gone the minute Johnny snatched the word "billhook" out of my mouth. But he stood there, in amaze like a pig doing its wee-wee, as Crip Quigley would say. Maybe he was stuck to the floor like I was. But when Johnny called him a blackguard, Paddy became unstuck at last. He never said a word, but the look on his face was terrible, like the face of a man looking down into a grave at a rotting body. He stood there in the same doorway he'd often walked through to eat his meals, to play cards on a Sunday night, and to chat. He didn't even try to answer the mad accusations Johnny had fired at him. He knew it was all over, that nothing could change things back to the way they used to be. He just turned on his heel and left like a dog with his tail between its legs. At that point I began to cry.

Paddy was gone and the four children were bawling, with Johnny standing there looking around as if he'd landed in his own kitchen all of a sudden, like a time traveller ending up in a place he wasn't supposed to be. Then, I declare to God, if Johnny himself didn't start. He plonked down on to his chair and put his head between his hands. When the children saw his shoulders jerking up and down, they got worse, just sat there with their hands under the table and bawled like calves looking for milk, the water dropping off their chins on to their laps.

There's the lights of Rathmount. That means I'll be passing Feeneys' yard in a minute. There's a terrible dog in there that barks like you were a murderer when you pass by. I'm always afraid he'll manage to get out through the gate. Another three miles to the hospital. The dog must be asleep; maybe he died.

It was the worst day of my life, except for the day my poor mother died roaring from the pain of the cancer, may the Lord have mercy on her. I can still feel the feeling in my stomach as I watched Paddy sloping out of the kitchen like a beaten dog that had never got a beating before. Poor Paddy, poor Lizzie – although Johnny says it was Lizzie who made Paddy come out to see which way the wind was blowing. He says Lizzie would have cursed at Paddy when he went home, and Paddy would have gone to bed and covered his head in shame. Johnny never liked Lizzie, but after what Johnny thinks she made Paddy do, will and all, he hates her now like she was a snake.

I never liked Rathmount or the people in it, and I hardly know anyone who lives there, except for Johnny's brother-in-law, of course. I've always heard it said that Rathmount is right in the middle of the Cretin Belt, that there's a big swath of the county hereabouts with a lot of people whose eyes are too close together and with buckteeth as crooked as a ram's horn.

In twenty minutes I'll be standing beside Missus Brady's

bed. I'm longing to take one of the sweets out of the bag, but I'd be afraid she'd know I'd disturbed the special fold Eamon gives to the bags he uses in his Emporium. She'd tell me, too, if she thought I'd taken one. Anyhow, she'll give me a sweet the minute I give her the bag.

I wonder will she have twisted the whole thing of the ditch into a funny story yet. Suffering duck! I'll never forget it. The sight of her! And of course we couldn't leave the children by themselves when we brought her home to Jim. I'll never forget the faces of the lads as they came out of the parlour in a line, the way they looked at her, not knowing whether to laugh or cry or be frightened.

There she was sitting in the priest's armchair, with her grey hair out of its bun and hanging down her back till it was nearly touching the floor; and the stink of her! I could see the lads' noses crinkling when the smell of the rotting potatoes got them.

"Do I look like a witch?" she asked them in a sharp voice, and they all jumped back. Then she gave a low cackle. She was more embarrassed than they were, only she was trying to pretend her way out of the embarrassment by being funny, by pretending it was normal to sit in the priest's chair looking like a witch and smelling like a dead ass.

Thank God Johnny came in at that very minute, and all the attention went to the two long poles he was carrying. When he announced what we were going to do, all the unease went out of the kitchen and, by the way everyone got excited, you'd think it was suddenly Halloween or Pancake Tuesday.

We tied the poles under Missus Brady's chair and made it into one of those litters you'd see fat people being carried in in story-books. The children laughed out loud and clapped their hands when Johnny and myself lifted Missus Brady off the floor, she making nervous noises but doing her best to pretend she wasn't afraid, Jayjay the youngest wanting to get up on her lap so he could go for a jaunt with her.

Out through the back door we went, me first, to where Becky was already holding the white-faced mare by the winkers, the mare with her ears laid down crossly on her head, the wind whipping her mane and the flame of the yard lamp jumping up and down when the breeze got into the glass globe.

We put the litter down, and Johnny and myself faced each other. Johnny counted to three, and in one great burst of energy we lifted the litter clear over the side of the cart and put the chair down gently on the floor. The minute she landed, Missus Brady said, "Sweet Jesus," as if she'd unexpectedly met her saviour.

I held the mare's head while the chaps helped Johnny with the gates, it was getting so windy. Every now and then a beam of moonlight swept across the yard as the clouds were broken apart and whipped off the face of the moon by the fierce winds in the sky. Clouds the size of prairies were being torn into pieces the size of fields, that flew across the sky as if the devil was after them.

Johnny came and took the mare from me and led her out through the gate on to the lane. With my hand on the wingboard, I walked along beside Missus Brady to keep her company, to give her the impression I was ready to catch her if she started to fall out of the chair. The girls walked in front, one of then holding the swinging yard lamp, holding hands like they never do, forgetting their spikiness towards each other in the excitement of the moment. Behind us came the two boys with the beam of the flash lamp all over the place, they jumping into loughs of water and not feeling the cold of the water on their legs.

There was Johnny in front of me leading the mare by the winkers, and Missus Brady high up in the cart on her throne, her unloosed bun flying behind her in the wind. She was out of a picture book, like something that one of those Italian carvers with the long quare names had carved, or like a picture you'd see on a bank note; the mane of the white-faced mare glinting in the moonlight, giving her a sheen, the huge head going up and down full of determination, as if she knew she was drawing the passenger of her lifetime, her ears laid down along her skull to warn off any enemy that would try to ambush the royal progress. I was reminded of a picture on a postcard I once saw of Queen Victoria on an elephant in India surrounded by lads with funny hats waving big feathery fans at her to keep the flies away.

There's the high walls of Saint Dympna's lunatic asylum. The next thing will be the white walls of the hospital. Thank God, I'm nearly there. I'm winded, and I'm nearly dizzy from letting my eyes get caught up in the light of the flash lamp glinting off the spinning spokes of the new bike Johnny gave me for our wedding anniversary. He's a quare fellow; a lunatic if he thinks he's been made a fool of, but a real thoughtful person behind it all. I think he's the best man in the world.

31. Liam Glanvil

Dear Sister de Monfort,

Thanks for *The Dog Caruso*. I read it in four days. It was a great adventure. I learned a lot about dogs. Daddy said *Riders of the Purple Sage* is the best book he ever read.

The name of the composition is "The Pig".

I remain, Your nephew, Liam

THE PIG

Through the kitchen window, the children peep at the men backing out of the pighouse pulling the rope. Then the pig comes, the rope tied to a back leg, and it pawing the ground with its other feet trying to get a grip; and the squeals of it! They pull it across the haggard to the edge of the slope so the blood will run down into the dunghill.

In my father's hand, the sharpened blade of the long knife glitters, and we all run away with our fingers in our ears.

Once the pig's terrible squealing and Rover's terrified barking is over and we have come out from under the beds, the worst has happened. But, even so, we still look only from a distance, peeping from behind gates or doors or windows or through spread fingers so our eyes won't have far to go if we have to look away quickly.

When the men carry the boiling water from the boiler house to the haggard, the steam rolls off the tops of the buckets like clouds tumbling down the mountain when there's heavy rain coming. Through the window of the middlehouse the children watch as the scalding water is poured over the pig, raising blisters on the skin to make it easy for the men with the scraping knives to take off the hair.

When the pig is dragged on a sheet of canvas into the yard to the boiler house, clumps of bristles surround the bare spot where it died, like beads of a broken glass necklace. On the canvas, the pig, as pink as a baby just washed in hot water, looks like it's asleep. By the time the men and the pig get to the boiler house, we have run up to the stable to hide in the arched doorway.

A rope, hanging from the pulley-wheel that's tied to a rafter, is tied around the pig's two back feet. The men stop pulling when the pig's head swings up off the canvas. For a few minutes a trickle of red water runs off the nose and Mister-Cavanagh-of-the-shop puts on a red rubber apron and ties it behind his back. The galvanised bath which the children wash in every Saturday night is pushed into place, and Mister Cavanagh opens the pig's belly between the two rows of teats with one swipe of a hooked knife.

Grey and purple glistening tubes, like squirming, fat eels, bulge out through the slit. When Mister Cavanagh pulls the cut apart with his hands, the whole glob of purple-grey begins to slide down into the bath, and, to help it out, Mister Cavanagh nicks the places where the guts is attached to the inside of the pig. There's a big slop sound, and the purple-grey eels almost come spilling out of the bath into Mister Cavanagh's boots. When the steam comes up off the guts in a cloud, the men move back from the terrible smell.

The children hold their noses, too, afraid a breeze might blow the fresh gut-smell over to the stable door.

Even though I've seen the pig being slit open four times, I still expect the guts to be red, and when they are grey and purple I am always surprised.

Everyone's teeth go mad when my father drags the bath of guts out from under the pig, the galvanised rim tearing along the concrete floor like a deaf nun's nails on a blackboard. Mister Cavanagh sticks his bare hand into the bath and we move nearer, sidle up along the wall of the houses to the cowhouse doorway. When Mister Cavanagh finds the liver, he pulls it to the top of the pile and snips it out. My father holds out the big blue willow dish that's used on the table for the potatoes at dinner time. The liver is so big it hangs over the edges.

I'm the only one of the children who will eat the liver, and my sisters make vomiting sounds when they see me eating it, the place where the liver came from still in their memories.

Mister Cavanagh dives into the bath again and comes up with the heart. I always think the heart's going to be as big as a football, but it's only as big as a big potato. The heart is put in the glass bowl my mother uses to shape jelly for after dinner on Sundays.

We all step out of the cowhouse doorway when Mister Cavanagh bends down over the bath again, because we know he's after the most important part. When he pulls out the bladder, other guts still attached to it, he holds it up. Then, in an English accent, he says the same thing every year, "Behold the bladder of a traitor." Then he says, "Whose turn is it this year, lads?" And all call out, "Jayjay." It will be Jayjay's turn to blow up the bladder and make it into a football, after it has dried in the kitchen chimney for a week.

Mister Cavanagh is very careful when he removes the bladder to be sure he doesn't nick it. A sow's bladder is the best because it is so big. Sometimes, we only get to play with the blown-up bladder for a few minutes before the wind blows it into a thorny hedge. But, no matter how short a time it lasts, our hands and clothes smell sharply like old pig water for a long time afterwards and my mother complains. The smell is like a long, thin knife that plunges into your insides every time you breathe.

Even though Mister Cavanagh holds out the bladder and tries to coax Jayjay to come and get it, we all stay where we are. My father takes the bladder and, for now, hangs it on a high nail in the boiler house wall out of the reach of the cat.

The children cringe back into the cowhouse doorway again, peep around the corner of the wall, their spread fingers over their eyes. They know what's coming.

My father holds one pig ear, and this year – because Paddy Burns tried to make my father tell a lie – Benny Cosgrove holds the other. Mister Cavanagh gets down on his knees in front of the pig and begins to cut off the head. When he has cut a deep line all around the neck that looks like a ribbon around a girl's neck, he puts down the knife and picks up the bushman's saw that's used to cut sticks for the fire. When the teeth of the saw grind into the neckbone, Becky cannot bear it any more. When she runs back down the yard to the middlehouse, the rest of us run with her, everyone like little pups whimpering at their mother for going too fast, stepping on each other's heels. Into the far corner of the middlehouse we crowd, fingers in ears, eyes squeezed tightly shut, still whimpering.

By the time we sidle back up to the cowhouse door, the head is gone, the feet have been sawed off, and two short sticks are keeping the slit in the belly wide open. The bathful of guts is gone too, buried in the hole that was dug in the garden yesterday to keep it safe from stray dogs. Mister Cavanagh calls to us, tells us everything is finished for the day, that the pig will have to hang for two days before the salt is rubbed in.

It's much easier to look at the pig now because it doesn't look too much like a dead pig; no head, no feet, no insides. But when we push each other through the boiler house door we see the head lying on sheets of butter paper on a board across the top of the bran barrel. It's nearly funny to look at the pig's head with its eyes closed, its ears falling forward, and the three big rings in its snout above the nose holes. Mister Cavanagh takes the pig's head home with him every year. Paddy Burns used to get half of the liver and the four crubeens, but this year Missus Brady will get them, along with her pile of rashers.

After Mister Cavanagh has lined his big bucket with butter paper, he picks up the head by the ears and lowers it in, the two-holed snout and the rings sticking up over the rim. When he gets on his bike, my father stands on the lane holding up the handle of the bucket and, as he goes by, Mister Cavanagh grabs it. The bike waddles around on the lane until he gets up speed, and for a long time it looks like Mister Cavanagh will end up in a ditch. When he gets the bike going straight, my father cheers and claps. The children join in.

Jayjay asks my father to bring in the bladder and hang it in the kitchen chimney.

For the two days the pig hangs waiting to be salted, the children are afraid to go to the boiler house. It's almost like there's a body hanging in there, and if you touch the pig by accident it would feel cold and damp and soft and dead.

But this year, because my father gave me an important job to do, I went into the boiler house by myself and touched the dead pig.

Once he told me he had an important job for me, my father wouldn't tell me any more, except that I was to go with him. He brought the stepladder to the boiler house and put it against the wall beside the pig. Then he brought me into the far room, to his shaving table. He unscrewed the handle from his razor and took out the Gillette blade. He replaced it with one of the rusty blades which he took off the cracked doll's-set saucer near the mirror. Back out to the boiler house we went, and he showed me the hair in the creases of the pig's skin that had been missed by the scraping knives. He showed me how to use the razor. Then, as he left to cut hedges across the fields with the billhook over his shoulder and the red handle of the sharpening stone sticking out of his pocket, he told me not to fall off the ladder when I climbed up to look for hairs.

For a long time, I stood there looking at the pig, looking at where one of the front legs, sawed off at the knee, joined the body. There was a lot of hair in there. To get at the hair I would have to bend the leg away from the body. I stared at the hair, and I wanted my father to know that I could do the job he had given me. The dead pig flesh looked very like the flesh of a person, and I began to think of all the boys in my class in school with their shirts off, and their galluses on their bare shoulders holding up their trousers, their bodies the same colour as the pig's, not even much warmer in the cold classroom.

I took the pig's leg in my left hand and bent it away from the body. Once a year we have the county doctor's examination day in the school. The night before the examination everyone is supposed to wash themselves. On examination day all the desks get pushed back to the classroom walls. The minute the doctor arrives, all the boys take off their shirts so the doctor won't be kept waiting when it's the next person's turn. The townie boys point at us and say we are so thin the harp could be played on our ribs. We could point to some of the townies and tell them they are so dirty potato seeds could be sown on the backs of their necks, but they would only beat us up later in the schoolyard.

My father's sharp razor slices through the stiff pig hair. This is what they make toothbrushes out of, Billy Bates told me one time. "Imagine putting dirty old pig hair in your mouth," he said. I think he was trying to be funny.

The strange smell of the blue flames under the silver pots fills up the classroom. The clean nurse in her white clothes puts the doctor's instruments in the pots and lets them boil while she weighs everyone. It's like the school is no longer a school: no desks, the doctor, the nurse, the smell, everyone with his shirt off, all the pink flesh, the teacher gone somewhere. In a straight line, we move slowly towards the thin, white weighing scales on the floor with the spinning numbers. The nurse says the same thing to everyone. "Step up. Don't move." Then she fills in a little box in a white card, and she says, "Step off. Stand over there." When she has weighed five boys, she measures them to see how tall they are, presses their bare backs against the cold, green wall, and puts a ruler on top of their heads. She says the same thing to everyone: "Put your back to the wall. Put your toes to the line. Stand up straight." She fills in another box on the card and says, "Stand over there." We wait our turn with the doctor.

When I pulled the second front leg out from the body, the pig swung on its rope, twisted, and rubbed up against me. I jumped back, thought for a second that the pig had come back to life, and it with no guts or head. It took a few seconds to get my breath back, took a minute before I could touch the pig again. In the boiler house chimney I thought I heard moaning, but it was only Crip Quigley's cow bawling.

The doctor pokes each boy in a whole lot of places as if feeling a pig to see how fat it is. He feels the arms, lifts them up, and feels the armpits. When the boy squirms at the tickling, the doctor says, "Stop that!" He looks at the fingernails. "Stick out your tongue." Then, like magic, a tongue depressor is in his hand, and before he even puts it in the boy's mouth there's the sound of throwing-up noises. "Stop that! Say aah." The tongue depressor makes the eyes water. While the boy is trying not to throw up, the doctor has already taken the depressor away from the throat and he's moving it around the mouth as if he's looking for something he lost. He pushes the cheeks out, lifts the top lip, taps teeth, looks up the nose, pulls the ears back and looks in. The doctor does everything very quick. The worst thing he can ask is, "When was the last time you washed yourself?" because that means he knows the boy he's asking hasn't washed for ages.

I moved the stepladder a little bit, and while I was climbing up to get at the pig's back legs I was thinking about how the doctor, without even asking me to open the buttons of my fork, suddenly had his hand in my trousers. "Stop that!" he commanded when I doubled over and pulled away from him. "Look that way and cough," he said. I looked towards the window and coughed. He took his hand out, and while he was filling in a lot of boxes on my card he asked, "Are you a farmer's son?" Before I could answer, he asked me another question, "Is that mark on your face from ringworm?" Before I could answer, he said, "Tell your

mother not to let you near calves with ringworm. Next."
The next boy was Sean Delaney, who was turned around
talking to the boy behind him. Sean Delaney jumped when
the doctor shouted "Next!" at the top of his voice, his face
so red it looked like it could burst. Then the doctor said,
"Nurse, are you doing your job?" The nurse blushed and
said, "I'm sorry, doctor." She went to the boys who were
queued up for the doctor and hissed at them like a goose
standing up to a dog, "The next boy who talks will get an
injection."

Sean Delaney made a noise when the doctor poked him
in the ribs real hard. "Stop that!"

There was a lot of hair around the pig's backside, and I
had to balance myself on the ladder so I could hold the tail
out of the way with one hand and shave with the other. The
tail was the worst part to touch because it hadn't been
scraped at all. It was still covered with fine hairs, and it was
as dirty as the rest of the pig had been before it was scraped.
I caught the tail between my thumb and finger and moved
it to one side, and then scraped the razor along. Suddenly,
I got a terrible fright. I didn't know what was happening
until it was all over. And when it was over, my feet were on
the ground, and my two arms were around the pig. That
was how I saved myself when I began to fall: wrapped my
arms around the pig and held on while I slithered down to
the floor, my face against the pig's side all the way down. I
could hardly catch my breath, and black patches floated
across my eyes like thin clouds in front of the moon on a
windy night. I didn't know what happened to the razor.

It was only when I heard a laughing voice saying
something about hugging a dead pig that everything began
to come clear. Bigword Bates was standing in the boiler
house doorway, with his face pointed to the roof and he

laughing so much he was shaking. Like someone who has been caught doing something wrong, I pulled away my arms, rubbed my sleeve on my face where it had been touching the pig, and cleaned my hands on the back of my trousers. I wanted to burst out crying, but I wouldn't please Bigword. The more he laughed, the more I wanted to hurt him with something hard.

"That's the best one yet," Bigword said, when he calmed down. "I never saw anyone with his arms around a pig before, and I'd swear you were kissing it."

Before I could stop myself, and because I knew Bigword would go around telling everyone he saw me kissing a dead pig, I shouted, "I wasn't kissing the pig. I wasn't. I wasn't," and I began to cry. All I could think of was the boys from the town surrounding me in the school playground shouting, "Glanvil kisses dead pigs! Glanvil kisses dead pigs!"

I ran past Bigword, out of the boiler house, across the yard and into the kitchen. I sprung up on the little hob in the dark of the corner.

My mother always knows when something is wrong.

I told her about falling off the ladder when Bigword Bates frightened me. My mother thought I had hurt myself when I started to bawl all over again, and it took a long time to explain to her about the boys in the schoolyard. She was running her hand through my hair the way she does to calm me down, when the kitchen door opened.

"Are you in, Missus?" It was Bigword Bates.

My mother looked around the corner at him. "Liam wasn't kissing the pig, Billy," she said. "He was only trying to save himself when he fell after you frightened him."

"Oh, of course, Missus, he wasn't kissing the pig at all. I was only codding him."

"Well, don't say it to anyone," my mother said. "Even if you only say it for a laugh, someone will believe he was kissing the pig, and then they'll all be jeering him."

"Ah, sure, I didn't mean to frighten the lad, Missus. I didn't even know he was in the boiler house. I came to look for the loan of the second billhook. Dunkle says Paddy Burns won't be working for Johnny any more."

"You know where Johnny keeps the tools, Billy. I'll tell him you took the billhook."

Through the kitchen window, I peeped and watched until Bigword Billy went out of the yard, the billhook over his shoulder. I still wanted to hurt him.

I couldn't make myself go back to the boiler house to look for the razor. When my father came back from cutting the hedges, my mother went out to the yard and talked to him. He found the razor on the floor between the bonemeal and the bran.

He told me what a good job I had done, but he didn't ask me to finish shaving the pig.

32. Missus Brady

I was sorry to be leaving the hospital, the nurses, the fresh sheets, the food and all.

But, like Crip would say, even a monkey's tail comes to an end sometime. And so, after I had spent four weeks in traction and aiming at bedpans, and one week puttering around the wards with a walking stick, they brought me out in a wheelchair, my stiff, plastered leg sticking out in front of me like I was one of those old knights on a horse with a long spear out in front.

Everyone I met in the corridors said goodbye and wished me luck. "Good luck, Missus." Luck!

Luck! says I to myself. If they only knew! The best bit of luck I've had in the last thirty years was breaking the leg that got me in here in the first place. Does everyone else in the world live in such luxury that they thought I would be going to a better place when I went home from the hospital? – the turf fire on the hearth breaking my back whenever a body tries to cook something; keeping the fire going around the baker when I do a bit of bread, more often than not it coming out too well done or half done; the chimney so wide at the top that half the kitchen floor gets covered with wet soot when it rains; every bit of heat given off by the fire sucked up the chimney and spread to the four winds; and

God forbid it rains when I'm cooking – umbrella time, and Jim shouting at me about how it's bad luck to raise an umbrella inside a house.

"Good luck, Missus," the people called, and I leaving every bit of luck behind me in the hospital. Good luck, Missus! I felt like saying to them, "Do ya want to know the luck I'm going home to? No lavatory, and me with a stiff leg having to try to squat – to say nothing of me gimpy hip; the drinking water to be carried from someone else's pump a quarter of a mile away; a man in the house who's as crooked as the hind leg of a jennet in his contrariness; the turf to be carried in, the ashes to be carried out; the washing to be done and spread out on the whitethorn hedge to dry; the food to be got ready; the onions to be minded; the doctor's office to be cleaned; Paddy and Lizzie Burns to be fought; and yer wishing me luck! What yer wishing me is bad luck."

Down the bright, clean, dry, smooth, warm corridor I sailed in the wheelchair, the leg leading the way, one of Johnny Glanvil's thick socks on the foot. Kate brought it in to keep the foot warm when I was in traction, the foot hanging up in the sky, sticking out of the plaster.

The man stopped outside a door in the wall and waited. I hadn't a notion what he was talking about. The feelings about the place I was going to were washing over me, and I was too full of pity for myself to even care what the man was saying.

Then I nearly jumped out of my skin when, all of a sudden, the door opened by itself, but not like any door I'd ever seen before. It disappeared into the wall with a swoosh. There I was, sitting looking straight into this little room as bare as a robin's nest in winter, not even a picture hanging on a wall. I got into a bit of a panic when your man pushed me. It's a torture chamber like the Communists in Poland have for Cardinal Mindszenty, I thought to myself.

"What are you going to do to me in here, Mick?" says I.

"Nothing at all, Missus Brady," says he, and I heard the door closing behind me. The next minute didn't my stomach jump into my mouth and I nearly died with the fright; I thought we were falling straight down through the ground. Then my head nearly fell off my neck with a sudden jerk.

"In the name of the sweet Jesus, Mick," says I, "but what's happening to us at all?"

"Sure, the lift comes to such a sudden stop sometimes, Missus Brady, t'would nearly knock a fella's guggs out of his bag," says he, and the door wheezed open.

Well, I never in my life felt like such an eegit, and I very nearly letting your man, Mick, know that I didn't know what a lift is. I must have been so distracted when I came into the hospital that I never even knew I'd been in the lift. The fright was still on me and my stomach was still settling back into its place, when they pushed me up the ramp into the back of the ambulance. The minute they closed the door, the inside of the ambulance got dark, and I started thinking again about facing back into Derrycloney, into my own house, into Jim's house, into the house we rent from Johnny for half a crown a month. My own house! My own nothing, except the clothes I wear and my good topcoat with the fox heads.

I knew by the turns on the road and the feel of the wheels in the potholes when we got to Derrycloney. I knew by the stopping and the backing and the driving, that the driver was getting the ambulance as close as he could to the house. When the door swung open the light rushed in, and I took a deep breath and held it, like I do when I'm going to splash cold water on my face in the winter.

I was in such a state that I must have had my eyes shut tight while they were unloading me. When the wheelchair landed on the ground, the first thing I saw was Jim standing in the kitchen door, and I had to give him a second look because I thought he was crying. Jim crying, mind you! And sure enough, he was – the water running down his face like rain off a duck's back. He hadn't seen me since I went in to the hospital.

Well, I don't know what happened to me when I saw him crying. Right away, I remembered Benny Cosgrove holding my hand when his mother's coffin was lowered into the grave – it was the same feeling that swept over me. It was the first time in Jim's life, even from the time he was a child, that he gave any sign he was fond of me – standing there in the doorway so glad to see me he was crying. I don't know whether it was the memory of Benny's little hand in mine, or all the pent-up dread of coming home from the hospital, or the sight of Jim crying that started me off, too. Big fat tears fell down into my lap just as the two ambulance men put their hands under my arms and stood me on my feet. "Ah, Jim," says I, "sure, it's all right now. I'm home again."

Just before he turned around and went into the house, Jim made a loud snuffle and wiped his nose with his sleeve.

The ambulance men let me stand there in the yard until I got my bearings. I took a few steps, just myself and the walking stick, and I started thinking that maybe it wasn't so bad to be out of the hospital; that I was beginning to know I was appreciated, needed – the first time since that day at Kitty Cosgrove's funeral.

When I took a step towards the door, the ambulance men closed in on me real quick to help. "It's all right, men, thank ye," says I, and I feeling stronger and better with every step I took. The men followed me into the kitchen, their hands out to catch me in case I fell. They were a nice couple of lads. One of them pulled a chair out to the middle of the floor and then they stood there like two nervous hens looking at a cock strutting towards them, while I lowered myself, the plastered leg bent a little bit at the knee. I was a bit breathy.

There was no sign of Jim.

"I'd make yee a cup of tea if I could," says I, and the two men talked at the same time and said thank you and not to bother yourself Missus and we're grateful and all that kind of stuff. Then they asked me was I comfortable? Would my husband be able to look after me? Did I want them to put me on the bed? Would they leave a mug of water near me in case I needed it? And I thought they'd never go away and leave me in peace. Too much niceness can kill a person.

When the noise of the ambulance was gone up the road, I expected Jim to come out of the bedroom; that's where I thought he'd gone so the ambulance people wouldn't see him crying.

"Jim," I called out after a while. I waited. "Jim, they're gone now. Come on out here and tell me all the news."

I looked around the kitchen: ashes everywhere, the usual half of the floor thick with black soot, dirty plates and mugs all over the table, the water bucket nearly empty. "Sweet Jesus tonight," says I to myself, and my heart began to sink back to where it was when I was leaving the hospital. The more I looked around, the more sorry I felt for myself. Everything was worse than I had imagined, and I started to get cross. Where the hell was Jim?

"Jim," I shouted, "will ya get in here and get me a mug of water." I wasn't even thirsty.

I listened, thinking I might hear him crying. And, sure

enough, I could hear him in the bedroom, and he sobbing. My heart collapsed into softness again. "The poor old bugger," I said to myself.

"Will you come on out here, Jim?" says I. "Come on out here and tell me everything."

I waited.

There was the sound of something being dragged along the floor towards the bedroom door. And sure enough, after a few minutes Jim's backside appeared around the windbreaker wall. He was bent over and walking backwards, pulling something along the floor, and, I declare to God, I thought to myself, "He made me a rocking chair so I'll be comfortable with me broken leg," and never once in his life did he make anything for himself or anyone else.

He backed his way across the kitchen floor, bent over like an old woman picking potatoes – her arse in the air – his two hands near the floor pulling a sack by the two corners. He nearly backed on to my lap, and when he stood up and stepped aside there was Cinders with his head on his paws looking like he was asleep. And Jim says, "Poor Cinders died." And off he goes crying again.

In the end I laughed, but before I laughed I nearly cried, nearly lifted the walking stick to whack Jim across the shoulders. And just as I was about to drop into a deep pit of self-pity, didn't it cross my mind that I was a terrible eegit for even thinking things would be different, could be different. I must have been a bit daft. A rocking chair! "Ya big eegit," I shouted at myself. Jim so happy to see me, he's crying! "Ya big eegit of a woman!"

I nearly fell off the chair with the laughing, the dead dog at my feet, Jim slobbering. I think I became hysterical for a while, water running down my face into my mouth and down along my wattles under my blouse. I'd never tell anyone, but I think in my laughing I went to the very edge of madness and looked over the side.

Jim must have thought my laughing was crying for Cinders. He slobbered a few things that I didn't understand but which sounded as if he approved of the noises I was making, as if he knew how I felt about the loss of the mangy cur.

"I've his grave dug in the garden," he says, and I nearly said, "Not in one of me onion beds, I hope." But I didn't. I just sat there and watched Jim wrapping the sack around the dog, like the dog was a Christian and the sack was a shroud.

And Jim must have only stepped into the back garden when I heard laughing and talking, the voices of children. It was Kate below with the four children and they all carrying something: a bucket of water, a jug of milk, a hot shepherd's pie, two loaves, cabbage, a stone of spuds, a six-inch-thick piece of boiled bacon, an apple cake and a jug of Bird's custard, the steam still rising off it. For about one minute, the children were real shy, but, when one of them asked the first question about the hospital, that was the end of the shyness.

Kate never said a word about the state of the place; she never would. She cleaned everything, took out the ashes, got the fire going, swept the floor, and made a pot of tea. They were gone before Jim came back from the burial, and if he noticed any difference in the kitchen he didn't say a word. Maybe he thought I had cleaned and cooked while he was at the funeral of that pisser of pee into other people's pots. When I gave him a plate of apple cake and custard, he said, "This is better than a wake for a person."

When he drank the last mouthful of sweet tea, Jim said he was going out to visit the grave, and I said to myself, "This is how I'm going to be able to forget the hospital – all this stuff that'll be funny when I get the cast off me leg." I stood up and leaned against the table while I piled up the delft and knives and forks, all the time thinking to myself about Derrycloney. "Everything that happens here, no matter how bad it is, turns out to be funny in the end; even the reason why Cha Finley killed his sister is funny. He didn't kill her for money or because he hated her – he just had to get the threshing done. But it's only by looking for the funny things that ya can keep going. There's even something funny about Paddy and Lizzie thinking they could forge a will to steal Benny's bit of a farm; they couldn't even write a real will, never mind forge one." And, I declare to God, at that very second, when I was thinking of Paddy and Lizzie and the will, didn't I hear the noise of Paddy's ass-and-cart in the chimney, and right away I forgot about the hospital and the crinkling sheets and the nice nurses and the good food. "I have to take up me post," I said to myself and, with the walking stick in my hand, I hobbled over to the door.

For a second, it seemed my eyes were not attached to my brain. What I was seeing wasn't making sense. Paddy and d'ass-and-cart were just coming past my flower garden, and never in my life have I ever seen such a big load on an ass's cart. For a minute I thought I was looking at a bit of Duffys' Circus; there were chairs and bits of beds, mattresses, the kitchen table, even the kitchen dresser for all the plates and mugs, the chest of drawers that used to be in poor Kitty's room, bikes. One thing was piled on top of the other, all so high that I was sure they had to use a ladder to get it up there. Everything was tied on with ropes, and, sure enough, the ladder was sticking out at the back.

As I stepped out into the yard to lay into Paddy, didn't I see Lizzie and the two daughters walking behind the load, the two young ones helping her on her bad feet.

And then the whole thing hit me like a ton of bricks; they were leaving Benny's and they were taking everything with them, all the furniture, anything they could get on the ass's cart. The crossness that welled up in me! I wanted to run out on the lane and block their way. I wanted to shout at them, call them all the worst names I could think of. But there was so much crossness in me, I couldn't move, I couldn't even speak.

None of them looked at me as they went by, and I was glad because they might have thought I was having a fit, or choking on my own spit. But they were not looking at the ground as if they were beaten or doing something shameful. They were looking straight ahead, their heads up in the air, and they stepping into every pothole and cow shite on the road. When they had gone by, I went out on to the lane and looked after them until they went around the corner at the Fiery Hill, the chair on the top of the load the last thing I saw.

"Ye crowd of mane hures," I thought to myself. "That bad luck may follow ye wherever ye go."

I don't know how long I stood there leaning on the stick, looking at the ground at my feet, thinking about the hardness of Lizzie. "She must have a heart like a stone," I said to myself, and I turned around to go back into the house. And when I looked down the lane, there was Crissy the Widda outside her house, and all the Glanvils outside their house, and Benny outside his house and Crip out too, and they all looking up the lane at the passage of the meanest meanness they had ever seen in their lives.

I waved my stick in the air and everyone waved back and, as I left the lane, all the others turned back to their own houses too.

"They might have stolen the furniture," I said to myself, "but at least Benny has his farm."

As I raised my plastered leg to lift it over the step into the kitchen, didn't the words that your man, Mick, said to me in the morning finally get through to my brain. "T'would nearly knock a fella's guggs out of his bag." Wasn't it a quaint way he had of saying it – guggs out of his bag? I smiled and I thought to myself, "Sure, the English mustn't know half the time what we're talking about in this country."

33. Kate Glanvil

The whole thing with Paddy and Lizzie seemed to have come to a sudden end when we saw them all going up Derrycloney with d'ass-and-cart full of furniture; what a sad parade that was – a funeral more than a parade.

The four children came galloping into the turkeyhouse all shouting at the same time, me telling them not to step on the turkeys' feet, they all trying to tell me that every one of the Burnses had gone up the lane with d'ass-and-cart full of chairs and beds and tables and bikes.

"Didgee tell yeer father?" I asked them, and the four of them fled like terriers to the cowhouse where Johnny was under Threespin trying to drag the milk out of her.

We all met at the same time at the wicket door, the children on top of each other's heels trying to be the first on to the lane. By then, the Burnses were up at the bog field gate, and all we could see was the three women walking behind the high load of furniture. The minute my eyes lit on Lizzie hobbling along on her bad feet between the two daughters, I started to cry. Of course, I wouldn't have cried at all if I'd known then what they'd done to Benny's house.

With my back to the high yard wall, I buried my face in my hands and cried like I cried the night poor mother died. All I could think of was how the Burnses and ourselves had been such good neighbours, and now we would never be able to talk again. On the far side of the anger at each other was still the memory of how nice we were to each other once upon a time, and this made the separation between us all the more terrible. Why is it that the bitterness between people who have once trusted each other, but no longer do, is the worst bitterness of all?

Some of the children stood around me pulling on my apron, not knowing what else to do with a crying mother. When I heard Johnny saying, "Bad cess to the lot of ye," I came out of myself, and I was annoyed at Johnny. I reminded him that the children were listening, but I was really cross at him for only being cross at the Burnses and not sad at all. Sometimes I don't understand men.

We all stood there looking after them as they got smaller in the distance.

An ass takes very short steps when it's walking, and it took the Burnses a long time to go up the lane. After they passed her house, Crissy the Widda came out and stood at the side of the lane looking after them, a long strip of knitted stuff in one hand, the needles and ball of wool in the other.

When they went by the next house, I was surprised to see Missus Brady shuffling on to the lane with her walking stick. She stood there leaning to one side, looking after the load of furniture until it disappeared down the Fiery Hill. When Lizzie and the daughters disappeared, Missus Brady turned around and looked down the lane. She waved her stick in the air, and we all waved to her. So did Crissy the Widda. When we turned to go back into the farmyard, we saw Benny standing against the wall of the henhouse, and further down the road Crip Quigley was out in the middle of the lane, squinting himself blind. Johnny told us to go on in, that he was going to talk to Benny for a minute.

A quarter of an hour later, I was mixing the mash for the calves when Johnny came into the boiler house; he was white in the face. "They took everything," he said. He sat down on an upside-down bucket and pushed his cap back off his forehead. With elbows on knees, he parcelled his face between his hands. He looked as if he'd just found one of his cows dead.

I was still feeling some sympathy for the hobbling Lizzie. "They brought some yokes with them when they moved in," I said. "I suppose they were entitled to take them with them."

"They took everything except the walls and the roof," Johnny said. "There's nothing in the house; they even ripped the grate out of the fireplace, nothing left but the ashpit; they took the curtains, the pictures off the walls."

As Johnny went on, any tenderness I had for the Burnses began to ooze out of my heart.

"They took the mantelshelf and the kitchen clothesline. They took the doors off the two rooms. There's not one piece of furniture left. They even swept the floors to show how bare they left the place. And they even took Benny's wreck of a bike."

In Johnny's voice, I could clearly hear the satisfaction that he had been proved right about Lizzie's viciousness.

"Benny has the farm all right, but he hasn't one tool and he hasn't even one animal. He didn't get any of the money when Paddy sold the cow and the two calves last month. D'ass-and-cart was Benny's, too, but he's never going to see it again."

The more Johnny talked, the weaker I felt at the knees. I sat on the edge of the bran barrel. The depth to which the Burnses had gone to get their revenge was sickening. What the Burnses had done to Benny, they had done to us.

I had brought Lizzie to Mass in the pony-and-trap, had even gone down the lane to pick her up at her own door every Sunday morning. We had given her a pair of plucked chickens every Christmas; I'd even taken the insides out because I knew Lizzie didn't like doing it. We'd given them apples and rhubarb, half the pig's liver and the crubeens every year, to say nothing about the piece of salted bacon two feet long at Easter. Paddy had played cards at our kitchen table on Sunday nights during the winters. He had taught our children how to play rings in his own kitchen. He'd made whistles for them, made them spinning tops and whips, too; he even made the little wooden man who danced on a board when he whistled.

"There's not a bit of winter firing in the place. There's not a sod of turf in the barn; not even a bit of mull left. Benny says Paddy made a gap in the hedge down the fields at the tarred road and took the turf out that way in d'ass-and-cart in the night."

I was glad the children were in the kitchen at their homework when Johnny started with his cursing – the real kind.

"I hope they never have a happy day in their lives," he said quietly.

"Ah, Johnny," I said, afraid of the curse he was laying on the Burnses. "Don't wish bad things for them. It'll only come back at ya."

"I don't care," he said. "I'd be willing to live in misery if it meant they'd live in misery for the rest of their lives. I hope what they did to Benny sticks in their craws and chokes them, never lets them have one good day to the day they die."

I knew that the best thing to do was to let Johnny's words sail on past me, not stop them and wrestle with them. So, after a long silence in the darkening boiler house, the two of us stood up at the same time.

"We'll have to help out Benny," Johnny said. "It's hard to know where to start."

"I'll bring him out his supper and try to figure out what's the best thing to do."

Johnny went back to Threespin.

The children fought with each other over who would carry what out to Benny's; there was the mug, the jug of tea with the sugar and milk mixed in, and the plate of bread — buttered and jammed. I gave Jayjay a saucer to keep him happy. Before we left, I told them about the empty house, warned them not to pass any remarks and not to ask any questions.

Benny was standing in the middle of the kitchen looking at the ashpit when we walked in, his hands buried in the topcoat pockets. When he turned towards us, his face had the same look as it always has, not showing crossness, pain, disappointment or anything else, just the blankness of a child who has suffered from the casual cruelty of grown-ups.

The children stood gaping at the emptiness, and they didn't even know it when I took Benny's supper out of their hands. I put everything on the wide windowsill and poured the tea.

"Here's yer supper, Benny," I said, and I handed him the mug.

Carefully, he sipped, testing the hotness loudly.

In the corner of my eye, the fireplace looked like a mouth with all the teeth ripped out. Bright patches on the walls showed where the pictures and the calendar used to hang. A shape like a shield in the smoke-stained far wall was where Paddy's homemade ringboard had been. Two jagged-edged holes in the chimney breast showed how savagely the mantelshelf had been pulled out – a piece of rough-hewn wood that couldn't be of any use except for burning.

I put my hand on Benny's shoulder and, through the catch in my throat, told him that we'd come out later with some things.

We left him where we'd found him, the mug to his lips, his eyes on the destroyed fireplace. On the way back to our house, the children fought for my hands, the two smallest winning, the two oldest settling for the security they got from holding the other hands of the younger ones.

34. Billy Bates

News has the quarest way of travelling, and that's a fact beyond a doubt.

It was up the town in Eamon's Emporium I was, telling Eamon about the horsewoman galloping up after Johnny Glanvil's mare stumbled and went down, sending me flying over the front creel out of the cart. Johnny's mare was back on her feet as soon as I landed on the road on my hands and knees. Before I'd skidded to a stop, your one was off her horse asking me if the mare was hurt.

"Feck the mare," says I, and I shouting at her, "Look at my hands and knees. They're skint."

"My good man," says she in her horsewoman's accent, "I have a good mind to report you to the Irish Society for the Prevention of Cruelty to Animals. You were galloping that mare."

"My good woman," says I, the hands and knees falling off me with the pain. "And how would you get twelve loads of beet up to the station in one day if ya didn't gallop yer horses?"

"My husband doesn't grow sugar beet," says she.

"Well, law-di-fecking-daw," says I. I climbed back into the cart, nearly drove the wheel over her feet. "Get out of me fecking way," says I, would have said "fucking" only it was a woman.

"You didn't!" says Eamon, and he in the stitches of laughing.

"Be gob, I did," says I, and a woman walked in through d'Emporium door. Before she even got to the counter and without as much as an "excuse me", she said, "Gimme five Woodbines, Eamon."

"Certainly, Miss Hippwell," Eamon said and he took a cigarette box off the shelf behind him.

Miss Hippwell! The Hippwell One! "Oh, good shag," says I to myself and I breathless all of a sudden. Here I was standing beside the woman that gave life to my dragon, the woman I rode regularly, the one I wrestled with down at the lake, she in her skin. My mouth was dry. The dragon stirred in his cave and beads of sweat popped out on my forehead. I got itchy under the arms. I was standing within a foot of the palace of pleasure and I was afraid to turn and look at her.

When she threw five pennies on the counter, she bumped against my arm and I got the smell of her! She was as bad as a dead ass in a ditch after a month.

Eamon wrapped five Woodbines in a piece of brown paper and handed them to Miss Hippwell. It was only when she turned to leave that I looked at her. Her steatopygia was the first thing to fill my eyes, and she was so big that the hem of her dress in the back was six inches higher than the front. She'd have been a Hottentot if she'd been yellow. Her hair was like a bunch of last year's binder twine soaking for a month in a bucket of old engine oil. She went out into the dark.

I knew that if I ever introduced her to the dragon again, the dragon would slink away, probably disappear. I thought of the old plans I had once hatched, full of spuds and chickens, that might have eased me into her place of pleasure. But, now, as I looked after her, my nose still full of her unpleasant odours, I thanked God I had been saved from being swallowed alive in her stygian interstice.

When the door closed behind her, I gaped at Eamon. "Is that . . .?" I didn't have to go any further.

He nodded. "That's her, poor soul," he said. He looked around for a box to put my messages in, and I was left with my mouth open, silent questions drooling out over my bottom teeth. I had just mustered enough saliva to ask Eamon if the Hippwell One had always looked this way, when I heard the strangest sound, and it was only strange because it was seven o'clock on a November night. What was it, but the sound of Johnny Glanvil's pony-and-cart coming to a stop outside d'Emporium.

Johnny came in, and that's how I found out that Benny's house had been stripped clean. While he talked, Johnny started buying sugar and tea and bread like it was the last day before a war. He even bought a frying pan. Of course, I didn't know how clean a job Paddy and Lizzie had done till I went into the house on the way home from town with my messages on the back of the bike in a cardboard box.

All the way down Derrycloney I was thinking about the Hippwell One, about how different she looked from the Hippwell One I had fantasised my dragon into so many times. The difference between the imagined and the real was staggering. But just imagine the staggering I would have done if the real one had jumped up on my back naked, down at the lake. She would have broken my legs.

I had to step around the windbreaker wall in the kitchen before I saw what devastation Paddy and Lizzie had wrought, as the bible might put it. The sight of the place made me speechless; it was the first time I'd ever seen a bare house. Kate Glanvil and the children were there, Kate hanging curtains on the windows with bits of twine and thumbtacks. The children were sitting on a bag of straw on the floor against the far wall where the ringboard used to be. I often wondered would Paddy ever have made the ringboard at all if he hadn't been so good at the game himself. "Seven," he'd say, and the next second the ring would be swaying on the seven hook. He won money off everyone on Derrycloney Lane on that ringboard

A double-wicked paraffin-oil lamp, on the wide windowsill in the front wall, gave off all the light there was.

Benny was standing on an upside-down bucket, hammering at a piece of wood high on the chimney breast. Looking at Benny swinging a hammer is like looking at a one-handed woman knitting a sock.

"What are ya doing, Benny?" I asked. Benny looked at me with those sheepy eyes of his, but he didn't say anything.

Kate gave me a look as if I'd put my two feet in it up to the hips, and Becky said, "They took the mantelshelf."

"What did they want the mantelshelf for?" I asked, and I heard Cha Finley's ass-and-cart outside on the lane, heard Cha shouting deafly at d'ass to stop. The next minute the constipated midget was standing in the doorway; he's five foot nothing but he's a midget in the brain too. "Run out the two pigs till I count them," he shouts, when Benny is down there earning a shilling on Sunday mornings.

"I brung a bed in d'ass-and-cart," Cha shouted. From where he was standing he could only see me. "Where's Benny?" he shouted.

I didn't want to get into five minutes of non sequiturs with hard-of-hearing Cha.

"Do ya want a hand with the bed?" I asked him.

It was only when I was going in with a black-iron bed-end under each arm that I saw the bedroom door was gone. Cha was behind me with the spring frame. "How's yerself, Missus Glanvil?" he shouted, when he saw Kate at the window.

When I came back into the kitchen, who walks in but Dunkle, wearing the new hat with the feather in the band and the secondhand gabardine coat that he bought at a fair twenty years ago for two-and-thruppence, a trace of everything he's eaten or drunk ever since on the front of it. The Deadman's Coat, he calls it. With the new hat and the old coat he looked like a pile of shite with a green linnet sitting on top.

Dunkle saw Cha in the bedroom doorway. "What are ya doing out so late with d'ass-and-cart, Cha?" he asked, like he was the emperor of China.

"I brung up the sister's oul bed for Benny to sleep on," Cha said.

"The one ya . . ." young Liam Glanvil started to gasp, until Kate stuck him to the wall with spears from her eyes.

"Where's himself, the victim of the whole plot?" Dunkle asked. "Where's Benjamin?" Even when a poor hure is up to his arse in trouble, Dunkle will jeer.

"Benny's fixing the mantelshelf," a child said.

Dunkle stepped around the windbreaker. "Hello, Missus," he said to Kate. "Is it curtains yer hanging up for yer man?"

"Aye, Murt," Kate said, as much as to say, No Murt. Can't ya see I'm hanging up dead chickens, ya bloody eegit.

"We better get the mattress before it rains," Cha shouted.

"It's not going to rain," Dunkle pronounced.

"It's always going to rain," Cha said. "Give me a hand to rassle it into the house, Billy. It's worse than rassling a sack of beet-pulp."

As we went out again, I heard Dunkle asking, "Why are ya fixing the mantelshelf, Benny? Ya can't ate off it and ya can't sleep on it. What's wrong with it anyhow?"

Cha and myself were wrestling the mattress out of d'ass's cart when we heard something scraping along the lane. Then Crip Quigley, dragging a chair behind him, came into the light shining out through the kitchen window.

"Be gob, Crip," says I. "Fer a minute there, I thought a naeroplane was swooping down out of the stratosphere to beat the shite out of me."

"Is yer head stuck up in yer arse again, Billy?" Crip-brave-in-the-dark says, and to tell the truth I was taken aback a bit. Crip was never the one to stand up for himself. He dragged the chair into Benny's, leaving a trail of edgy noise after him.

"What happened yer head, Billy?" Cha shouted.

"Nothing at all, Cha," I shouted back. "Crip thought for a minute there I had it up in me arse."

"That'd be sore if it festered," Cha said, and he led the way back into the house, one of us at each end of the mattress.

By the time we got into the kitchen, Dunkle had enthroned himself on Crip's chair in the middle of the kitchen floor. He was coming to the end of one of his windy stories.

"'Shure,' says I," says he, "'in my day a woman didn't go to the hospital at all. When I was a young lad, the woman took a batter of flour and water the night before and the next day she put the babby from her like a snot. Hospital, me arse!'"

At the window behind him I saw Kate Glanvil giving Dunkle a look. "Ya should try that with a calving cow, Murt," she said, "but make sure you stand out of the way so the calf won't kill ya when it comes shooting out."

Murt took her seriously. "I tried it once, Missus," he said, "but it only made the cow sick."

I saw Kate rolling her eyes as she turned back to the curtains.

While Dunkle was holding forth on obstetrics, Cha had stopped for a second to adjust his grip on the mattress. "Be janey, Murt," he shouted, "rassling a tick is like rassling a sack of beet-pulp."

When we threw the mattress on the bedspring, I heard Johnny's pony-and-cart out on the lane. "Be gob," says I to myself, "all the birds are flocking together tonight." And from the kitchen I heard Kate Glanvil's voice. "G'out there lads and help yer father with the stuff."

In the end, everyone except Dunkle helped to carry in the things Johnny brought: table, chair, frying pan, kettle, teapot, tea, sugar, bread, butter, milk, spoon, knife, fork, sheets, pillowcase, blanket, and two iron grills, one for the bottom of the fireplace and one for the front. Johnny had brought turf too, in beet-pulp sacks, and Cha and myself carried them down to the barn while young Jayjay held a flash lamp.

"Do yeh see what I mean about rassling a beet-pulp sack?" the vindicated Cha shouted.

Johnny had wedged the iron grills into the fireplace by the time we got back to the kitchen. The emperor of China was still enthroned in the middle of the floor, his legs stretched out in front and everyone having to step around him. He issued an edict: "Bring in an armful of that turf, lads," he pronounced. "It's not going to do anyone any good down in the barn. Are ye a pack of eegits or what? Go on with ye."

Like two sheep, Cha and myself turned back to the door, but Johnny stopped us. "I'll get the turf, lads," he said, and as he went out with Jayjay he stepped on Dunkle's foot with the iron-shod heel of his leather boot. Dunkle yelped, "Oh, shag, me shagging toes."

As Johnny was profusely expressing his apologies to Dunkle, Missus Brady and her walking stick hobbled in around the windbreaker wall. Her homemade shopping bag was hanging out of her free hand.

"Sweet Jesus tonight," says she, and she looking around the kitchen, "is there a wake or what? Who's dead?" Then she saw Benny standing on the upside-down bucket and he still trying to put up a new mantelshelf. Missus Brady clicked her tongue as if to say, "Hures, cunts and fuckers is all they are – the Burnses." She put her bag on the table beside the stuff Johnny had brought, and hung the walking stick off the edge of the table. One of the Glanvil children took it and started limping around the kitchen. Missus Brady took out a jar full of her homemade raspberry jam, a piece of butter paper tied on the top with a piece of yellow wool. She put in her hand again and, when it came out with a shank of brown-skinned onions, Dunkle made eyes at everyone, as if to say, "Isn't she a terrible eegit of a woman, bringing onions."

Crip Quigley had ensconced himself at the dead fireplace on the small hob. Crip tries to make himself disappear when Cha's around, because he and Cha haven't spoken to each other for a million years, since Crip's cow broke into Cha's field of young barley and Cha shouted at Crip. But, the quare thing is, they still go to each other's threshing and help each other to round up loose animals.

Johnny had a blazing fire going quicker than I've ever seen a fire getting lit. Amazement at the bitterness of the Burnses kept cropping up in the conversation that was going on about the weather. "And they took the knives and forks, too!" someone would say out of the blue. "They didn't even leave a stump of a candle!" Then, more talk about the weather until someone would say, "I can't believe they took the grate; the grate, mind you!"

Missus Brady told Johnny to boil the new kettle and we'd all have a cup of tea.

"There's no mugs," Ruthie Glanvil said.

Kate counted everyone by nodding her head at them. "Twelve," she said. She looked at Johnny.

Johnny stuck the filled kettle down into the blazing turf and moved it around to make sure it wouldn't turn over. He took Becky and Liam with him to go home for the twelve mugs. Dunkle pulled his feet home real quick as Johnny went by, and there, standing at the windbreak, was Crissy the Widda with her hump, the shape of her body saying, as usual, "Here's me head, me arse'll be here tomorrow." She had a bag in her hand, and a purple ribbon in her black hair. As Johnny went out through the door, Kate called after him, "Thirteen, Johnny."

Crissy the Widda looked up at Benny and said, "I brought ya something, Benny." She put in her hand and took out a jam jar full of honey, bits of wax suspended in the amber; butter paper for a lid tied on with a piece of red wool. "There yar, Benny," she says, and she put the jar on the table. "I've something else fer ya, too." She pulled out a knitted scarf six feet long and two feet wide, yellow, blue and purple. Crissy was beaming as if she'd won a prize.

"That'll keep yer feet warm in the bed," Dunkle said, and he winked at everyone behind Crissy's back.

It suddenly struck me that everyone had brought something for Benny except myself and Dunkle, and, real quick, I began to feel very quare. I had nothing to give Benny. It was Dunkle who had the money, and it would be from Dunkle that something should be coming. Then I remembered my box of messages on the back of my bike, and at the same instant it struck me like a ton of bricks that, if I did give something to Benny, the meanness of Dunkle would stand out like a sore thumb for everyone to see.

Out to the cardboard box I tore and came back in with a loaf of bread and a jar of Bovril. Everyone looked at me, and Dunkle said, "Jazus, don't you think you could a got a bigger bottle of Bovril than that?" Oh, shagging Jesus! I wanted to skull the fucker. But I never said a word, because I knew if I did he'd only tear d'arse off me in front of everyone.

The teapot was too small for thirteen mugs, so Johnny made the tea in the kettle. By the time the mugs were milked and sugared, Missus Brady and Kate had two loaves of bread buttered. Crissy the Widda got as much honey and jam on the table and the floor as she got on the bread.

Benny stepped off the upside-down bucket and looked at his handiwork. The piece of wood he'd used for the new shelf had been a slat in the asshouse manger, and it still looked like it belonged in the asshouse. But everyone complimented Benny on his craftsmanship, Dunkle observing that the shelf was crooked.

Everyone was dying to get at the bread and jam, but at the same time everyone wanted Benny to be the first to get his tea and bread. But he stood there looking around the kitchen for so long that Dunkle finally said, "What's wrong with ya, Benny?"

"I want something to put on the mantelshelf," Benny said, and hardly anyone heard him. Jay handed him the new two-mugger teapot.

You'd have thought Benny was a priest holding up the host after the consecration at Mass, the way he put that teapot on the shelf. It wouldn't have surprised me at all if he'd genuflected.

The mantelshelf must have meant something to Benny, but, whatever it was, it was lost on me.

Crissy the Widda gave Benny a cut of bread dripping with honey, and then she made noises like an oul sow when she licked her fingers. Missus Brady gave him his mug, and then the rest of us got ours. A silence fell into the kitchen for a minute while everyone chewed, and then Crip Quigley said, "This is the nicest tea and bread I've ever tasted in me life." And then, carried away with his own enthusiasm for the tea and bread, and forgetting he was not talking to Quigley, Cha Finley said, "I couldn't agree with ya more, Crip."

Give Crissy the Widda half a chance and she's off talking about bees and beehives. She loves saying "Langstroth" even though she cannot get her fat tongue around it. Crip's and Cha's compliments about the tea and bread gave Crissy the Widda the narrow opening she needed and she said, "Langstroth was a priest, ya know, and . . ."

Dunkle cut her dead. "I've a riddle," he said. "What did Blessed Oliver Plunkett say when he got to heaven?" Everyone knew the joke about Crissy's head and arse. Missus Brady and Kate Glanvil glared at Dunkle for skating on such thin ice. He didn't seem to notice. "Here's me arse, me head will be here tomorrow," he said and he roared laughing, yellow teeth hanging out.

There was a loud knock on the door and everyone looked at each other, because no one was missing.

"What time is it?" Johnny whispered.

"After nine."

"Who could it be at all at this hour of the night?" Kate asked.

"Yearrah, for Christ's sake!" Dunkle said, as if the rest of us were children. He stood up and went around the windbreaker to the door. Missus Brady sat down in the chair.

Everyone had stopped eating. Everyone was listening. The

children slipped over to Johnny. Then we all heard Dunkle saying, "Is it yerself that's in it? Come in, sir, come on in." And who steps around the windbreaker but Mister Parkingston-Shaw-the-solicitor and his hat in his hand. He looked so clean with a nice suit and topcoat on, shining shoes. We all gaped at him as if he'd caught us doing something wrong. It was like a priest had walked in. Of course, Dunkle was all over him.

"Will ya have a cup of tea, Mister Parkingston-Shaw, and a cut of bread in yer hand."

The solicitor didn't seem to hear the old arselicker. He was so surprised to see all the people standing around with mugs in their hands that he was rendered speechless for a second.

"Hello," he said. Everyone muttered something back at him. Then he saw Johnny. "Hello, Mister Glanvil."

"Have a chair, Mister Parkingston-Shaw," Dunkle said, and he pointed to where Missus Brady was sitting. Missus Brady didn't budge, just looked at Dunkle as if he were a hen shite stuck to her heel.

"I'm looking for Benjamin Cosgrove," the solicitor said.

"That's Benny there," Dunkle said, and he pointed.

Mister Parkingston-Shaw took an envelope out of his topcoat pocket. He looked at the envelope for a minute as if a fit of shyness had come upon him suddenly. "I was afraid Mister Burns and his wife might take the farm animals with them when they left," he said into his boots. But then he lifted his head and looked from face to face as he spoke. "I found out from Mister Glanvil what the three animals were worth. Then I told Mister Burns that he owed me that amount for consulting with me about the will. I knew the only way he could get that kind of money was to sell the cow and the two calves."

Mister Parkingston-Shaw took a sheaf of blue notes out of the envelope. "Hold out your hand, Benjamin," he said.

Of course, Benny held out the hand with the bandage and the fingerless glove on it. What a claw it was. By the time Mister Parkingston-Shaw had reached twenty, we were all counting with him. When he got to the one-pound note, the solicitor put his hand up in the air and brought it down slowly. "Fifty-one," everyone said together, and then everyone began to cheer. And when the cheering was over, everyone was smiling, but nobody knew what to say or do next. Mister Parkingston-Shaw backed over towards the windbreaker.

"Yer a daycent and an honest man, Mister Parkingston-Shaw," Cha shouted.

"A real gentleman," Dunkle said quickly, as if he wished he'd said what Cha had said. "Daycent and honest."

"You are all decent people yourselves," Mister Parkingston-Shaw said. "I see you're all helping Benjamin to get back on his feet. If you don't mind, I'd like to help out too." He opened his topcoat and took his wallet out. He stepped over to the jam-and-honey-splattered table and put down three green one-pound notes.

Everyone heard Missus Brady hissing at Benny to say thanks. But if Benny did say thanks, no one heard him because Dunkle grabbed at the limelight again.

"Be gob," says he, "I nearly forgot." He took a wad of notes out of his trouser pocket, and everyone in the kitchen could see him slipping back twenties and tens until he got to the fives. I couldn't take my eyes off the roll of money, couldn't believe one person could have so much, couldn't stop thinking of all the times Dunkle had counted out pennies into my palm for me to buy a bit of bread. "Here's a fiver for yerself, Benny," he said, as he plonked the brown

Irish five-pound note down beside the solicitor's three singles. "Shure, maybe ya could get a calf or an ass fer yerself."

The big eegit! Everyone in the kitchen could see what Dunkle was doing. But if the solicitor was impressed, he didn't let on; if he thought he had been outdone in generosity, he didn't give himself away.

"Goodnight," Mister Parkingston-Shaw said, and as he went around the windbreaker he put on his hat. We heard a motor car starting and driving away.

There was silence in the kitchen until Dunkle said, "Never let a Protestant think he can give more to charity than a Catholic." He went over to the table and picked up the fiver, took the roll of notes out of his pocket, flicked through it till he found the right place, and then he put the whole thing into his pocket.

I couldn't hold back any longer. I put my empty mug on the table and faced up to him. "Murt McHugh, yer the meanest man that ever lived and yer a terrible eegit and everyone knows it and everyone laughs at ya behind yer back and ya can take yer farm and push it up yer arse as far as it goes. Yer nothing but a spavined oul hure."

I don't know how I got out through the door, I was so blinded with crossness. I was even past Crip's house before I remembered the bike. Back I went and grabbed it, but I was so put out I never even thought of getting up on it. I felt like I was drunk, and I've never been drunk in my life to know what drunk is.

35. Liam Glanvil

Dear Sister de Monfort,

Thanks for *The Snow Goose*. I read it in six days. It is the best story I ever read. Daddy is reading *Great Expectations*. Mammy is reading *The Nine Tailors*.

The name of the composition is "The Swans".

I remain, Your nephew, Liam

THE SWANS

Every year, the swans came back to the lake when the swimming season was over, when the heat had gone out of the sun for the year.

Someone always heard the swans coming. The music their wings made was like the sound of the leaking bellows in Sean Delaney's forge when it's pumped quickly to redden the horseshoes. If we were home from school, we all ran down to the lake, trying to get there before the swans landed. We'd hide in the bushes.

On the last part of their journey, the swans sailed down the sky on silent wings, wobbling in the air as they steered themselves in for a safe landing. Their feet drew two lines across the water and then, when their bodies touched the lake, they split the water like a plough opening the first furrow in a field of grass.

I loved the swans.

I loved the way they could glide around the surface as if they were moved by magic, leaving no ripple behind them. I loved the shape of them; the neck curved and the orange-billed face tucked down, as if they were shy about being so beautiful.

When the swans put their heads under the water and tipped up their bodies until their tail feathers pointed to the sky, we counted to see how long they could hold their breaths. If one came up from feeding on the bottom with a piece of water-grass hanging from its beak, the other swan stretched out and took it.

Murt McHugh said he could foretell the weather from looking at the swans' nest. If the top of the nest was far above the surface of the water, it meant the swans knew the lake would rise before their eggs hatched. That meant there was going to be a wet spring.

There are times when it is good to be afraid of swans. They do not like anyone going near their nests and I only know they can have up to eight eggs because that's the biggest clutch of cygnets I've ever seen. If anything tries to harm the young ones, the swans will attack with their wings and beaks. A swan is so heavy it could easily knock a man down.

Even before I heard Mister Saint-Saëns' picture of a swan on the gramophone, I had always thought swans were sad. Maybe it was because of the story of the Children of Lir that I imagined the swans were waiting for the magic moment when they would lose their feathers and become little children again; maybe it was because of their loneliness out there on the water, just the two of them after the young ones had grown up and flown away to find their own patch of water; maybe it was just because they have a sadness about them, even though they look beautiful. But the minute I heard Mister Saint-Saëns' *The Swan*, I knew he felt exactly the same way about them as I do.

And the morning I went down to the lake to look at them before I went to school and found the two of them shot dead and thrown up in the bushes, the first thing that came into my head was the sad, beautiful music that Mister Saint-Saëns wrote. I stood there looking at where the red blood had run across the white feathers, had run down the hanging necks and down along the orange beaks; and *The Swan* got softer in my ears the more I cried for the dead Children of Lir.

It was the very same when we all went running out on to the lane later that day, when the Burnses went by with the ass-and-cart full high with furniture and bikes and doors. I knew from my father's anger they were going out of our lives for ever; and I remembered the spinning tops and the whips and the painted whistles that Paddy Burns made for us; and how he carved the little wooden man who tap-danced on a board when there was whistling; and how Paddy had made us laugh when we would ask him the time – catching the cat's straight-up tail, looking at its bottom and saying it was half-past.

Maybe it was because the swans were killed and the Burnses left Derrycloney on the same day that the same sadness I felt when I saw the dead swans came rushing back into me as the Burnses went away. As they sank out of sight at the Fiery Hill, I heard Mister Saint-Saëns' music, again.

I held my father's hand and I cried again.

P.S. Daddy said to tell you Billy Bates went to America last Monday. He had two suitcases and new shoes. Daddy brought him up to the bus in the pony-and-cart. When they were going past Missus Brady's house, Billy shouted, "*Arrivederci!*"

FICTION
from
BRANDON

TOM PHELAN

Iscariot

"This is a novel about religion, families, sex, guilt and joy – with a 'whodunnit' narrative that keeps you reading to the last page. It is written by a writer who understands the concept of craft." *Examiner*

"Tom Phelan's second novel leaves us in no doubt about his talents as a keen, indeed harsh, observer of humanity . . . By weaving a litany of characters rendered in a composite of opposites he mirrors the balancing of argument that is his peculiar horn of a dilemma. One on which sex predominantly features. But ultimately one on which Tom Phelan's world view is tempered with a warm, forgiving, humanity with the exception, that is, of the Catholic Church." *Sunday Tribune*

"Tom Phelan's impressive second novel is sometimes moving, intermittently erotic, at times bleak and foreboding, but always gripping . . . *Iscariot* would be a worthwhile addition to any Christmas stocking." *An Phoblacht*

"An outstanding novel reflecting the human realities of priestly celibacy today." *The Leinster Express*

"Universal in its dark, intense exploration of the underside of a parish and the life of its priest." *The Irish Times*

"Moving . . . erotic . . . always gripping." *The Irish Globe*

ISBN 0 86322 246 3
Paperback £6.99

J. M. O'NEILL

Rellighan, Undertaker

A dark, intriguing modern gothic tale. The final novel by a writer who was a master of his craft.

In a small rural town in Ireland, nothing is as it appears. Ester Machen brings with her a mystery, and death is stalking the young people of the town. Though 'the town is talking', the only person determined to get to the bottom of the mystery is the detective Coleman. He has few allies, but Rellighan the undertaker gradually assists him in attempting to reveal and rid the town of the terror that has grown within it. They both risk death but unfalteringly continue to unveil the mystery, becoming deeply embroiled in the dark world of the occult as they strive to eradicate evil.

ISBN 0 86322 260 9

Original Paperback £8.99

J. M. O'NEILL
Bennett & Company

Winner of the 1999 Kerry Ingredients Book of the Year award

"O'Neill's world owes something to the sagas of Forsyte and Onedin, and his plotting has, at times, some of the pace and complexity of John Buchan, but the novel is, nonetheless, uniquely Irish with its sanctuary lamps, street-children, moving statues and bitter memories, and it is a contribution to an overdue examination of Irish conscience. The poor and the middle classes are indeed those of Frank McCourt and Kate O'Brien, but O'Neill's is a strictly modern and undeluded vision of the past. The writing is shockingly credible." *Times Literary Supplement*

"He is an exceptional writer, and one we must take very seriously." *Sunday Independent*

ISBN 1 90201 106 6

Original paperback £7.99

J. M. O'NEILL
Duffy Is Dead

"A book written sparingly, with wit and without sentimentality, yet the effect can be like poetry. . . An exceptional novel." *Guardian*

"The atmosphere is indescribable but absolutely right: as if the world of Samuel Beckett had crossed with that of George V. Higgins." *Observer*

"Not a single word out of place. . . Every word of it rings true." *Daily Telegraph*

Duffy is Dead is mournful, funny, warm – a marvellous comedy of Irish low-life, lovingly set among the streets, shops, pubs and people of London's East End. With its quirky, quicksilver wit, this remarkable novel has come to be regarded as a classic of its kind.

ISBN 0 86322 261 7

Paperback £6.99

J. M. O'NEILL
Open Cut

"A hard and squalid world depicted economically and evocatively. . . the tension in the slang-spotted dialogue and the mean prose creates effective atmosphere." *Hampstead & Highgate Express*

"A powerful thriller." *Radio Times*

"O'Neill's prose, like the winter wind is cutting and sharp." *British Book News*

"Fascinating." *Yorkshire Post*

"An uncannily exacting and accomplished novelist." *Observer*

"Exciting and dangerous, with a touch of the poet." *Sunday Times*

Hennessy lived in London: grafted, struggled and eked out his days in a London respectable people are careful never to see. A construction site world of 'kerbside sweat, open-cut trenches, timbered shafts'. A bleak, desolate world of whisky-dulled pain, casual brutality and corruption.

But Hennessy planned a change to his station in life. An abrupt and violent change.

ISBN 0 86322 264 1

Paperback £6.99

JOHN TROLAN

Slow Punctures

"Compelling. . . his writing, with its mix of brutal social realism, irony and humour, reads like a cross between Roddy Doyle and Irvine Welsh." *Sunday Independent*

"Three hundred manic, readable pages. . . *Slow Punctures* is grim, funny and bawdy in equal measure." *The Irish Times*

"Fast-moving and hilarious in the tradition of Roddy Doyle." *Sunday Business Post*

"Trolan writes in a crisp and consistent style. He handles the delicate subject of young suicide with a sensitive practicality and complete lack of sentiment. His novel is a brittle working-class rites of passage that tells a story about Dublin that probably should have been told a long time ago." *Irish Post*

ISBN 0 86322 252 8

Original Paperback £8.99

DAVID RICE

Song of Tiananmen Square

"Ten years after the killings in and around Tiananmen, David Rice has recreated the sights, sounds, smells and above all the emotions of Beijing in the spring of 1989." Jonathan Mirsky, who reported Tiananmen for the *Observer*

"Utterly fascinating. . . powerfully affecting." *The Irish Times*

"A story of love in the time of trouble: love between an Irish lecturer Peter John O'Connor and a beautiful young Chinese student Song Lan. . . A racy novel. . . [and] a worthwhile reminder. . . that when the shooting stopped in Tiananmen Square in 1989 the torture did not end." *Sunday Tribune*

"Bringing alive the struggle for freedom and human rights, this tale has at its heart a story of love and friendship pushed to breaking point." *Irish News*

ISBN 0 86322 251 X

Original Paperback £8.99

STEVE MACDONOGH (ED)

The Brandon Book of Irish Short Stories

"This impressive collection." *Times Literary Supplement*

"Ranges hugely in setting, style and tone. The confident internationalism of these mostly young writers reflects something of the spirit of the new Ireland but it is grounded in an undeceived realism . . . On the evidence here, the future of Irish fiction is in good hands." *Observer*

"This exciting collection of short fiction." *The Irish Times*

"A host of the best contemporary Irish writers." *Ireland on Sunday*

ISBN 0 86322 237 4

Paperback £6.99

KITTY FITZGERALD

Snapdragons

Sometimes shocking, frequently humorous, often surreal, *Snapdragons* is a unique and extremely engaging rites of passage novel about a young woman who grows up unhappily in rural Ireland after World War II. She is disliked – for reasons she cannot understand – by her parents, and has a running feud with her sister. Yet the mood of this story is strangely light-hearted, frequently comic and absolutely memorable.

She makes her escape to the English midlands, and works and lives in a pub in Digbeth, Birmingham, where her sister has settled with her husband. Her already difficult relationship with her sister is further strained when she discovers how she is living. She also learns the sad reason for her parents' hostility towards her.

A captivating story of a young girl in Birmingham and the North of England in the 1950s, its main protagonist, Bernadette, who carries on a constant angry dialogue with God, is one of the most delightfully drawn characters in recent Irish fiction.

ISBN 0 86322 258 7

Original Paperback £8.99

DAVID THOMAS

Anger's Violin

"There are many settings in which to base a novel and this has got to be one of the most original ideas . . . *Anger's Violin* is not an ordinary book.

It is something different altogether – that rare commodity in these days of mass publishing, a good book with a good story and good characters . . .

Thomas has genuine talent and his career as a writer should know no bounds . . . He writes with power and grit, yet maintains a soft touch." *The Irish World*

"The writing here is intelligent, erudite, witty, entertaining and rewarding. Even though one would normally regard a thin premise as a plot, and a denouement which is explained rather than discovered as being weaknesses, both are easily forgiven and forgotten such is the quality of the prose throughout this 'European' novel." *Examiner*

"Interwoven with stories of European myth as well as its rich history, which work especially well mixed in with the narrative. . . Most satisfyingly, its lead charcter and narrator finish up with a new outlook on life, conveyed by an author whose perspective is singular and refreshing." *Irish Post*

ISBN 1 902011 04 X

Original Paperback £7.99

CHET RAYMO

In The Falcon's Claw

"A metaphysical thriller comparable to Umberto Eco's *In the Name of the Rose,* but more poetic, more moving, and more sensual." *Lire*

"Raymo's gift is to bring to life that distant time, vividly but without straining the reader's credulity, in a brief 200 pages or so. There are many strands in this fine novel – love, religion, the stars and the nature of time, church politics, Latin and Irish verse – and they are skillfully put together in a vigorous language that invokes a fresh, unexplored Europe of 1,000 years ago." *Sunday Tribune*

"An astonishing text that reminds us of Umberto Eco's *In the Name of the Rose*. . . with Chet Raymo, this generation of American literature has found one of its most profound philosophers." *Dernieres Nouvelles d'Alsace*

"The French critics were right when they saw in Chet Raymo, author of *The Dork of Cork,* a writer of exceptional culture and erudition, which in no way diminishes the strength and originality of his wit, nor the vivacity of his novel . . . *In The Falcon's Claw* is a novel of never-ending pleasure. . . superbly innovative. It is a work of rare and irreverent intelligence." *Le Figaro Litteraire*

ISBN 0 86322 204 8

Original paperback £6.95